the
good
sister

the
good
sister

jamie kain

St. Martin's Griffin
New York

THE GOOD SISTER. Copyright © 2014 by Jamie Kain. All rights reserved. Printed in the United States of America. For information, address St. Martin's Press, 175 Fifth Avenue, New York, N.Y. 10010.

www.stmartins.com

The Library of Congress Cataloging-in-Publication Data is available upon request.

ISBN 978-1-250-04773-1 (hardcover)
ISBN 978-1-250-04778-6 (e-book)

St. Martin's Griffin books may be purchased for educational, business, or promotional use. For information on bulk purchases, please contact Macmillan Corporate and Premium Sales Department at 1-800-221-7945, extension 5442, or write specialmarkets@macmillan.com.

First Edition: October 2014

10 9 8 7 6 5 4 3 2 1

To Zac

Acknowledgments

This novel might never have made it into print without the support of some of the generous people in my life. Years ago, when I was in the midst of creative burnout, my friend Bethany Griffin suggested I try writing something different, maybe a novel for teens, and that suggestion led to my sitting down and putting into words on the page the story I most wanted to write. My agent, Annelise Robey, was the first person to read the book and give it an enthusiastic vote of confidence. Without her ideas and advice, I would have been lost. I also owe a debt of gratitude to everyone at the Jane Rotrosen Agency who gave feedback on *The Good Sister* throughout the creative process. In addition, I wish I could have given my thanks to the late Matthew Shear of St. Martin's Press, who first read the story there and passed it along to my editor. I never had the pleasure of meeting him. I am deeply grateful to my editor, Sara Goodman, for taking a chance on this novel and helping it find its way into the world. Every day, I'm thankful to my children, Alex and Annabella, for reminding me that life is about more than sitting in front of a keyboard telling stories. Finally, my husband, Zachary Kain, believed in me—and in this book—even when I didn't, and for that I can never thank him enough.

Be humble, for you are made of earth.
Be noble, for you are made of stars.
—SERBIAN PROVERB

the
good
sister

One

Sarah Jade Kinsey

It's strange how someone you never knew and will never know can change the course of your life forever.

For me that someone's name was Brandon.

But before I can explain about him, I have to explain about me.

And what is there to say about me?

The truth is vastly more complicated than it ever was before the night a guy named Brandon, whom I never knew and would never know, appeared in my life and disappeared again in a brief and violent instant.

Life, it turns on a complicated array of delicate gears we cannot see. A heart that beats can go still in the space of a moment. Breath can vanish before we've had a chance to say good-bye.

My name is Sarah Kinsey.

I am, or was, the oldest of three sisters.

To tell my story, I must wrestle with this question of verb

tense, past or present, tedious and mundane as it is. I don't know if I, the person, still exist in any way I can explain, so I stumble over mere words, desperate in death—as in life—to understand and to be understood.

Death is the twist of the knife that makes life so sweet, some say, though I am not sure I would agree.

Imagine a place where you neither sleep nor wake up. Imagine the life you would have lived, could have lived, playing before your eyes like a movie, only not.

Imagine none of this, or all of it.

The truth—if such a thing exists—eludes me.

Death has cut clean through my life, so that now I am no longer Sarah. I am the bloodred tulip tilting in the wind, I am the brown-black earth of a thousand years, I am the welcome rain on a parched day. I am a grain of sand, and I am the entire ocean. I am the beginning and the end of me.

Here is what you have to understand. Although I spent much of my life imagining what dying would be like in a far more concrete way than most people ever do, when it finally happened, it wasn't for the reason anyone expected. It wasn't at all how I imagined it would be.

It did not come from the slow decay of my body, not from cancer eating me away from the inside or wearing down my body's ability to fight. It came from gravity, that simple force we all take for granted, the one that binds us to the earth and all we hold dear.

A moment before, my feet were planted on the earth, and a moment later, they were not. It was that simple.

No, that's not exactly true. It is not so simple, not really. Love had a lot to do with it. Also grief, guilt, and no small amount of reckless, youthful foolishness.

And then there was Brandon, a horrible twist of fate I did not see coming.

But gravity, not cancer, brought me here, wherever here may be.

Two

Asha Nadine Kinsey

Today, March 29, is the day of my sister's funeral, and I am getting a new tattoo. I hold dead still as I watch the needle pierce my skin, laying down black ink in a straight line along the edge of a stenciled star. It stings like hell, and like so much of my life lately, I watch and consider the pain as if it were happening to someone else.

The needle's buzzing sound reminds me of bees.

Bees, bees, we need to save the bees. Life as we know it will end if we don't, or at least that's what I hear. They are a keystone species, holding our world in the balance with their tiny acts of pollination. And Sarah was the keystone of our family—the one who held us together.

Remove her, and we fall apart.

But actually the needle and the bees don't sound alike. Mostly it's the sensation, so much like a bee sting that won't stop, that makes me think of industrious flying insects, and honey, and hives, and the fate of the world. Lavender honey on fresh sourdough bread was Sarah's favorite treat in the world.

Was.

This word sounds wrong in my head, and I blink away barely-there tears that won't come anyway. I am an emotional desert—bereft, barren, possessing little sign that anything here survives.

Here is something no one tells you about what happens when the person you love most dies. You all of a sudden start to see how pointless most moments are. We are so busy with bullshit, we fail to stop and recognize the profound. So busy with brushing teeth and buying groceries and washing dishes and watching YouTube and checking Facebook and texting and putting on makeup and driving to here or there and looking for lost keys, it starts to feel like what we are really doing is hiding from how totally fucking scary life is.

Like one minute you have a sister and the next you don't. That kind of scary.

Isn't that what we should all be stopping and noticing?

Doesn't our profoundly precarious existence deserve most of our attention?

I think it's just too big for us to hold in our mushy brains for long.

Too big for me, definitely.

I stare at the top of Sin's head, bent over my leg resting in his lap, as he focuses on the black star he is drawing there, just above my right ankle. It is the largest of a spray of stars that he has inked there over the past hour. His dark brown hair is a jumble of clumsy spikes today, the result of a haircut I gave him and his own affection for styling products. He is wearing a pink shirt with a white rabbit on the front, above the caption PLEASE DON'T EAT ME.

We have not talked in the minutes since he started the tattoo because he has to give the work all his concentration. He's still learning not to screw up, and I'm the perfect practice dummy since I don't really care if he does. The buzzing drone is accented by the sounds coming from the other room, of a stereo playing Bob Marley's "Could You Be Loved?"

Could I? I think I could if the right guy was asking the question.

To Sin's left is the funky wooden kitchen table that his mother, the not-so-famed artist Jess Lowenstein, has painted in a rainbow of colors and patterns, and on top of the table are his inks and the tattoo equipment he inherited after Jess gave up her short stint as a tattoo artist (turns out skin wasn't her medium, nor was the kitchen table).

Midday light pours through the sliding glass doors on the other side of the room. Outside, it's an offensively sunny day, as is often the case in this part of Northern California, even though it's still technically the rainy season. We have micro-climates here, as Mr. Tobias, the geography teacher at school, would say. Which means that while it might be a foggy, cold day across the Golden Gate Bridge in San Francisco, or even a bit west in the San Geronimo Valley, here on this side of Mount Tam, in the little, Marin County, stuck-in-the-1970s hippie town where most of the members of my parents' old commune settled after their guru fled the country and everything fell apart, we have six months of warmth and sunshine from mid-April to mid-October and often long into the winter, regardless of the weather anywhere else.

Most of the time, I am fine with this, but today, I wish for a storm. I wish the sky would turn dark and rain would fall until no one could see anything and the streets were awash in an epic flood.

This only seems appropriate.

Sin hits a particularly sensitive spot with the buzzing needle, and I wince. Tears well up in my eyes once again, but a movement outside distracts me. On the other side of the sliding glass door sits Sin's cat, Buddha, who is neither Buddha-like nor catlike. His long, mangy gray fur and blue eyes remind me of some kind of northern sled dog, and he's nearly the size of a dog too. He stares at me vacantly, not in the reproachful way cats so often do, but in a way that suggests he doesn't really see me.

Maybe I am a ghost. Maybe the week since Sarah's death has actually been a horrible dream, and I am the one who died. I often imagined this, in the many years that we were as close as two sisters could be. I imagined what it would be like to take her place, to be the one with cancer, to die so she could live. I admit, I never wanted to do it, but I also could not imagine her gone.

I had never known—and do not want to know—a world without Sarah.

Another stabbing pain jars me back to the present, and I exhale a curse. It's real now, this pain, it's happening to me, and I'm relieved to at least be feeling something. He's working over bone now, where there's no layer of fat to dull the sensation of the needle.

Sin stops and looks up at me. "You need a break?"

"No, keep going. I'm fine," I lie, because I want to keep feeling the pain, or at least watch myself sort of feeling it.

Whatever it is I'm doing here.

Although Sinclair Tyler is my best friend, he is probably not someone I should trust to give me a tattoo. Not because he's inexperienced so much as because he is someone I shouldn't allow to leave any more permanent marks on my body. And yet I do. Again.

Something about our friendship feels almost dangerous, almost self-destructive, but I can never quite put my finger on what it is. It probably has something to do with the bottle of whiskey he has hidden under his bed. Or the way I feel a little frantic about the idea of him vanishing from my life.

I don't even know why I torture myself with the idea of him suddenly deciding not to be my friend, but I do. Often. I guess it's another of those things that make me feel something. And I was always so close to Sarah, I didn't make much effort to gather a big collection of friends.

Another stabbing pain, and another wince. I jerk my leg a little this time, and Sin has to stop and wait for me to be still again.

I'm only fifteen—turning sixteen this summer—but it's my third time going under the needle. The first was an infinity symbol my parents had tattooed on the bottom of my foot when I was five years old. I can still remember how hard I cried, how I tried to squirm away from the pain, but my dad (whom I now only call by his old hippie name, Ravi, because it pisses him off) held my leg tight and promised me all the ice cream I could eat when we were done.

Afterward, I ate an entire carton of rocky road from the 7-Eleven, then threw up—an event that to this day I'm sure my mother would deny having allowed. These days she's too aware of the evils of processed food to admit having ever entered a convenience store.

The second tattoo I had done a few months ago, a half-moon on my upper thigh that my mother does not know about. Sin put it there, his slight fingers working over areas no other guy has really touched. There was Ben Thomas, but he only groped me through my jeans in the backseat of his car before I wised up and got the hell out, which in my opinion doesn't count.

But Sin, he doesn't count either. I've never been attracted to him the way I am to other guys, the way I am to his brother. Sure, there is a little of the inevitable guy-girl tension between us, I guess, but from the time I first met him at the start of freshman year sitting in the row across from me in Honors English, I've never thought of him as a guy the way I do other guys. It's probably because he was wearing a purple dress that day, and he looked better in it than I would have.

Not that Sin is a full-time cross-dresser, but he is totally comfortable wearing girls' clothes whenever the mood strikes him. Mainly he does it to confuse people.

Our friendship feels natural, if a bit addictive. I'm used to being the unnoticed one because having a sister with cancer means you learn to get over yourself, and Sin is used to attracting attention. It's what he does best. He's teaching me things.

Also, I just like that in a sea of freaks, he manages to stand out from the crowd.

"I found one of Sarah's hairs in the sink this morning," I say out of the blue, and Sin takes this news in stride.

For days now he's been listening to me recount all the ways I can't believe my sister is gone.

"It was a really long one, so blond it looked white."

"God, I'd kill for her hair."

"You don't have to now—she doesn't need it anymore," I try to joke, but it falls flat, and I loathe the sound of my own words.

An image of her body, all burned up now, rendered into ash and crammed into an urn, invades my head, and I torture myself with it a little. How could my sister be inside an urn? It makes no sense.

Sarah had survived two battles with leukemia, and she'd been in remission for nearly five years. Miraculously, her hair had grown back even more beautiful than it had been before, long, silvery blond, capable of turning heads a mile away.

"I kept the hair and put it in my treasure chest. Is that weird?"

Sin stops his work and glances up at me for a half second. "It's only weird if you collect a bunch of them and crochet a memorial bikini with it."

He prides himself on topping my weirdness. I don't reward him with a response.

My treasure chest is one of those old-fashioned hope chests people used to give their daughters to store stuff in that they'd need when they got married. Mine is a carved Asian one that used to be my mother's, given to her by her parents before she rebelled and ran off to the commune. Years later, she gave it to me because my name means "hope" in Hindi, and she thought a hope chest would be the kind of thing I'd like.

It's the only nice thing I own, which is why I screamed

and raged when Lena (that's my mother, but she's not the kind of woman who enjoys being called Mom—she considers it a restrictive and unnecessary label) tried to pawn it a few years ago to help pay the rent. In it, I store the things I don't want anyone else to take from me: my journals, a collection of coins my grandfather gave me before he died, and an odd selection of crap I've collected over the years.

Sin is filling in the largest star now, wiping blood away and inking in black. Over and over, he repeats the pattern. Ink, wipe, ink, wipe.

The stars are for Sarah, who liked to lie outside on the roof at night with me and stare up at the sky. She would say things that made my head hurt, things I could barely understand. Like "How can the universe go on forever?"

I never had an answer to that one, though I always wanted to. I didn't believe it went on forever because I couldn't wrap my mind around it, the same way I can't wrap my mind around my sister's being rendered into ash and stuck inside an urn.

In my childish head, when I considered her question, the universe stopped on the edge of heaven. Wherever that was.

But for Sarah's sake, I'd stay quiet and try to imagine how something could have no end. Was the universe a big circle? Did it close in on itself, like my own life often felt as if it would at any moment? Did it collapse somewhere out there, unable to bear the weight of its own complexity?

So, stars for Sarah, who should have gone on forever, and maybe she does. Maybe now she's just a part of the endless universe she loved to talk about.

I close my eyes and wonder where my grief is. Except for an occasional welling up of tears, I've been dry-eyed since my sister's body was discovered washed up on Agate Beach in

Bolinas, bloated, tangled in seaweed, and stuck facedown in the same tide pool I'd once visited on a field trip with my second-grade class.

This makes no sense. It's like a thunderstorm raging overhead, clouds black and heavy with water, but no rain coming down.

I want to cry, need to cry, but the storm won't come.

"You still okay?" Sin says, more solicitous than usual, as he wipes the tattoo clean one last time.

I leave my foot propped up on his lap because I know he still needs to put some antibacterial stuff on it.

"I'm fine," I lie.

He knows I'm not. "I mean about Sarah. You gotta go to the funeral after this, right?"

I don't know what to say. Do I have to go? What will happen if I don't?

If I don't mourn Sarah's death, does that mean she's not really dead?

If only I had such control.

Before I left the house this morning, Lena had given me a business card with the address of the memorial service and told me to be there at noon. It was already twelve thirty.

"You can't skip your own sister's funeral."

"Yes, I can."

He stops putting away his supplies and gives me a look. "That's messed up."

"I don't believe she's really dead, so I'm not going to mourn."

I sound ridiculous now, and I'm not fooling Sin for a second, but I don't want to say the stuff that needs to be said. Instead, I shrug and try to look defiant.

"You mean like you think someone else's body was just

found out at the coast, and that someone just happened to look exactly like Sarah?"

I don't expect him to argue with me, and it takes me by surprise. I guess I was hoping I'd get sympathy, not a bitchy attitude.

"No, I mean . . . I don't know what I mean."

It was easy to love Sarah, with her angelic blond beauty and her sweet, long-suffering nature. If I had been creating her life, the movie version, I couldn't have cast anyone more perfect for the role of cancer sufferer than Sarah Kinsey. And in the movie version, if Sarah had to die, it would have been from cancer, just like she was supposed to, or else she'd live on happily ever after. She would not have died unexpectedly from a fall off a cliff.

Sarah couldn't be gone. She had to still be out there somewhere, even if it was only her disembodied spirit, floating off into forever.

"I've been wondering something," he says. "But don't get mad at me for saying it, okay?"

"What?"

"Do you think she really fell by accident?"

"Of *course*," I say, the one sounding bitchy now. "She wouldn't like . . . jump, or anything. And Rachel was there. She saw her fall."

"Maybe she faked it. Like maybe her cancer came back, or she was worried it had returned, and she didn't tell anyone. That would be a pretty good reason to be depressed and jump off a cliff."

But Lena would have known if Sarah had been sick again.

Even if it had been true, it wasn't a good reason for Sarah. She'd lived with the disease for so much of her life, for her it was as much a fact about herself as having blue eyes and blond hair. She was thankful for each day she had alive in a way that only a cancer survivor could be.

"She. Wasn't. Depressed."

But I am not as convinced as I try to sound. The police—and everyone else—took Rachel's story of Sarah's accidental fall at face value. They'd had no reason to question it, and no evidence suggested anything but yet another tragic accident on the treacherous Marin coast. The newspaper reported such stories with horrible regularity.

Our conversation is interrupted by the aroma of weed and Tristan's entrance into the room. All the air whooshes from my lungs as I take in the sight of him, shirtless and stoned, his dreadlocked, brown hair pulled back into a messy pony-tail.

I am so in love with him, I never manage to produce a coherent sentence when he's around. Yes, in love. It's true. For me and nearly every other girl in this corner of Marin County.

Though I'm at a distinct disadvantage to the rest of them since I've only known him for two years, and I'm not even sure he realizes in any concrete way that I exist.

He goes to the refrigerator without saying a word, removes a glass of something green and sludgy that I know from experience is the barely palatable spinach smoothie their mother, Jess, makes as her specialty breakfast drink, then leaves the room without looking at or acknowledging either of us.

I'd strip naked for him in a second. I know this about myself. I'm presently, officially, a virgin, but I'd give it up for him. That's sort of been my secret plan since the first time I laid eyes on him.

Totally inappropriate thoughts, given the occasion, and

that at this very moment I'm supposed to be standing around near my sister's urn and contemplating the brevity of life.

Now that Tristan is gone, Sin says, "Have you ever thought it was possible somebody pushed her?"

This idea startles me, then makes me want to throw up, because I haven't considered it for even a second. I'm still stuck in the denial stage, looking for some way to make Sarah alive again.

But I know this is beyond stupid. "No! Of course not. *Rachel* was there with her, for God's sake."

Sin says nothing because he thinks my sister Rachel is about as trustworthy as a rattlesnake. She may have a petty, vindictive streak, but she's not a murderer. Not in a million years.

"Hmm," he finally murmurs.

"What? What does that mean?"

"The trail where she fell isn't all that narrow, at least not that I can remember. It's hard to imagine her falling accidentally."

I want to stab him in the hand with one of the tattoo needles for saying that.

Since this isn't an option, I finally bring up the other reason I've come here today besides getting a tattoo. "Will you go with me, to the funeral?"

"Sure," Sin says casually as he digs around for something in his tackle box full of tattoo stuff. "Thought you'd never ask."

He pulls out a little packet of antibacterial ointment, and a bandage.

"No bandage," I say. "I want to be able to see it."

He rubs the ointment on my skin, and when he's done, a

large, glistening black star, two inches around, surrounded by a spray of smaller stars, adorns my ankle.

Black, like darkness. Black, like Tristan's eyes. Black, like the weight in my chest that feels as if it might bury me alive.

Three

Rachel Anne Kinsey

I've never been to a funeral before. I look at the little crap brochure someone has handed me with my sister's name printed on the front in fancy script. Sarah Jade Kinsey. Printed below that are the dates of her birth and death, dates I know too damn well and don't want to be reminded of.

Then, a quote somebody must have thought to write down for just this occasion while Sarah was still alive, or maybe it was something she'd written herself in a journal (it would be just our mother's style to read it) or a school essay. It was some shit she'd once said when asked how she felt about dying: *I'm not afraid of death. I'm afraid of forgetting to live.*

Right on, Sis. That Sarah. She always knew how to produce a cliché inspirational quote for her own funeral handout.

No, not a funeral. It's a memorial service, I read, when I flip to the second page. You see, even our free-loving, acid-dropping, idol-worshipping parents can fall for the sales pitches of the funeral-industry assholes, who must have convinced them to print up this little keepsake I am staring at now.

I'd have expected something more bohemian from them than this lame-ass assembly at the Spirit Friends Temple of every goddamn person who knows us. Maybe a gathering to toss flower petals into the ocean where Sarah drowned while someone plays the guitar and sings "Kumbaya." But whatever. I'm glad we're here and not there, and probably the suddenness of Sarah's death caught them so off guard, they just went into robot mode and started doing whatever the funeral people told them to do.

The petal tossing will come later, and in private, for each of us, along with our own guilty baggage we may or may not attempt to throw into the Pacific along with the flowers.

Guilt. It's my new best friend, my hobby, maybe even my full-time job.

I'm sitting in the front row of the temple, with an empty seat to my left where Asha is supposed to be, and my whimpering, sniffling mother to the right. Next to her is her asshole boyfriend, Ron, and beside him sits our dad, Ravi, alone.

He must be pissed Lena brought her boyfriend, but I am working hard at not giving a crap.

Candles flicker at the temple altar around the dark blue urn that contains the ashes of what used to be Sarah (when the coast guard found her body, it was already too bloated and wrecked from being in the ocean to make an open-casket service possible, or so I've been told).

As a form of self-torture, I've tried a few times to imagine what my sister must have looked like, her moon-pie face all stretched out like a balloon, seaweed tangled in her long hair, her body no longer the 110 pounds of perfection her cheatin'-ass boyfriend probably once thought it was.

From the corner of my eye, if I turn my head just so, I can sort of see David. He cries freely, tears streaming down his face and getting soaked up by his beard. His body shakes occasionally with the intensity of his grief, and I kind of envy that. I sort of want to wail and throw myself on the floor and show everyone how much pain I am in, but that shit is pretty hard to fake.

Because what I feel is not grief, exactly. It's more like horror at what I—and my life—have suddenly become.

I'm not sure I ever loved David. I realized, as soon as Sarah died, that what I'd loved was taking him from her. I had a guy of my own. Still have him. AJ couldn't be here today, mostly because I didn't ask him to come and also because I couldn't have him and David in the same room without some crazy daytime-talk-show brawl going down.

Weird how love works—or doesn't work in this case.

David is not my type. He's the kind of guy who sits in the park playing his conga whether anyone is listening or not, likes to talk about the meaning of life, and is just as happy with the girl's paying as anyone. He is not what most people would call a real man.

He believes in free love because it looks good on paper and not just because it's convenient for him.

But Sarah was clearly crazy about him, and he probably loved her about as much as any dude could love a girl who might drop dead of cancer in the near or distant future.

If I weren't such a player, I'd have left well enough alone. But I saw the way he looked at me.

My stomach growls, but no one seems to notice. I wish I at least had a piece of gum or something in my purse, and I wonder how long this crap is going to last, and will there be food after?

I know this is not something I'm supposed to be thinking now. I'm supposed to be so wracked with grief that I can't eat. I'm supposed to get nauseous at the thought of food, not be fantasizing about a chicken burrito.

I wish I had a watch so I could see the time, and then I wonder if I can get away with sliding my hand into my purse and pulling out my cell phone to look at the clock on it. Better not. The little brochure thing I'm holding says that there will be a slide show of images from Sarah's life, along with a chance for loved ones to speak about her. How long can that shit last? All day, knowing these motherfuckers.

Lena asked me if I wanted to speak here, and I said no, and she got pissed, and I said, well, maybe I'll change my mind so chill the fuck out. But it's not going to happen. I can't get up there and spew half-truths about how much I loved my sister, how tragic her death is, blah blah blah.

It's tragic, okay, whatever. But just as my feelings about David are complicated, so are my feelings for Sarah. I mean, is being forced to live in the same family for eighteen years the same thing as love?

And speaking of family, where the hell is Asha? Leave it to her to skip out on her own sister's funeral. My thought vibes must have reached our mother, because she looks up from her sniffling to the empty seat on my left and whispers, "Where is she?"

I shrug. Don't meet her eyes. She looks away.

Asha's probably somewhere getting drunk with that little shitbag best friend of hers. He creeps me out, the way he doesn't seem all that much like a guy, and yet he doesn't act all flaming gay either. He's like a sexual in-between.

The lights go dim in the room, and somewhere, someone turns on some music. The sound of Sarah's all-time-favorite makes-me-roll-my-eyes-and-gag song, "Both Sides, Now" by Joni Mitchell, comes through unseen speakers, and the slide show begins on the wall in front of us. I try not to engage in any eye rolling or pre-vomiting. An image of Sarah from what looks like maybe a few months before she died is the first to appear along with Joni's voice singing about angel hair and ice-cream castles in the air.

Yeah, yeah. Here come the waterworks all around me. I feel sad too, but for none of the right reasons.

From behind me, I hear more sniffling. Soon it's coming from all directions.

I look away from the image on the wall and down at my skirt, which I spent half of last week's paycheck on just for this occasion. I smooth my hands over it, until I reach the hem, and I cross one leg over the other. I don't smoke a pack a day or anything, but right now I'd give anything for a cigarette, or a shot of tequila, or both.

That is what I spent the other half of last week's paycheck on. Serving up coffee drinks at Sacred Grounds is not exactly the glamorous life I'm destined for, but it and my fake ID keep me steadily supplied with my vices, making it hard to quit. Most of my more ambitious friends are eagerly awaiting acceptance letters from the colleges of their dreams, but at the age of eighteen, I graduated a semester early thanks to not failing any classes and not giving a crap about college prep, and I'm having a hard time figuring out what I want to do with my life past next weekend.

Not Sarah though. When I look up again, I see a picture of her at the age of five or six, wearing a stethoscope and an oversize white shirt she called her doctor shirt. She spent so much time in the hospital, it wasn't any big mystery why she always knew she wanted to be a doctor or a nurse.

One year one thing, the next year the other. Back and forth endlessly, except for that one year when her cancer came back and Lena decided it was time to give alternative medicine another shot. Sarah developed a short-lived fascination with studying Chinese medicine and becoming an acupuncturist before she went back to the nurse career path.

It was both sweet and pathetic, this girl who likely wasn't going to make it to adulthood, busily planning for her future. Part of me always wanted to point out to her that she might as well slack off and have some fun, not go around acting like she had a big future to live for. And another bitchy part of me enjoyed watching her waste her time.

Yes, I am a bad sister. The absolute worst you will ever meet.

But this is what you have to understand about me—I became invisible when Sarah was diagnosed with leukemia. I was not a genetic match for donation purposes, but Asha was. So she got to be the hero, and I got to be the dumb little kid everyone forgot about. Not that I'm bitter or anything. These days, I know how to get what I need.

I look back up at the slide show and am stunned to finally feel a wave of grief wash over me as big as any natural disaster. It's crazy; what finally gets me is the image of Sarah in a sort of nurse's uniform, standing on the front porch smiling wide. I'm pretty sure David took that picture. It's from last summer, when Little Miss Perfect did a volunteer stint at the hospital taking people's blood pressure and writing down vital signs. My eyes burn with furious tears, and I might let out a few good sobs, except that a loud door-slamming noise interrupts the flow of my grief.

I turn with most of the other people in the room and see Asha stumble through the double doorway, followed by her weird-ass friend Sinclair. She looks drunk, and not at all dressed for the occasion, in her ripped jeans and faded green tank top. Her long, dark hair spills over her shoulders looking like it hasn't been brushed in days—like me, she inherited Dad's dark hair and green eyes, but unlike me, she doesn't know what to do with herself.

Because almost every other seat is full now, she is forced to weave her way up the aisle to the front row, to her designated seat, but Sin follows her, so there's an awkward scrambling for a second chair. Someone two rows behind gives up his aisle chair, moving it forward to be next to Asha's, then takes another seat that requires much shuffling and apologizing.

All the while, the Sarah slide show plays on, but I am unable to look at it now, not when I have my reeking-of-whiskey sister beside me, taking up all the space in the room.

She has a crazy way of doing that. I've never figured out what her game is, or where she gets her nerve, but she is an energy vortex. When she's near, I feel like I need to go take a nap.

I glare at her, and she looks back at me through eyes that appear not to give a damn about anything. I think, maybe this is her thing, that she never seems to care just how catastrophic she is.

I don't even bother looking at the emo. Instead, I let my gaze travel over Asha's inappropriate attire, but it stops at her ankle. She has the legs of her jeans rolled up to capri length, and a new tattoo—a cascade of black stars—is on the outside of her right leg, the one closest to me. I can see that it's real by the way her skin is red and raised around the edges of the fresh ink.

I know she has done this on purpose. She has figured out a way to create maximum drama even in silence.

She used to call Sarah Starlight. It was one of their many cutesy habits, coming up with tongue-in-cheek hippie nicknames for each other.

My stomach cramps, and I start to sweat. If I try hard enough, I might be able to lose my breakfast croissant right there all over Asha's fresh tattoo.

I wonder if Lena or Ravi sees the tattoo. It's impossible not to notice, since Asha is not wearing shoes or socks, only a ratty, old pair of gold-embroidered thong sandals, and a silver toe ring on one toe. She has her toenails painted dark blue, and this, I know, is also for Sarah, the color of night sky.

Her strategy has worked. I am furious, though I don't quite know why. I'm going to kill her when we get out of here.

I want her to stop sucking the energy out of me, so I am forced to turn my attention back to the awful slide show. But I can still feel her there, sucking, sucking, sucking.

The image on the wall now is a family shot, all three of us sisters before we became teenagers, maybe ages eight to eleven. We are outside somewhere in the redwoods, I think at Samuel Taylor Park. I halfway remember the day, a gathering of Lena and our father's old friends from the commune.

We look like filthy little hippies, our hair messy and our

feet bare. Sarah is in the middle, the glowing wraith among us, her silvery-blond hair hanging only to her chin thanks to a recent round of chemo, her face oddly serene. Asha is on the left, tugging on Sarah's hand, looking as if she wants to escape the camera's lens. And I am on the right, the tallest even though I'm a year younger than Sarah, and definitely the prettiest of the three, my arm around Sarah's shoulders, a big, fake smile plastered on my face, looking as if I am trying to convince the world of my happiness.

Now, looking back, I can see the hint of everything to come after in my eyes. The lies, the guilt, the horrible end to our sisterhood of three.

And now the secrets that keep me up at night, staring at the ceiling.

Whoever said the camera never lies, well, maybe they were right. But you have to know what you're looking for, right there under your nose, to see the truth hidden in the details.

Four

Asha

If I had known getting drunk and jumping into the Tylers' hot tub naked would make Tristan Tyler notice I was alive, I would have done it a long time ago. Better late than never though, right?

But, no, wait, that's not how this part of the story starts. There was the funeral, which I do not remember because my brain-under-the-influence has mostly blacked out that part of the day. And then there was some debate about whether I should be forced to go home and sleep off my buzz or should attend the funeral after-party.

I remember Rachel glaring at me, maybe even threatening me, but this is nothing new and could have happened weeks ago or not at all. And I have a few fragmented memories of some horrible slide show, and some tearful speech given by my father, and that's all. I'm not even sure in which order these memories belong, or if they were but a dream within a dream, as my favorite poet, Edgar Allan Poe, once wrote.

Sin and I each did four shots of Jack Daniel's before hopping on our bikes and riding to the temple. This, I report with complete earnestness, was not a good idea. Between the two of us, I think we were nearly hit by four different cars, and for sure it wasn't the cars' fault.

Lena ended up furious enough to ban us from the after-party—I remember that part—leaving Sin and I drunk with no place to go. So we went back to his house, a little steadier on our bikes now that we'd had some time to sit and sober up in the temple.

Sin fell asleep on his bed, and I found myself bored and still a little wasted. It seemed wrong to ruin a perfectly good buzz alone in Sin's bleak little room, so I wandered outside, noticed that the hot tub was open, stripped off my clothes, and got into the bubbling, hot water.

Which brings us back to right now.

It is late afternoon, and a ridiculously warm, breezy day. Global warming at work, I guess. I lie with my head back, staring up at the light dancing on the leaves of the huge oak tree that stretches its branches partway over the deck where the hot tub sits.

I hear the back door of the house open, and I assume Sin has woken up and is coming out to find me, so I don't look toward the sound. We were alone in the house last I checked. My head tilted back and my arms outstretched to my sides on the edges of the tub, I am aware that my bare chest hovers at the waterline for whoever cares to look, but Sin has seen me naked enough times when we're changing clothes that it doesn't matter anymore.

And besides, he's decided again as of last month that he isn't into girls anyway.

But when I hear a low voice say, "Hey, nice day, huh?" I know it isn't Sin's.

It's Tristan's.

I rarely hear him speak, so the sound startles me out of my leaf gazing, and I sit up fast, then slide deeper into the water to conceal as much as I can of my nakedness.

When I look at him, he's got a lazy half smile on his lips that seems kind of . . . flirtatious, I guess is the right word.

Flirtatious. My brain does a double take.

I allow a moment for the idea to sink in.

No way is Tristan flirting with me.

Something about his smile gives him a kind of devilish appearance. Normally his face is angelically handsome, and this vision of him now thrills me.

I am still drunk enough to say out loud, "It feels good in here. You should come in."

"I was just about to."

My whole body melts into the water, or at least it feels that way. Tristan is about to get in the hot tub with me, and we've just had our longest conversation ever. These facts are almost too stunning to be believed.

I watch him pull off his red T-shirt, my gaze landing on his abs and chest. Oh, God. He's beautiful, no doubt. A little too thin to be calendar-boy material, he's nonetheless better looking than anyone else I've ever seen this close to naked.

I am starting to panic. What if I say something that makes me sound like a complete dork? What if I don't? What if I say nothing at all?

Then I remember my favorite question for times such as this—what would Sin do?

Since Tristan is his brother, the question might not make

perfect sense, but if he was about to be naked in a hot tub with the star of his fantasies, he'd definitely find a way to be cool or, even better, startlingly weird, about it. Perhaps he'd act like he didn't care. He might even ignore the other person. He'd let the person do all the work. Or else he'd make uncomfortable comments about their anatomy.

I'm not at all sure I have the guts to try either approach.

But then Tristan starts taking off his pants, and I am transported to this whole other mental place where my mind is truly blank and my mouth feels as if the dentist has just stuck one of those suction-hose things in it and sucked me dry.

I try my best to look everywhere but at his crotch, even though that's the place I most want to look. I've seen plenty of guys naked—my dad, guys swimming at the nude beach— but none of them were guys I wanted to see, not like this. I'm pretty sure, by the time his pants are down around his ankles, that he wasn't—or isn't—wearing any underwear, and I find this idea intriguing.

Then he sits down across from me in the tub, and I am able to meet his gaze again.

"Hey, I, uh, heard about your sister. I'm sorry. It must be hard."

I've been subject to this kind of comment about a thousand times in the past week since Sarah's death. But something about Tristan saying this now makes me tear up. He has pulled me out of my hormonal reverie for his body and reminded me that I'm supposed to be in mourning.

I mean, I *am* in mourning. It's just that the process doesn't necessarily look like it's supposed to. My body and mind are refusing to cooperate.

"Yeah," I say. "I still can't believe it."

"You wanna smoke?" He produces a joint and a little red lighter from his jeans lying nearby on the deck.

"No thanks," I surprise myself by saying.

The truth is, I'm feeling a little sick now from the whiskey and perhaps the horrifying funeral thing that I've blocked out, and I don't want to be any more fuzzy headed for my first real encounter with the guy of my dreams.

He lights up and takes a long, deep hit, then sits there holding his breath until he's red in the face.

In the queasy haze of my impending hangover, it's hard to remember what exactly I find so irresistible about Tristan. Aside from his being gorgeous, I mean. Okay, so maybe it's mostly that he's gorgeous. But he's also a good guitarist, and he plays in a popular local reggae band even though he's only seventeen and all the other band members are in their twenties.

But it occurs to me now that I finally have him captive, I don't have a clue what to say to him. I don't have a plan. I'm still the same awkward, mute dork as always—not the cool, witty girl of my fantasies who actually gets with Tristan.

Tristan exhales a long, slow cloud of smoke, coughs a little, and smiles at me.

"So you and my little brother—you guys don't, like, get it on, do you?"

I am mortified. It never occurred to me that he might think this. Equally mortifying is the idea of Sin's finding out that I'm in love with his brother. I've never told Sin, though I guess I've sort of always assumed he could tell. Yet if he comes out here now and sees us, I'm not sure what he'll think.

"No, we're just friends. Best friends."

"You don't dig dudes in dresses?"

Mildly amused by his alliteration, I smile. "It depends on the dude, I guess."

He takes another hit as he lets his gaze fall to my chest, which I've forgotten is nearly exposed now that I've allowed myself to sit up a bit. I force myself not to slide down in the water again, and to my extreme surprise, I get the distinct feeling he's liking what he sees.

Oh, God.

This is quite possibly the most exciting thing that's ever happened to me, and I'm terrified by all the possibilities of what might happen next.

I feel his foot brush against my leg under the water.

"Sorry," he says, exhaling smoke again, but he doesn't move his foot away.

Instead, he eases it up my calf to my thigh, eyeing me to see how I'll react.

Oh, God.

Oh. My. God.

Oh my freaking God.

This is so not happening.

But it is.

I straighten my leg and let my own foot drift toward him, bumping against what I think is his hip, and that's pretty much all the permission he needs to slide across the hot tub to sit next to me.

Here, time and space start doing weird things, speeding up and slowing down at the same time, like in a movie when the good guy is about to shoot the bad guy, or vice versa.

I'm crazily aware of his thigh against mine, the hairs poking me in a way that's not unpleasant. And I stare for what seems like a long time at his biceps, where there's a group of three moles gathered as if having a meeting. But it was probably just a second or two, I realize, when I look up at him.

Then I notice his mouth, which I've never all the way noticed before. I have not ever been close enough to study the lines in his pink lips, or the way his lower lip is exactly the same size as his upper.

I look into his eyes finally and am surprised by the flecks of gold there, among the brown of his irises. I'd always thought his eyes were black, but no. What does he see? Does he see me, or am I just here, convenient, a nice diversion in the hot tub?

I don't want that to be true.

His gaze locked on mine, he leans forward, closes his eyes, and kisses me.

Warmth like a drink of whiskey flows through me, and time does a funny thing again, speeding up now, making what I want to last become infinitely too short already, too close to ending even if it doesn't.

I taste marijuana and feel his tongue flick against my lips. At the same time, his hand is sliding up my thigh, navigating the same territory Ben Thomas attempted to chart last year.

I am thrilled and terrified, too much so to relax for a second of what is happening.

"What the hell?" I hear, and I break the kiss as I glance up to see Sin standing over us, looking as furious as I have ever seen him.

He is glaring at me, only me, as if he doesn't even see his brother sitting there. I want to point out to him that I didn't start it.

I understand instantly that I have betrayed him somehow, but it makes no sense. None at all. Maybe he's just angry that I went into the hot tub with my new tattoo, I think stupidly, right before he storms away.

Five

Sarah

Murder.

It's not something most people have to contemplate in any real way. It's a vague Ten Commandments kind of idea.

Thou shalt not, we are told, so we don't.

But what if we do? Then what? Can life as we know it even go on?

Consider these three sisters: Sarah, Rachel, Asha.

We three girls.
Only two now.
No mathematician am I,
So I ask:
Take away one life,
Then take away the one that took it away.
Does that add up?
Does the universe come into balance then?

Can we call it multiplication of negatives,
A negative times a negative equals a positive
Each and every time?

Six

Asha

As best friends go, I am apparently the lowest of the low. I am the filthy residue clinging to the bottom of a bad friend's shoes.

But I'm still not sure about the why or what or how of it.

In the moments following Sin's storming away angry from the hot tub, I am still far too keenly interested in Tristan, naked and draped around me, to fully process the whole disaster.

I watch Sin retreat back into the house, and then I look at Tristan for confirmation that he is still there. That we have just kissed, with his hand charting new territory and all that.

He is staring at my mouth, intent on picking up where we left off. "Don't know what his problem is," he murmurs, then goes in for another kiss.

At first, I am into it. Relieved, even. My body is nearly as liquid as the bubbling water in which we sit. I feel as if I might at any moment ooze into Tristan, as if another kiss might turn into his drinking me up.

My brain, on a hazy delay, finally responds. "I . . . I'd better go make sure he's okay."

The words squeak out of me halfheartedly. I don't want to go, don't want to end this fantasy come true, don't want to stand up naked, get dressed in front of Tristan, put all that distance between us to face my pissed-off, crazy best friend.

"Don't go," Tristan whispers, his breath tickling my cheek and almost convincing me.

But could I face Sin later if I don't go after him now?

No.

Here my brain snaps all the way back to reality.

I reluctantly edge away from Tristan, and he looks at me through a glassy gaze that seems at ease with the situation. I feel bare in all the places we were touching that we now aren't.

"I thought you said you two aren't getting it on," he says, sounding confused rather than annoyed.

"We're not. I don't know why he's so mad."

"He wants you all to himself."

"No way. Not Sin. He doesn't even like girls."

Tristan smirks at this. "Is that his story this month?"

I shrug. It's true, Sin's sexual interests seem to lean which-ever way the wind is blowing, but I tend to take his proclama-tions at face value. He's always seemed to know better than anyone else exactly what he wants.

Now, I stand up and step out of the hot tub, trying to be

cool about Tristan's having a prime view of every naked inch of me. This is pure torture. I have peered at myself undressed in the mirror, wondering how my body will look to the opposite sex. And here I stand, in front of the object of my desire, wishing I were one of those girls who works out constantly.

But I'm not. I'm one of those girls who eats empty carbs and refined sugar and all the other stuff I'm not supposed to eat. And aside from riding my bike and my weekend hikes with Sin, I don't get tons of exercise. I don't do two hours of power yoga every day the way some girls at our school do—some of whom Tristan has surely seen naked.

My body is all wet—I haven't thought to bring a towel, and neither has he—so I'm stuck trying to tug on my clothes over wet skin. Panties and shirt, no problem, but my jeans prove more difficult and involve much bouncing around and tugging. I get the distinct feeling Tristan is enjoying the show, though maybe not in the way I'd like him to.

My ankle is burning now where the fresh tattoo is reacting to being immersed in hot water, then cold air. That's got to be why Sin is so pissed at me—the tattoo. He's scrupulous about aftercare. He doesn't want his work out there in the world looking shitty.

I know deep down I'm fooling myself.

I don't want to go inside and face him. Something tells me it's not going to be pretty. But I head for the back door, stepping around fallen leaves because I don't want them to poke my overly tender bare feet. I've left my sandals inside Sin's bedroom—another reason I have to face him.

At the door, the wolf-cat Buddha is waiting to be let out.

But when I open it, he turns and runs under the table. Whatever, dumb cat. I trudge through the kitchen and down the hallway to the closed door with the sickly sweet poster of kittens in a basket. Sin, always big on irony.

I knock on the forehead of a blue-eyed white Persian, and I call out, "Sin?"

I expect this to be a long, painful process, but he jerks the door open immediately and there we are, face-to-face. Before I can say a word, he throws my sandals down the hallway, slams the door, and I hear the lock click.

"Sin?" I say stupidly. "Can we talk?"

Suddenly my whiskey buzz has worn all the way off, and I am feeling a little queasy again. But I know I won't throw up. I never do unless I drink cheap tequila.

"Get the fuck out of my house!" he yells through the door.

I blink at the kitten poster, stunned. This definitely isn't about my not following the tattoo-care rules. Don't I get a little leeway for having a dead sister? For today's being the day of her freaking funeral? For having to face the horrible question of how she died?

Isn't this my best friend who just sat with me through the most grueling hour of my life, saying good-bye to the only member of my family that I love without hating too?

She can't be gone. She can't be gone. *She can't be gone.*

And if she is, and if Sin hates me now, I am alone in the world. Totally fucking alone.

I feel tears prickling at my eyes, blurring my view of the kittens and their little paws perched on the edge of the basket. Immensely sorry for myself now, I turn and leave.

I can't go home, so I ride my bike to the park in the center of town, find the sleeping bag I keep stashed in a tree for hanging out at the park, lie down under the shade of a redwood, and stay there for the rest of the day staring up at the branches, as if waiting for them to reach down and lift me into the sky, away from all of this.

Seven

Sarah

Ticktock goes the clock—
We wait and plan
for our lives to begin
Never realizing all the while
Life is half-done, and before we can catch our breath
It will be gone.
Ticktock
Goes the clock.

I sometimes think in poetry here in the great Whatever. The words arrive, neither good nor bad. Like snowflakes they drift into my mind and come out, little bits of the truth I am beginning to grasp.

Eight

Rachel

In the weeks after Sarah's memorial or funeral or whatever it was, I feel like I'm stoned all the time, but not the good kind of stoned. More like a bad trip where you want to tell every dumbass you see what you don't like about them, and when you're not feeling like that, you just want to go to sleep.

I avoid David, which is fine because he must be avoiding me too. He sends me a couple of texts but doesn't call or anything when I never answer. I am not sure what to do with him now, and I just fucking don't think about it.

AJ, my Official Boyfriend, comes over a few times but says I'm acting like a bitch so he leaves, and I haven't seen him in a week. He'll come back whenever I call and say I'm sorry, which will be I don't know the fuck when.

I just want everyone to disappear. Or I want to disappear. Or both. I go to work, I come home, I smoke, I sleep. I am losing weight. AJ pointed this out to me, said I'm getting too damn skinny, but whatever. Who cares?

The worst part though is the nightmares. Ever since the memorial service, I wake up every night, my body drenched in sweat, my throat closed up even though I'm trying to scream. In the dream, which is always the same, I am with Sarah on the trail where she died, and we are arguing about whose turn it is to have the car for the night. I am so angry at her, I could hit her, and when we round a bend in the trail, and rain has washed away a hillside, Sarah slips, loses her balance, and in one swift, horrible instant, I push her, and she goes over the cliff.

That's when I wake up.

I don't often go back to sleep after that dream.

Then something changes. I meet someone who wakes me up from this weird haze I've been in, and I don't know why. He is the last person on earth I would think could wake me.

The first time I see Krishna, he is walking past me on the sidewalk. I am leaning against the wall outside Sacred Grounds, the coffee shop where I work, smoking a cigarette. Just off my shift, I feel on edge, shaky from lack of sleep. I can't stop thinking about Sarah. I am haunted by the nightmare, the frightening realness of it.

So he walks past me, and he is wearing a loose white shirt that sets off his olive skin and dark hair. He is gorgeous, but he is also definitely a hippie type, which I am officially swearing off after David. I know he's a hippie or some kind of freak because he's wearing an orange sarong below his white shirt. He even looks a little like David, which is the first thing I notice about him.

When I catch his eye, I don't smile. Instead I take a drag on my cigarette.

"That's not going to make you feel any better," he says, and keeps walking.

I stop midpuff. I wasn't expecting a lecture on smoking, and he has my attention now for some reason I can't imagine. Some part of me wonders if he can read my thoughts or feel the darkness of my nightmares. Seeming to sense it, he turns and looks at me over his shoulder, smiling like freaking Gandhi.

Any other day I would have rolled my eyes and told him to go blow himself. Today though, haunted as I am, I just stare at him with the cigarette dangling from my lips.

He stops in the middle of the sidewalk and seems to make a decision. Then he comes back and says, "I'm on my way to a community dinner at the meditation center over the hill. Any chance you'd like to join me?"

I am so caught off guard I laugh. "Really? You want me to fucking go to dinner with you?"

"Yes. I do."

"How do you know I'm not a serial killer?"

He smiles, revealing straight, white teeth. Jesus teeth. "I have faith."

"You shouldn't."

"I'll take my chances." He says all this without even the slightest vibe of flirtation, which is confusing as hell. He has the sort of mellow energy that reminds me of the guy my parents used to call their spiritual leader.

I underestimated his attractiveness when I first saw him. Now that I see him full on, he has these beautiful green eyes that seem unreal next to his olive skin. That he doesn't seem to be flirting makes him all the more attractive. I've always loved a challenge.

"Okay, sure," I say. "Why not?"

He smiles broadly. "Great."

Almost laughing again, and also thinking I've lost my mind, I follow him. I get in the car that he has parked in the town's main lot across the street. The rusty, burgundy car is so old I can't even tell what kind of Toyota it is. The cloth seats maybe used to be red but are now faded to pink. The inside is clean though and smells like that incense shit Lena is always burning. From the rearview mirror hangs a string of brass beads that have some Asian-looking symbols etched into them.

As he gets in the driver's seat, I note his firm muscles and lightly hairy legs beneath the orange sarong thing.

What if *he's* the serial killer? I don't think I care all that much. I just want to see what happens next.

"My name is Krishna," he says before starting the car.

Of course it is. "Hi, Krishna. I'm Rachel."

"It's nice to meet you, Rachel."

"So what's your real name? Mike? Steve?"

"It's Krishna."

So his parents were spiritual seekers too. Of course. Everyone around here was twenty years ago.

As he drives, he asks me about myself, and I tell him about things I haven't said aloud to anyone else. About my family, my dead sister, my stupid relationships with guys, my job, and my graduating last December. It all just comes out of my mouth. He listens, taking in all that shit without judging it, which feels good. I can't remember the last time anyone listened to me like that.

Definitely not a guy.

By the time I'm finished talking, we've made it out of town

and are on the winding road that heads toward the coast. I can hardly believe myself, confessing my life story to a stranger. But there's something about this guy, something so open and free of bullshit, that I feel as if complete honesty is the only option.

It doesn't make much sense, but nothing about Krishna does. He catches me off guard in a way I've never experienced before.

He starts telling me all about himself, how he was a heroin addict and a drummer until he found Buddha or whatever. He tells me about his family back in a small logging town in Washington, how he has two older brothers, but he hasn't seen them in years because they think he's a freak for becoming a monk.

This logging-town childhood doesn't mesh with his having a name like Krishna, but I don't bring it up.

"Do you miss them?" I ask, not sure why I even care.

"Sometimes, but I know the part of them I miss, I can find anytime I recall our childhood together."

Oh, yeah. Right on, Mr. Hallmark cards. "So you're like a real monk? Does that mean you don't have sex?"

He smiles like he's remembering something. "Yep. I'm celibate."

"For how long?" All my hopes about me and Krishna naked start to fizzle out, and I didn't even realize I was hoping.

"Forever."

"Are you a virgin?"

"No, I gave up sex a year ago to help myself stay focused on my spiritual development."

Oh, whew. "So was it hard to stop having sex?"

He smiles. "Sometimes. I've been immersed in meditation

for a good part of the past year. Bodily urges interrupt sometimes, but meditation takes me back to where I need to be. I
think of meditating as the question and the answer."

I say nothing, disappointed. I'm not used to this.

We arrive at the meditation center and get out of the car
to follow a winding path up to its front entrance. It's a low,
brown-wood-shingle building of the kind people like my parents think is groovy. Big windows, big trees. Krishna holds the
door open for me, and I feel for a moment as if I might float
up off the ground and into the sky.

Nine

Sarah

This doesn't seem like heaven or hell, I suppose. More and more I think I am stuck in some in-between place, a nowhere land.

It's strange how time folds in on itself now, free from the artificial, linear labels we impose on it. I have no sense of whether moments, days, or weeks have passed. I can only get a frame of reference by watching my family. I see my mother, Lena, going to her therapist, so I know it's Tuesday. I hear her say it's been three weeks since my death, so I know time drifts on without me.

And still, lingering like a whisper, like a ghost, there is always Brandon.

Three days before I died, I went with Lena to my grandmother's house in Tiberon. Her understated mansion was built to blend into the hills and trees that surround it. Walls of windows look out on San Francisco Bay and the city across it wearing a cloak of fog.

My grandmother is an heiress to a Dutch shipping company, and thanks to her my parents (who used to not believe in things like health insurance) were able to pay for my medical bills for so many years. On this day, we'd come to her house for the sort of obligatory visit that means my mom needs some money.

In the time since she and my father split up ten years ago, my father has prospered as a sell-out advertising executive. He cut off his hair, shaved off his beard, bought a bunch of suits and ties, and started driving a BMW. He also stopped going by his hippie name, Ravi, and started going by his birth name, John, to newcomers in his life.

Meanwhile, my mother has clung stubbornly to her latter-day ideals, probably because it's easier that way. She can call herself a musician, artist, dancer, massage therapist, or yoga instructor—whatever she feels like being that week—and my grandmother will give her money to support her.

It's a pretty sweet deal, with the only catch that Lena has to show up and ingratiate herself to her mother, whom she hates. This is why I've come along, because Grandma de Graas doesn't get as mean when I'm around. A self-proclaimed in-valid, she feels a bond with me and my infirm body—or at least she did when I was alive.

And here's another weird thing—that Grandma de Graas has outlived me. Here in this wherever place, all I have to do is think of Grandma and I can see her in my mind's eye clear as if I were in the room with her, frail and wispy, tooling around her bedroom, getting assistance from her long-suffering nurse in and out of the wheelchair, and I realize that life makes no sense. There is no sense of balance or fairness, no universal force that makes good things happen to good people and bad things happen to bad.

If any assholes ever get their comeuppance, it's purely by accident. I know that for sure now.

Case in point: racist, arrogant, selfish, narcissistic, abusive Grandma de Graas, still alive and perversely happy as she has ever been. She doesn't donate money to charity (unless you count my mother—and you can't since their money exchanges are more about her exerting control over Lena than anything else) or do kind things for her neighbors or even have a fondness for animals. Far as I know, she mostly spreads unhappiness to whatever she touches. She lives a charmed life if I've ever seen one.

When we first moved to Marin County from the commune, we stayed here, at her house, for several weeks while we looked for a place of our own. I remember distinctly the smell of the house back then, a scent of ocean air mixed with expensive wood and the orange oil a silent, brown-skinned maid named Lupe used when she cleaned the furniture.

For most of our stay, Asha, Rachel, and I played outside in the gardens, careful to heed our mother's warning not to disturb Grandmother by being noisy in the house. Our grandfather had already been long dead by then, having suffered a massive heart attack at the age of forty, so Grandmother de Graas was unaccustomed to noise or even people in the house. So said Lena.

Outside, we concocted elaborate games and scenarios, pretending we were a group of princesses lost in a garden, or that we'd been shipwrecked and were exploring the grounds of an abandoned but haunted castle. Forced to play together in unfamiliar circumstances, we three sisters were capable of being the best of playmates.

Not until the end of our stay, when a rainstorm forced us indoors, did we finally get a taste of our grandmother's true nature. Asha, who was maybe four years old, accidentally bumped a table in the foyer and sent a fancy white vase crashing to the ground. Standing a few feet away, I remember watching as the shards of porcelain scattered, pelting my feet.

From the next room, Grandmother came to survey the damage, her dry lips pressed into a thin line. "You stupid, stupid girl," she said to Asha, who was on the verge of tears. "Get out of this house right now."

Our grandmother pointed to the front door, and Asha glared at her, astonished. It was pouring rain outside, cold, gray, not the sort of weather any sane person would banish a four-year-old into. We had never experienced anything like this in our young lives, and we were frozen, unsure whether such a demand was meant to be taken seriously.

"I'll clean it up," Rachel said. "Don't make her go outside." Until now she'd been the silent bystander, although it had been her game of leapfrog that had sent Asha careening into the table in the first place.

"All of you, outside now!" Our grandmother continued pointing at the door, her posture alone enough to convince us she wasn't joking.

So I took Asha's hand in mine and we went, shuffling one by one out onto the front entryway, which had a shallow overhang that provided almost no shelter from the slanting rain. Rachel was the last to exit, and she was unable to resist slamming the door behind her.

There we stayed, huddled against each other, teeth chattering until our father found us after what felt like hours but was probably not so long. He insisted we leave Grandmother's house that night, and we did. I've never stayed here again since, nor have I ever wanted to.

But that was years ago, before Lena and Ravi divorced, and before Lena discovered that her mother was our only reliable means of financial support.

So the last day that we visited her, I found myself sitting at her sleek, expensive teakwood dining-room table, staring out at the bay through the window, while my mother spoke in hushed tones to Grandma in the next room.

This was the drill. I had to stay out of things unless Grandma started getting angry. Lena didn't like being seen groveling.

I was thinking about David (the love of my short life), wondering if he was out of his printmaking class yet, about to get out my phone and send him a text, when my grandmother wheeled into the room. I wondered for a moment if she'd finally gotten fed up with my mother and pushed her off the balcony, but I later learned that Lena had, at the last second, decided to tell my grandmother that I was the reason she needed money this time.

It wasn't exactly a lie. I had outlived everyone's expectations, and my parents now found that their oldest daughter was about to go on to college after taking a year off from school to save some money, and they hadn't bothered creating a college fund for me since I was supposed to die anyway. I'd gotten an acceptance letter from UC Santa Cruz the day before, and it had prompted me to ask my mother if she'd be able to help me pay for school.

This simple question had sent her to bed in tears for the rest of the day, claiming she had a migraine. This was how Lena dealt with most problems. She wasn't cut out for life off the commune, or life as the mother of a child with leukemia, or life in general.

"So," my grandmother said to me in her slight Dutch accent, "you have defied all the odds and are going on to college. What a wonderful thing."

"I got accepted to three schools so far," I said, adopting the pleasant, deferent tone I always used with her.

"Your mother tells me you still want to be a nurse."

I nodded.

"Why not a doctor?"

People had never asked me questions like this before now—what do you want to be when you grow up? Being known as the Kid Who Has Cancer was, for a long time, my lot in life, and even when it wasn't, people still tiptoed around me, as if the shadow of death lingered near.

"I want to help people in a hands-on way." This was my simple, standard answer. I'd never had to try hard to make good grades in school, so perhaps my grandmother thought I should strive for the greatest academic challenge. Or maybe she was just being contrary.

She gave a curt nod. "You're too pretty to be a doctor anyway. No one could take you seriously."

I knew better than to react to this. Lena relied on me as the one who didn't let Grandma push her buttons.

"How are you feeling? Still sore from your fall?"

I didn't realize it at the time, but looking back, I can see that this was my subtle way of getting her back. While

Grandma loved to talk about her ailments, anyone else's bringing them up always made her feel weak and vulnerable. I watched her shrink back into her chair a bit, looking tired. Then I felt bad for my spite.

"No need to discuss an old woman's frailties," she surprised me by saying. "The more important matter is this issue of your college education. How do you intend to pay for it?"

"I'll work, I guess, and get college loans."

"And your father? Is he going to help?"

I hadn't been speaking to Ravi lately, not since I'd seen him walking down the street holding hands with a girl who looked to be about four years older than me at most.

"I'm not depending on it," I said, though I would likely ask him for help eventually, once I'd decided for sure which school to attend. He wasn't comfortable with loose ends.

"I'll be very upset if I pay for your education and you go and die before you get to use it."

I hadn't been expecting such a backhanded comment, and I sat there stunned, unsure what to say. How great did the risk of my cancer's relapsing have to be before I wasn't worth spending college-tuition money on?

Part of me wanted to stand up and leave, tell her to stick her money up her ass, but I knew the real reason we were there wasn't just about college money. It was about my mother needing money to pay the rent, and if I blew it now, we'd spend the next month eating nothing but ramen noodles and avoiding angry calls from the landlord.

Also, because this often meant my middle sister, Rachel, and I coughing up our own money to pay for food and other essentials, I was doubly motivated.

"I'll try my best not to die," I said evenly, meeting her eye and almost smiling as I said it.

Satisfied with that, she nodded and wheeled herself back out of the room. A minute later, I could hear her and Lena talking again in hushed tones, probably haggling over the amount of the check Grandma was writing.

Because no one was yelling or slamming doors, I knew this visit had been a success.

I got out my cell phone and began composing a text to David: *R u free?* I typed, then hit send.

I used to think I wanted to be a doctor, but the more time I spent in hospitals, the more I saw that the people who made a difference were the nurses. A few of those who'd helped me over the years were my heroes, angels who'd swooped in and offered soothing words and gentle touches when I'd been in the worst pain of my life.

I wanted to be one of them. When I was younger and still believed in God with a capital *G,* it was partly because I thought if I was a good enough person, maybe God would let me stay alive longer. Maybe he or she or it would make the cancer go away for good. I used to think we had to bargain our way through the world, trading good deeds for good luck, but now I know it's not that way at all.

I spent my whole life trying so hard to be good, and in the end it didn't matter.

My cell phone chirped to let me know that David had texted me back. I looked at the message: *We r all free*—his little bit of phonetically spelled philosophy.

I wished I could be as hopeful as he was, but I wasn't. I could hear Lena and Grandma de Graas still murmuring in the next room, two people bound by love and hate, tangled in family ties. Just like my sisters and me. Just like all of us.

And here I am now, where we are supposed to be truly free (or at least that's what we assume about death, don't we?), still bound to the people I left behind.

Ten

Rachel

I have spent most of my life rolling my eyes at the spiritual-seeking crap that surrounds us in Marin County. Meditation and chakras and all that.

But when I am sitting in the dining room of the meditation center with Krishna, and I look around at the people smiling and talking, I feel kind of curious about them. Like, who are they and why the hell are they here and not at the mall?

I stand in line and get a plate of food, then take a seat at a table where some other hippies are already sitting and talking. Krishna tells me he will be right back.

The scent of incense and curry are heavy in the air, which is probably a good thing since I doubt any of these people wear deodorant. I pretend to be interested in my food, take a few bites, stir it around.

"Are you enjoying the feast?" Krishna asks as he sits down beside me.

Why do vegetarians always call it a feast? It's not like any-one's roasted a goddamn pig or anything.

"Yeah, it's good. Thanks." The lentil stew is heavy on the spice and coconut milk, and it's served over the ever-present brown rice. But it's okay. It's the first thing I've eaten since Sarah's death that I think I've sort of tasted.

"What did you think of the meditation session?" he asks.

I would like to say it was stupid, that I got nothing out of sitting for a half hour trying not to think, but I feel . . . the opposite of that. Ever since the session ended, I've felt this sort of crazy calm, like I've been drugged.

"It was hard to do . . . but I liked it."

"Monkey mind. We all struggle with it. It's a term to de-scribe how our mind always wants to jump from thought to thought. We handle it by simply noticing when the mind starts to wander and gently returning to our focus on the mantra."

I can't believe I am seriously having a conversation with someone about meditating and mantras. Part of me wants to laugh, and part of me is just here.

Being.

I feel sort of good and not panicky for the first time in a long time.

"I'll try to remember that," I say.

"Does that mean you might join us again sometime?" he says with a little smile.

He is so freaking gorgeous, I'd probably agree to celibacy for the next year if I thought it might eventually lead to some-thing with him, but the way he asks me the question, it's not like he's trying to sell me on Buddhism or get in my pants. It's like he genuinely wants to know.

"I think so," I say, surprising myself.

"I'd like that. Would you like a tour of the center?"

I say I would, and we carry our dishes to the kitchen where we each wash and dry our stuff and put it all back in the cabinets like good little pseudo-Buddhists.

Then he leads me out of the dining room into the main entry area and through the front door. From there we head down a path that passes the parking lot and goes off into an open field dotted with boulders, trees, and cows. We are walking into a postcard of Marin.

"This is one of the paths where we do walking meditation," he says as he walks beside me. "It's a style of meditation that you can employ anywhere, but it helps if it's a quiet place, free of distraction."

"How did you end up here?" I ask him, genuinely curious.

He smiles, and my stomach does a flip. "I wasn't always disciplined about my spiritual path. I told you about my heroin-addict days. When I got clean, I knew I had to do something drastically different. I'd been a Buddhist since my teens but not serious about it, and then I signed up for a weekend meditation workshop here, and the rest is history."

"And now you run the place and never have sex?"

He laughs. "No, I'm just a resident instructor. My celibacy is part of my own self-directed spiritual path."

I say nothing because I feel stupid for bringing up his lack of a sex life now. Something about him is so serene, so open and genuine, it wipes away all my crap. He's not like anyone else I've ever met, and because I know we can't have sex, I kind of just want to observe him and see what kind of magic he has that might rub off on me.

We wander along the path and take a short walk back toward the main buildings. He shows me the dorm areas, the campground, and the main offices. We end up back at the main entrance where we started.

My gaze lands on a job-notice flyer sitting on the front counter.

"I don't suppose you're looking for work?" he says.

The flyer says they have an opening for a full-time front-desk receptionist. I don't know what to say. Could I be a receptionist, smiling and answering phones and being nice to neurotic rich people and hippies all day?

It is so far from my idea of the job I belong in, I almost laugh, but something about Krishna makes me not want to hurt his feelings, so I don't.

"Hmm, I don't really have any experience other than serving coffee."

He smiles. "Well, think about it and let me know if you decide you're interested. I have a feeling it would be a good fit for you."

I don't know what to say to this, so I say nothing. Part of me is flattered he wants to give me a job, and part of me is trying to imagine my future.

"What are your plans now that you've finished high school?" He leads me toward the meditation room where we spent a half hour before dinner sitting silently with our eyes closed.

It seems like an odd question for a Buddhist monk. Aren't they supposed to be all about the present moment? What does he care about my future?

But why don't *I* care? That's the bigger question. I think of Sarah, the hike, and everything that went so wrong so fast, and I know I don't believe I deserve to be planning for a future now.

"I don't know," I say, wishing I had a better answer.

We are alone in the meditation room now, and he sits down on a cushion and invites me to sit on one opposite him. In all my vast life experience, this is the part where we get naked and screw each other's brains out, and I would definitely go there with Krishna, but I am sure now that's not what he has in mind for me.

I feel the wall that I always have up between me and the rest of the world crumbling down, brick by brick.

The room is so quiet, in spite of the people still milling about the center outside the door. Early evening light comes through the large windows that line one wall and reflects off the shiny wood floor. Something about that light makes my chest ache like I just got some shitty news.

"Have you ever looked at someone and known they have an important purpose in your life?"

"No," I say without thinking about it. Then I think of the way I so easily went with Krishna and came out to this place, not a single eye roll the entire time, and I consider changing my answer.

But before I can, he says, "I saw you on the sidewalk, and I didn't know what sort of tragedy you were experiencing, but I knew I was supposed to stop and talk to you."

"You mean like little voices told you so?"

He smiles a Jesusy sort of smile. "Not exactly, no. One thing meditation does for me is it helps me listen to my inner voice. Whether you call that voice God or your subconscious or the universe or whatever, it's the part of us that speaks the truth."

If I didn't know better, I would think this guy was so full of bullshit we should be drowning in it right now, but Krishna . . . I don't know.

He's different.

For once in my life I just trust him without questioning it too damn much.

"Why me?"

"I don't know yet, but the more we've talked, the more I've become sure we are supposed to help each other. Maybe I'm supposed to help you, maybe you're supposed to help me, I don't know that part yet. But I think you might make a good receptionist for the time being," he says with a full-on grin now.

"When you asked about my future plans, I'm not sure because I don't really want to go to college, at least not yet. And I guess I always thought I'd become like . . ." I feel stupid saying the next part but want to tell him the whole truth. "Like a model or something, some kind of celebrity on TV."

"It's the dream of our generation," he says without any sarcasm, and I'm grateful he doesn't make fun of me.

"Do you want to know the whole truth?"

He nods.

"Before my sister died, when I wasn't working at the coffee shop, I spent all day taking photos of myself to post on Instagram, and putting videos on YouTube, and, you know, that kind of stuff."

"What kind of stuff?"

"Like sexy stuff. Wannabe-porn-star stuff, I guess."

"Is that what you want to be?"

"No," I say, surprised the answer comes out so easily. "It's just, I don't have any talent besides looking hot."

"I don't believe that."

"It's true." I look off to the side, out the window where a row of redwood trees rustle in the wind.

"Maybe you need to give yourself a chance to find out what else you're good at, what else you like to do."

"Maybe," but I can't think of what I'd do. "I like to dance, but I'm not good enough to get into music videos or anything."

I might be able to get myself a job swinging on a dance pole, I think, but don't say it out loud. The only thing that's stopped me from doing that yet is the lack of reliable transportation I have into the city, where all the strip clubs are.

For some reason, I want Krishna to think I'm not as awful as I am, but I also want him to know the truth. It's an impossible freaking balance to strike.

"What about your little sister? Do you think maybe she could use your help?"

"What does she have to do with this?"

"Sometimes the good we have to offer the world is most easily found in what we can do for the people around us."

"She hates me," I say, but I realize instantly that it's not true. Asha maybe doesn't hate me so much as she just puts up with me.

"Why does she?"

"Well, mostly, I haven't been so nice to her." Or to anyone. "Nice hasn't really been my style."

"Do you think you might be able to change her mind about you?"

What I think is, Asha is the least of my worries. She is not the sister making my life beyond miserable right now. Sarah is the one I have to worry about. Now that she's gone, it's as if my relationship with her—and her death—are the only things that matter.

I used to think that if I could just show the world how Sarah wasn't as perfect as everyone thought, then I'd be happy. Then life would be fair. But now I have all the dirt on her. Now I know just how imperfect she is, and I can't tell anyone. Telling her ugly secrets now would mean leaving out everything I did wrong.

My legs are starting to ache sitting in this cross-legged meditation position again, and I don't want to talk about Asha anymore. I shrug and give a little who-knows smile, hoping that's enough answer for him.

"Can I tell you something else?" I say.

"Sure, anything."

"Remember how I told you my sister died?"

He nods.

"I was there when it happened."

I don't say the rest. I don't tell him *my* big ugly secret—that I am the reason she is dead, or Sarah's secret, which I'm afraid would pale in comparison to mine. That stuff, I can't say aloud.

I'm not sure I ever will.

He stares at me with this crazy intensity that makes me think I'm going to burst into flames, but he seems to be waiting for me to continue.

I don't.

"That's why I had to stop and talk to you on the sidewalk," he finally says.

"It is?"

"You're carrying a burden too heavy for one person to bear."

I say nothing to that, not sure what the hell to say.

"But we can't solve the world's problems in a day, and you're probably wondering if I'm ever going to give you a ride home, right?"

I smile and stretch my legs. "Yeah, sort of."

"Let's get going then." He stands up and extends a hand to me.

I take his hand and stand up myself, feeling warm at the physical contact with him, but then I feel stupid, because, of course, it's not like we're ever going to get naked together.

Unless I can change his mind about that celibacy thing. But as I walk out to the beat-up, old Toyota with him, I realize that's not exactly what I want to do. Instead, I think I want Krishna to stay just as he is—not quite like any other guy I've ever met.

Maybe someday I could tell him the whole ugly truth about Sarah's death, and he might not hate me for it. He might just smile that Jesus smile and tell me everything has a purpose. Maybe he will tell me how to sleep through the night while remembering that kind of truth.

But I doubt it.

Eleven

Asha

Spring break comes and goes. I realized right away I couldn't stay in the park forever unless I want to spend all my time smelling bad and starving, so I went back home to the house where Sarah is not, where all the questions about her death that have no answers scream at me. Home, 414 Redwood Way, has a gaping, empty space where my sister should be, and that space threatens to swallow me up, the closer I get to it. I stay in bed for the entire week trying not to get swallowed while most people my age are living it up. I try to read, but I can't focus. I hear nothing from Sin, and I want to die.

Thoughts of Tristan, and that kiss, alternately torture and entertain me. I can focus for a minute maybe on how it felt to have his mouth on me, his hand traveling up my thigh, but then thoughts of Sin and his anger always interfere, and I've decided it's better to just put the whole thing out of my head as much as I can.

I also try not to think about Sarah, and what we would be

doing if she were around on this day or that day or the next day. I mostly fail.

Lena hassles me to get out of bed, to help her with things. I refuse, and she flips out, and then she either goes to bed too or she leaves and goes to her boyfriend Ron's house, where she is spending more and more time these days.

Rachel and I usually have a strict policy of not talking and staying the hell away from each other, but near the end of spring break, she passes my door, sees me lying in bed, and stops.

She looks like she's about to say something, but instead she just crosses her arms over her chest and leans against the doorframe, staring at me as if I were a strange bit of flotsam that had washed up on the beach.

"What?"

"You can't stay in bed forever," she points out, as if this is somehow a helpful piece of news.

"Actually, I can."

To this, she says nothing. Just keeps staring.

I consider telling her to go away, but it would take too much energy and would probably have the opposite effect of what I want.

I close my eyes, and a memory surfaces, one of Rachel taking care of me after the bone-marrow donation. I was in bed, achy and exhausted, while Lena and Ravi were at the hospital with Sarah. So we were home alone together, and it was probably Rachel's first time having to take care of someone else. She seemed to be enjoying the responsibility, which surprised me even back then.

I remember her bringing Lena's laptop into the room, since we didn't own a television, and looking up online games for us to play while we sat side by side in bed. And she read to me from *A Wrinkle in Time* until it started giving me a headache. Then she went downstairs and came up a half hour later with a tray that held a bowl of soup and a cup of hot tea. The soup, a strange concoction of brown broth and floating food objects that she'd made from scratch herself, tasted so salty I gagged at the first mouthful.

But when Rachel looked hurt, I made up some lie about its going down the wrong pipe and forced myself to eat the whole bowl, claiming it was delicious. I got a horrible stomachache after, but it was worth it to have a night of Rachel and me getting along.

Nowadays, if Rachel brought me soup, I'd have to worry that she'd spit in it, or worse.

Without a word, she finally disappears from my doorway, leaving me to wonder what, if anything, she had to say.

The Monday after spring break, I go back to school but wonder why I've bothered to show up at all. My attendance has been spotty for the past month since Sarah died—a few days in school here and there, zombielike, and the rest not. My sister is still dead. This must be worth at least a couple more weeks of skipping classes. Maybe the rest of the semester.

But Lena has launched a campaign to get me into therapy, so now I'm doing whatever I can to stay away from home. I don't want to face Lena now, or Rachel, or a therapist, or any more reminders that Sarah isn't here or there or anywhere.

I realize, when I sit down in first period, I am hoping Sin will be here and acting normal again. I'm hoping he'll just pretend that horrible day of the funeral never happened, and if he does, then maybe I'll feel okay enough to go home and take a shower and sleep in my own bed.

Last night, after a fight with Lena over the Therapy Issue, I slept in the park in my sleeping bag again. I woke up with a bunch of dried-up redwood leaves tangled in my hair and a couple of itchy, red bug bites on my arm. I look like hell—I know because I checked in the girls' restroom a few minutes ago—and there wasn't much I could do to repair myself in the few minutes I had splashing water on my face and trying to untangle leaves from my hair.

I don't care what anyone thinks though.

Mostly.

The girl sitting next to me, Andy something or other, is looking me up and down. I can tell she wants to ask me something—what happened to you? Or, why do you look like such a wreck?—but she doesn't. She probably remembers about Sarah.

"Cool tattoo," she finally says.

I've forgotten about it. I should be washing it and putting lotion on it. It doesn't hurt anymore. I look down at the stars. My jeans are rolled up, though one pant leg is now longer than the other. For a moment, I hate the tattoo. It looks trendy, like something I'll regret when I'm old. I should have gotten something a little more timeless, I think. Maybe a dragon, or a bird.

But it's for Sarah, and there isn't anything more right for her, even if it is ridiculously trendy.

"Thanks," I say so quietly I'm not sure she can hear me.

Her attention slowly fades to the front of the room, where not much of anything is happening, just Mrs. Riggs shuffling through some papers. I sit through the first period in a stupor, and Sin never shows up. This isn't unusual for him, but I find myself staring at the door the entire time, willing him to appear.

Later, I wait at his locker, knowing his second-period class is geometry and he is beyond screwed if he fails it. He can't afford to miss another class, and sure enough, he comes ambling down the hallway toward me three minutes before he has to show.

I can tell by his expression though that nothing has changed. He doesn't look at me so much as he looks through me, intent on retrieving his geometry book from the locker I'm leaning on.

"Move," he says without even a hello.

"Are we ever going to talk about why you're mad at me?"

He half looks at me and rolls his eyes. "I don't have anything to say. Now move."

I step aside, but I don't leave. I watch as he attempts his combination, screws it up, and tries again. He gets the numbers wrong a second time.

"It's four, ten, seven." I can remember his combination better than my own.

He sighs heavily. Drama queen, I want to say, but I can't. I'm too afraid of pissing him off even more when I'm not even sure what's wrong.

I swallow my pride. "I'm sorry."

I need him, and he knows this. I'm not even sure I'll make it through the rest of the day without breaking down if he doesn't stop this and be nice to me again.

Still, he says nothing. He jerks his locker open so hard it almost hits me in the face, and I have to step back to avoid it.

This shocks me even more than his silent treatment, because Sin is not violent. He's not the hit-me-in-the-face-with-a-locker-door type. Throwing my sandals at me the day of the funeral was the most aggressive thing I've ever seen him do.

Without saying a word, he grabs his books, slams his locker shut, and walks away.

I watch his thin shoulders, covered in a black cotton cardigan that I'm pretty sure belongs to me, moving as he walks. He moves like a cat, stalking down the hall in a way that's half-natural and half-practiced.

He's wearing his dark brown hair free of product today, overgrown and shaggy. Not really a hairstyle at all. It suits him. With his hair unstyled, he looks a lot like Tristan, only smaller and more tense, less numb to the world.

What does he think of me? That I'm fake? A user? That I'll just take advantage of whoever is nearby to distract myself from real life?

Maybe he's right.

I grapple with this as I head in the opposite direction. The bell rings, marking me late for art class. The teacher won't care though. She rarely arrives on time, and we're all supposed to retrieve the previous day's work and get started on it when we get to class.

I enter the large classroom, and someone throws a paper airplane that narrowly misses my cheek as I make my way around tables toward the drawing rack.

I thumb through until I see a paper covered in black pencil lines. The effect is a nearly solid black page, with only the slightest hints of white peeking through. I'm not sure where I'm going with this, but I have a feeling some heavy erasing is going to take place soon.

I'd originally intended to call the piece *Night Sky* and leave it black, but I've tired of that idea. It seems cliché and lazy.

I turn to head toward my table, and it strikes me that I just can't do this. I'm surrounded by kids I know. Happy, sullen, belligerent, dazed—they are every kind of kid, and I don't want to see any of them. I don't know why I'm here. I don't know why I thought I could do this.

So I put away my crappy work in progress, and I walk back out the door. I keep going and going until I am off campus, free again, with no idea where to go or what to do.

Back to my sleeping bag in the park? Back home to battle Lena's agenda?

I don't know, I don't know, I don't know.

I wear my trousers rolled.

And I suffer the same malaise of spirit that we read about earlier this year in T. S. Eliot's "Prufrock" poem. I may not have understood most of it, but this feeling, I got that much.

I am walking toward the park, hungry and wishing I had some money to get a burger, when a silver car pulls up beside me. I look over to see Ravi, my so-called father, with his window rolled down. I haven't seen him since the funeral, and that event is fuzzy in my memory, but I'm pretty sure the barely-a-beard he's sporting is a new look.

"Shouldn't you be in school right now?" he says with a half smile.

He doesn't much believe in formal education, so I know he's not concerned about my skipping class, but still I feel a surge of panic that he might make me go back.

"I left early, citing emotional issues," I lie, as if I actually consulted someone before walking out the door.

"I've been meaning to talk to you. Would you like to go somewhere for lunch?"

Although the thought of having a heart-to-heart with dear old Ravi doesn't thrill me, I am hungry enough to nod and get in the car. I haven't eaten more than a few bites at a time in days, I think, and my body is finally telling me that's not going to fly.

Without my even asking, he drives us to my favorite burger joint on the edge of town, where I order a double cheeseburger, large fries, and a large chocolate milk shake. While we wait for the food, we go sit outside at one of the tables that's shaded by a red umbrella.

Ravi, I notice, is not wearing the thin leather bracelet he has worn for as long as I can remember, a gift his own father gave him before he died. "Where's your bracelet?"

He looks down at his wrist, then back up at me, surprised. "You remember that?"

I nod, and my stomach growls at the scent of fried food wafting past us in the breeze.

"I lost it a few months ago." The two lines that form between his eyebrows are the only indication of how much I know this saddens him.

"I'm sorry."

"I guess it's a lesson not to cling to anything, right?"

Except people, I think. We are supposed to cling to people. I look away, watching a familiar VW van painted to look like van Gogh's *Starry Night* as it heads toward town.

"What is it?" he asks when I say nothing.

"Maybe not things, but people. We need people."

"Yes. The trouble is, our expectations get in the way of appreciating what they have to offer."

I feel like screaming at him because I think he is talking about us. Our family. How our expectations of him to behave like an actual adult, like our dad, are just too much for him. But I want to stick around long enough to get my cheeseburger, so I try as best I can to sit there and not say anything.

"I get the feeling this little chat isn't going so well," he says with his crooked smile.

I shrug.

He cocks his head to the side, and his smile vanishes. "As hard as Sarah's death is on me and your mother . . ." He pauses, trying to steady his shaky voice. "I think it might be harder on you. I'm worried about you, Asha."

"Don't be. I'm fine."

"You don't look fine. You look like a homeless kid on drugs. *Are* you doing any drugs?"

"What do you care? You wouldn't want me to go and have any expectations of you to take care of your family, now would you?"

He winces at that, and I know I've hit him where it hurts most. I didn't exactly mean to, or maybe I did, but as soon as the words are out of my mouth, I wish I could take them back.

"That's not what I meant about expectations," he says carefully.

Our number, fourteen, is called over the loudspeaker, so Ravi gets up and goes inside for our food. When he comes back out carrying a tray of burgers, fries, and shakes, I am less hungry than I was before. Thinking about Sarah leaves me with a giant feeling of soul-deep emptiness that obliterates hunger.

Ravi places my food in front of me, and I stare down at it.

Slowly, I unwrap the burger and dump the fries on the make-shift paper plate created by the burger wrapper. Then I poke my straw into the lid on the shake and take a drink. I focus on the food in front of me, force Sarah out of my thoughts, one mouthful of chocolate shake at a time.

"I want you to know I am sorry if I've left you with the feeling that I don't want to be your dad."

"You didn't even *want* kids."

"Is that what your mother told you?"

I shrug and take a bite of my burger. It is huge and un-wieldy, cheese and tomato and lettuce and special sauce squeezing out every which way.

"I've wanted and loved each of you, Asha. I promise you that," Ravi says, all serious now. "Whatever fears I had as a young man, worrying about losing my freedom, they vanished the moment I held Sarah in my arms."

I stare hard at my fries, getting serious about selecting the perfect one to eat next. Not Sarah, not thinking about her.

"And when Rachel was born, and then you, I was thrilled each time. The days of your births were the best days of my life. I can't imagine what kind of shitbag I would have become if I hadn't had my three girls." He falters on those last two words, and I know he is thinking there are only two girls now.

Only two.

I blink and blink and blink. A wind is coming from the coast, drying out my eyes, thank God.

"Are you going to eat that?" I nod to his fries because mine are gone as if I have sucked them up in one giant inhalation.

He pushes them toward me, and I pick one up.

"How's your sister?"

"Which one?"

He gives me a dark look, and I leave it alone. "Rachel is Rachel."

"Rachel is the one I worry about most."

I don't worry about Rachel. She is like the serpent in the Garden of Eden, perfectly fine watching the destruction all around her.

Ravi's cell phone beeps, and he looks at it and mutters a curse. "I have to take a business call in ten minutes. I'd better get home so I can be at my computer for it."

"Thanks for lunch."

"Will you be okay walking home?"

"Sure."

"Call me if you need anything? I mean it."

"Okay."

"I'm serious, Ash," he says, putting his hand on the back of my head and looking into my eyes the way he used to when I was little. "We need each now more than ever. Call me, night or day. I will always answer, even if it's three in the morning."

I endure his hug, then watch him go, simultaneously relieved and not quite ready for him to leave. I hadn't gotten comfortable enough with Ravi in that short time to say much of anything that mattered. But what would I have said?

That I wake up at night wondering why anything matters at all? That I don't know who I am anymore if I'm not Sarah's sister? That I am not as good as she was, and I don't matter as much as she did, so it makes no sense for her to be gone and not me?

I know I wouldn't have said any of that, no matter how long he'd stayed. We are not that kind of father and daughter.

We are the kind who bump into each other on the street, have lunch, and part ways again, off to our separate lives. Me to my new home in a sleeping bag at the park, him to his A-frame, hillside bachelor cottage, free of the messiness of a family. From his living-room window, he can see for miles, nearly the entire town laid out below, but he can't see our old house, the one where we still live and he doesn't.

I have only been to his new house once since he moved back to Marin, but I wondered, did he choose that view on purpose?

Twelve

Asha

I am lying in the park again, in the shade of a towering red-wood grove, reading a five-year-old *People* magazine I found on a bench, learning all about Brad and Angelina's parenting skills, when someone plops down beside me.

I look up and find Sin. It's after three, so he must be on his way home from school.

"You're not sleeping here, are you?"

My first reaction is relief, but then I realize he still sounds mad at me. "Yeah, I am."

"That's why your hair looks so jacked-up."

"Yeah."

"You can't keep sleeping here. Something bad could happen."

I laugh at this. "What bad stuff could happen? Could my best friend hate me? Could my sister die? Could my life be fucked?"

"You know what I mean."

"Whatever." Turns out, Brad and Angelina's French château is a mess from all those kids running around trashing it and no one cleaning up after them.

"It's going to rain any day now."

"I don't care."

"I know you don't, but I do."

Relief floods my chest, and for a moment I can hardly breathe, I'm so happy. "I thought you hated me," I say, pretending to still be reading the magazine.

He grabs it and tosses it aside, so I roll off my stomach and sit up to face him.

"You have to stay away from Tristan." He looks at me all serious, like he means it.

I feel my cheeks flush because this is the first time we've discussed this Tristan thing, and I feel like I've been dishonest. Except I don't think I have been. Not exactly, anyway.

"Why'd you get so mad?" I finally dare to ask.

"He's a user, Asha. He doesn't care about you. He'll screw you and toss you aside like a piece of garbage. Is that the kind of thing you want?"

I'm insulted, but I have to choose my words carefully because Sin is talking to me and I don't want him to stop again.

"I don't want anything. It was just a stupid kiss. I was drunk, and sad, and there he was, wanting to kiss me. That's all."

Okay, so now I'm being dishonest. I'm being a big, fat, shitty liar. I want to stop but I can't. The truth doesn't seem worth telling.

"I know you think he's hot, Asha. I'm not stupid. Girls dig him, but I thought you were smart enough to just leave it at that."

"Whatever. I am. I mean, it's like I said . . ."

"Look, I'm sorry I passed out and left you alone, and got pissed off and threw your sandals, and slammed the locker in your face."

"Thanks." I study a blade of grass resting on my fingertips.

"You can stay with me. No more sleeping in the park, okay?"

"Your mom won't mind?"

"She probably won't notice, but if she does, she won't care."

I wonder if Tristan will notice or care.

"Listen. You have to promise to stay away from my brother though, okay? I can't be your friend unless you leave him alone. He's too skanky for you. And too old."

I wasn't expecting such harsh conditions, and this catches me by surprise. Sin's acting like he owns me or some shit? Telling me I have to choose between him and Tristan?

Stunned, I just nod. Then finally I choke out an "Okay."

Normally, leaving Tristan alone is never an issue, since he doesn't acknowledge I exist. But now that he has, now that we've kissed and been naked together, will he go back to ignoring me? I guess I'm about to find out because Sin grabs my hand and tugs me up off the ground, toward my impending doom.

Thirteen

Sarah

Memory is that trick by which we see the awful events of the past loom over the good, like mountains over mice. We don't recall life as it was. Instead, we remember what was different, frightening, or strange, and we turn our lives into fun-house mirror images of the truth.

Now though, I see what was lost.

I see what I've lost with such a stark, painful clarity, I can hardly grasp it.

We weren't always the family with the divorced parents and the screwed-up, broken sisters. We were once each parts of a whole. We fit together like puzzle pieces still fresh from the box, our crisp edges unmarred by time and neglect.

Consider the sort of picture we made, a beautiful family, not yet haunted by the specter of a sick child or the many small disappointments of life.

I felt the most hopeful the year we left the commune. When it became clear their guru would be leaving the country, Ravi and Lena decided to cut out sooner rather than later. With our wealthy grandmother in Marin County, and many former members of the ranch moving there, that seemed the most promising place to call our new home.

For a few years, life was kind of storybook nice. Or at least it seemed that way when I looked back on it.

I was almost ten years old when I got my first cancer diagnosis: acute lymphoblastic leukemia, or ALL for short. The symptoms had started with my feeling tired a lot, getting strange bruises that I couldn't remember a cause for, some of which my teacher saw and reported to the school nurse, suspecting I was being physically abused by someone. I remember their asking me if anyone hit or hurt me, promising I wouldn't get in trouble if the answer was yes.

If only it had been that simple.

So that is what I remember about fourth grade: missing the last three months of it, doing homework from a hospital bed, a strange visiting teacher named Ms. Rusk, who had sour breath and dark red hair cut too short for her round, fleshy face.

It had been, oddly enough, Grandma de Graas who insisted my parents take me to a real doctor and not the naturopath they used for allergies and colds and stomachaches. We went to a pediatrician in Corte Madera, who made me—a stranger to needles back then—cry by drawing blood into a syringe. Days later, she called and referred us to an oncologist.

When my parents told me what kind of doctor we had to see next, their expressions grave, I misheard them and thought they were taking me to a doctor for uncles. But I'm not an uncle, I almost pointed out, until my mother's dark gaze silenced me.

It took me months to realize that *oncologist* was just a fancy word for "cancer doctor" and that leukemia was the thing that would make my life take place for the next year in the slow motion that is illness and hospital beds.

I didn't respond well to treatment right away. Instead, I got sicker. The chemotherapy wasn't working; I had a bad form of ALL that required more aggressive treatment. The stuff people say to you when you are sick sounds oh so much worse when nothing is working. All the platitudes—you can fight this thing, you're going to come out on top, you can beat this, you're a winner—made it sound to me like I was playing an Olympic sport and not lying in bed watching cartoons and doing dumb worksheets assigned by Ms. Rusk.

Meanwhile, my parents' marriage was crumbling under the pressure of having a kid with ALL. Even then I knew it was my fault, though they insisted to us girls it wasn't anyone's fault.

But a few weeks after Ravi told us he was moving out of the house—that he and Lena needed to "explore other living situations" was how he said it—I did respond. It was as if my body had decided to fight my parents' divorce and was finally going to be victorious at something.

I'd undergone a bone-marrow transplant with Asha as my donor the month before, and according to the tests, I was finally cancer-free.

It had been almost a year since that first doctor visit.

My hair, only a few inches long and cut in a haphazard pixie do, would grow back, I was assured. In another few years I would have long hair again, and ridiculously this seemed like the best news of all.

Two years of occasional doctor visits to make sure I remained cancer-free passed before I got the news that cancer liked my body so much it had returned for a second stay. It's bad enough having cancer once, but twice? I had no symptoms and was halfway through eighth grade. So while my friends were looking forward to high school and hanging out with their first boyfriends, I was undergoing a second bone-marrow transplant.

The second round of stress was too much for Lena, who kind of stopped acting like a mother after that. From the haze of those years, I can now see just how dear a price we all paid for my life.

But what did I do with that life? Did I repay the family my cancer destroyed? Did I make the world a better place? Did I pass on my good fortune to those less fortunate than I?

None of the above.

I see the life I could have lived, the choices I could have made, laid out before me in my mind's eye, gleaming jewels on a table. And I see the ugly, rotting thing, the wasted life, I chose instead.

Fourteen

Asha

I wake up in Sin's bed, and it's dark outside, the gray-black darkness of just before dawn. I hear him breathing next to me, his warm body the only thing in the room that feels real at the moment while I'm still in a postdream haze.

I was just having a nightmare about Sarah. I've had them before, but in the others, she was alive, doing normal stuff, or talking to me, or whatever. They always feel like nightmares because then I wake up and have to remember all over again that she's gone.

In this one, I dreamed about her dying. I dreamed her cancer came back, and we all had to watch her waste away. But before she died, our mother decided she couldn't keep watching Sarah suffer and took her to a cliff and pushed her into the ocean.

In the dream, I was helpless to stop any of it. I could only watch from a distance, screaming for Lena to stop, with no sound coming from my throat. I tried to run toward them, but my feet wouldn't move.

Then I woke up.

I roll onto my side, scooting closer to Sin because it's cold in the room. My movement, or maybe my wakefulness, wakes him.

"Huh?" he says, as if I've said something.

I am so glad he's talking to me again. I successfully avoided Tristan all evening. It's been hell. I don't want to avoid him, but I can't go through another day of Sin's hating me.

"I didn't say anything," I whisper.

"Why aren't you asleep?"

"Nightmare."

"About what?"

"Sarah."

He is silent, waiting for further information, but I don't want to give it.

"What happened?"

I roll onto my back again and stare at the dark ceiling. Sin is facing me now, though since waking, he has adjusted himself so that no parts of our bodies touch. I wish he hadn't. I miss the warmth.

"She died," I say. "Lena pushed her off a cliff."

Silence again, then he finally says, "Freaky."

I am thinking about how it must have felt to fall. I almost can't think about it, but I have to. I can't let Sarah be in that awful place by herself. I have to feel it with her now, even if it's too late.

"I want to go to the place where she fell," I say. "I need to see it."

"We could bring flowers."

This is the best friend that I can't be without.

He thinks of things like this, in the middle of the night, without any help at all. And he says *we* when he could have just said *you*.

I shift my foot so that it's touching his. He doesn't move away.

"What if someone really did push her?" I say.

"That was just a nightmare. No one would push Sarah off a cliff. I'm sorry I ever said that might have happened."

"Something else doesn't make sense to me about that day." The idea forms in my head as the words come out.

"What?"

"Rachel. Why would Sarah have gone hiking with Rachel, of all people? Rachel never hikes."

"Did she ever say why they were together that day?"

My memory of the details surrounding that whole couple of weeks is fuzzy, like a nightmare I can only half remember. "I don't know."

"We'll ask her then."

"I guess."

"Maybe we should also talk to the people who saw Sarah last, find out what was going on that day."

"The police already talked to everyone."

"What about you? Weren't you one of the last people to see her alive?"

If only. I didn't have any significant last moments with Sarah. My last conversation with her, the last time I laid eyes on her, was the day before, a Friday afternoon after school. I'd told her we were out of vanilla soy milk, hoping she'd pick some up while she was out.

She'd said she was going to work, that she'd try to remember to buy some on her way home.

That was it, just one of those dumb, throwaway conversations.

"I didn't see her that day because I stayed overnight here, remember? By the time I went home, she was already gone."

"Was your mom around?"

"No. She was staying at her boyfriend's house."

"So Rachel's the one who knows all."

"I guess."

I'd already asked her about the day though. So had the police. And our parents.

No one doubted for a moment that Rachel was telling the truth. The police hear a story of two sisters hiking on the Marin coast and one falling, and the other one hurries to dial 911, gives a frantic report of her sister losing her footing, slipping off the trail, disappearing into the ocean below, no one questions it because people die by accident on that coast so often. Falling off trails, falling off rocks, or caught by sneaker waves. It's treacherous, and the ocean unforgiving.

Sarah was looking back at her to say something, Rachel had claimed. Didn't see the spot where the trail had eroded away. Fell before Rachel could even call out a warning.

So said Rachel, and so said the police report, swiftly wrapped up to spare our family any further grief.

So everyone believed.

But now, in this strange postdream haze, I can't imagine the scene my sister described ever having taken place.

Rachel would only get annoyed if I brought it all up again. But I had to. Maybe she'd recall some detail that she hadn't before.

What was I even hoping to learn?

The answer came to me, but I could never have said it out loud. I didn't believe Sarah fell by accident.

I just didn't believe it.

The idea took hold of me deep down, rendering me breathless. And if she hadn't fallen by accident . . .

The alternatives were unthinkable. I pushed the thoughts away.

"Can we go back to sleep now?" Sin says, yawning.

"Yeah, sorry."

"It's cold in here. Scoot over and warm me up."

He pulls me closer, tucks his body against mine, and I lie there wide-awake. His arm is draped over me. We have slept in the same bed plenty of times before, but never this close, never nested against each other like a pair of matching spoons.

I listen as he falls back to sleep, his breath slowing into a deeper, steadier rhythm, and try to summon some kind of pleasant thoughts I can fall asleep with, anything but thoughts of Sarah.

I think, what if Sin liked girls?

Fifteen

Asha

The next morning, Lena appears at Sin's house. I imagine she's gotten the calls from school that I haven't been showing up for classes, and she has apparently decided to play the responsible parent again. I am sitting at Sin's kitchen table eating a bowl of brown rice with milk and sugar. Sin is across from me doing the same. We aren't talking.

Tristan stumbled out the door a few minutes earlier without looking at us or saying good morning. Part of me is offended by this, and part of me relieved. I can't deal with him at all when Sin is around.

When I went to pee earlier this morning, he walked into the bathroom without knocking, just as I was pulling up my pants. He flashed a little half smile and said hi.

I tried to be all casual, not embarrassed, as I washed my hands.

"I've got a queen-size bed, if you ever get tired of sleeping in that twin."

Stunned, I didn't answer. Instead, I dried my hands in a hurry and left him there. If Sin had overheard that conversation, he'd never let me keep staying here, I thought at the time.

But now my mother is staring at me through the door, and I know it's all over.

"Aren't you going to let her in?" Sin says around a mouthful of rice.

"I thought you were."

Sin's own mother, Jess, never gets out of bed before eleven, and we're supposed to be extra quiet in the morning to keep from waking her. So when my mom lifts her fist to knock, which is kind of ridiculous since Sin and I both already see her, he jumps up from the table and opens the door for her.

"Hi, Lena."

"Hi, Sinclair. Do you realize you're harboring a wanted fugitive?"

Lena is wearing a pair of jeans I could never fit into, the expensive, skinny kind that hang in the windows of boutiques where I don't shop, the kind with $200 price tags. Probably a size two (my mom is thinner than I am, and this somehow seems wrong). Along with the jeans, she has on a green top that has all sorts of wraparound things happening and ties on one side, along with a pair of brown, high-heeled boots. Her hair is fresh from the salon, a lighter blond than what grows out of her head naturally, long and silky from probably some kind of chemical treatment.

She is a hippie only in spirit now, not appearance. This change has happened so fast I haven't even noticed it until now. I think she is trying to be upwardly mobile and wants to look the part. There isn't any other way to explain the way she looks now. If I didn't know she was broke, I'd also suspect from the lack of creases in her forehead that she'd been getting some Botox treatments. And yet, how could she afford the new outfit, or the salon hair?

Sin has slumped back into his chair.

My mother rounds the table to stand next to me. "Asha, I've been worried about you."

I don't believe her. Worry doesn't sound so calm, so rational. I savor the feel of her neglect. Poor me, no longer a useful daughter.

"I'm fine." I take my time scooping up the last few grains of rice floating in milk.

"You need to come with me now. You can't keep skipping school."

"I can't go back there. You can make an excuse for me. Tell them I'm still grieving."

She pulls out a chair and sits down next to me, placing a hand on my back. This is Lena being soulful, being real. Thinking if she can make physical and eye contact with me, she'll reach me.

This is when I notice a flash of sparkle on her other hand, the one resting on her lap. I look down and see a diamond ring there. It's a big one, a solitaire. On her ring finger.

"I don't want this to turn into a battle, darling."

"I don't either."

"Sin, could you give us a moment?"

Sin, a pro at dealing with my mother, ignores her and stares intently at his rice. I silently thank him for not leaving me alone. She glares at him for a moment, then gives up because she knows he has a stronger will than she does.

"I know this is the hardest thing our family has ever gone

through, but we need to stick together. We're going to scatter the ashes Sunday night, and I want you to be there."

This news comes to me as if she's kicked me in the chest. I am stunned and say nothing.

Scattering ashes. It can't be so. I am not going to scatter my sister in the wind.

"Asha, this will give you some closure. You need it, and I need my daughters there. This isn't easy for me either, you know."

"No. I'm not going."

Her lips get all thin. "Fine, if you're going to be a spoiled brat about it, I don't want you there ruining things the way you did at the funeral, but if you aren't going to be there, you *will* come to a therapy appointment with me next week."

"No way." I have been to mom's therapist exactly once. There will not be a repeat performance.

"This isn't up for debate, Asha. You can't keep staying here—you're going back to school, and you're coming home to sleep at our house tonight, and you're going to therapy with me. Do you understand?"

I think, if I relent on the school thing, which will at least be a distraction and will keep me from flunking out for the semester, she'll give in on the other two means of torture.

"I'll go to school. Just leave, okay?"

She sighs loudly. "Is that a real tattoo on your ankle?"

I ignore the question. I want to ask her about the ring she's wearing, but I'm afraid of the answer.

"That alone is reason enough not to let you stay here. You shouldn't be getting tattoos from your friends without my permission."

She knows about Sin's tattooing hobby from the tattoo of

a bluebird he put on his own foot. It's a beautiful piece, especially for someone with so little experience.

I say nothing. Her hand drops from my back. I look at her then because for a moment I wish I could bury my face in her chest and cry until her expensive new top is soaking wet. I want her to be the kind of mom who comforts me with kisses and cookies and commonsense advice, not therapy appointments.

"Our family is in crisis, Asha. It's not just you who's suffering. You should be home, not here."

She stands up, and I watch her leave. Something about her now is different, and it's not just the expensive clothes and the salon hair. She's walking with purpose, like she knows where she's going, for once.

Why couldn't she drag me out of here if it matters so much? Why couldn't she have showed up when I first disappeared?

Why now?

I'm wearing one of Sin's hoodies, a black one covered with little gray skulls. I tug it tighter around me, and I give him a look as my mom disappears out the door.

"Bye, Ms. Kinsey," Sin calls after her in an impressively genuine tone.

But she doesn't answer. She's gone, on her way somewhere more important than here.

Sixteen

Sarah

Love, my favorite four-letter word
And the official topic of all
Bad poetry
Do you know the difference
Between Love and lust?
Between Love and hate?
Between Love and death?
Have you ever felt the subtle twist of the knife
When one turns into the other?
It's a feeling that should need no past
Present or future tense
But tell that to the knife.

I am awake, but not Awake. Dreaming in slow motion.

I used to think that love could only be a good thing. I thought loving someone was like bestowing a gift upon them. And

I listened to all those love songs and believed them. Love is all we need, right?

It only occurred to me a few days before I died that maybe love wasn't such a wonderful gift. Maybe, sometimes, it was a curse, or a weapon, or an affliction, or all three.

Take my parents, for instance. If you met Lena and Ravi, you'd have a hard time believing they were once deeply in love. I only have a few early childhood memories to prove it. And you might not understand why they'd have had three kids. Ravi (aka John in his new and improved corporate, six-figure life) might point out that he never wanted children, and Lena, though she claims to love motherhood, is far more temperamental drama queen than nurturing maternal figure.

When you look around you though, really look, you start to see that all families are the crippled, imperfect by-products of our flawed attempts at love. Evolution created this weird chemical process to bind us together long enough to raise kids—in theory—and we in our infinite creativity decided to create a mythology around it. I see this now, and yet, I still don't understand it completely.

It still makes me ache.

Over the years, I pieced together the more or less complete story of my parents' falling in and out of love and having three daughters. It's a long, sordid tale, but these days I seem to have nothing but time to consider and reconsider the past.

And I like to think that having such a messy example at home is why I never quite got things right the one and only time I fell in love.

David was my first lover. We met at the bookstore where I worked two days a week after school. He was looking for a copy of the *Tao Te Ching* and I told him we were all out of stock. Crazy how well that little old book sells, I said.

He smiled at me and asked if I was interested in Eastern philosophy.

"My parents lived on a commune, so I kind of grew up with it." I shrugged.

"Really? Mine too. Which one?"

"The Peace Ranch." I already knew he wasn't a part of the same crowd because I'd have known him if he was.

"Cool. My mother was a follower of Osho."

So, there we had it, the common bond of growing up in the weird, upside-down world of a commune. And we talked for the rest of my shift, flirting, laughing, sizing each other up. I told him about my cancer, my family, and my lack of a boyfriend. He told me about how he'd graduated two years ago from a school in the city and was living with some friends, attending College of Marin part-time while he painted houses to earn a living. By the end of the night, I was dizzy from falling in love with him.

And even dizzier, probably, with the sensation of seeing myself through the eyes of someone who never knew me with cancer. To him, I was just the girl who worked in the bookstore. Every guy I'd ever known, to that point, had not seen me apart from my illness. I'd never had a real boyfriend before.

I didn't want anything from David. He's not the kind of guy you hook up with thinking forever or even next year. But then, I wasn't the kind of girl who needed long-term promises, given my slightly iffy health prospects. I just loved him in the pure, innocent way that is probably true of all first loves.

Funny how it works out though that when you expect

nothing from a person, they might just give you everything you didn't know you wanted. At least that's how it felt sometimes, when he'd show up at my house all excited because he'd written a song for me, or he'd spend hours braiding flowers into my hair and telling me a hundred ways he thought I was beautiful.

Really, I'm not making this stuff up. He was that sweet. And he did it all without the slightest bit of self-consciousness.

So I never saw it coming when he fell for my sister Rachel too.

Seventeen

Rachel

Sarah's urn, an ugly navy-blue thing with gold trim, has been sitting in our living room over the fireplace for weeks now. I find myself obsessing over the ashes. What do they look like? Will they smell bad? I sort of want to take a peek inside the urn and check it out, but I can't quite bring myself to do it.

Part of me imagines if I open the lid, her ghost will come seeping out of the bottle genie-style and spread the word about what an awful shitface of a sister I am.

We are supposed to take Sarah's ashes to the top of Mount Tam and scatter them, but Lena has been told this requires a permit. So, I guess we have to sneak and do it when no one is watching, because Lena doesn't believe in getting permits.

Also, she keeps saying we have to be united as a family when we do it. This is her go-to way for putting things off. Whenever Asha *is* around, she and our mother have these crazy fights like I've never seen. Asha's always been so whatever-I-don't-give-a-damn, it's hard to pick a fight with her, but Lena manages. My theory is the little donor-match sister reminds her too much of the dead daughter.

Everything reminds me too much of Sarah.

I'm not really mad at Asha anymore for showing up drunk at the memorial service. I kind of feel sorry for her since she is, after all, the one who's probably the most wrecked over Sarah's death. Even if I'm not sure she has the right to be.

Okay, I don't care if my stupid little sister has decided to live in the park with Barefoot Jack and the other local homeless and crazy, but it does make me curious. I imagine she's on a downward spiral, like we all are, but I don't think the parents realize how much closer she is to the edge than the rest of us. She loved Sarah more than anyone else did, and she's got to be taking her death the hardest.

You'd think any average parent could figure that out. But Lena, she's lost in her own world right now. She is taking the role of grieving mother seriously. She's been waiting a long time to play the role, ever since Sarah got her first cancer diagnosis all those years ago.

As I pass by the park on my way to David's house, I consider stopping and giving Asha a personal plea to come help spread the ashes. I think she'll want to be a part of it, even if she acts like she doesn't.

But she's not there now.

As I turn onto David's street, I see his car in the driveway of the house he shares with friends, and my stomach knots. It's been a long time since we've seen each other alone, and not just his stopping in to say hi while I'm working at Sacred Grounds, which he's started doing again lately. Problem is,

AJ stops in too when he's in town doing business, and if the two of them ever cross paths, some shit will go down.

I climb the front steps of his porch, and he must have seen me because he opens the door and comes out. "Hey, what a surprise."

He looks seriously fugly, his beard overgrown and his shirt off. He's wearing a drooping pair of jeans that stay up thanks only to a belt. His ribs and hip bones jut out in a way that isn't exactly attractive, reminding me of pictures of starving people in India.

He leans in for a hug, and I hug him back halfheartedly. When my sister disappeared over the edge of a cliff last month, whatever I felt for David went with her, I think. He just feels like a whole lot of nothing to me now.

I'm relieved when he doesn't try to kiss me.

"You doing okay?" he asks as we sit down on the front steps together.

"Yeah. You?"

"Not so much."

I nod and make a sad face. I guess I should be falling apart more—David and I united in our grief or some shit—but I can't muster the energy. I am remarkably calm, detached, waiting for some real emotions to come along.

I look away from David, at a house across the street, a run-down, blue cottage with faded Tibetan prayer flags hanging limp over the front porch.

"We're scattering her ashes Sunday night, around nine o'clock," I finally say when I feel enough time has passed.

He stares at a squirrel scurrying across the street.

"I could ask my mom if you can come along."

"That's okay. It's a family thing. I shouldn't be there."

"I don't think she'd care," I say, but I'm kind of relieved he said no.

Silence again.

When I'm about to change the subject to the reason I guess I've come, he says, "I went out to the spot. Where she fell. I did my own thing there . . . and scattered some flowers . . . you know."

"Oh. That's cool," I say lamely.

Some bitchy, little part of me feels jealous that he had this private moment for Sarah. And some part of me feels violated that he went there, to the spot that belongs to me and my own fucked-up feelings.

"I've been thinking . . ."

Before he can go on, I hold up my hand for him to stop talking. I have to be the one to say it. "I have too. I don't think we should see each other anymore."

I watch his face, not sure what I want to see there. Grief? Pain? Relief?

Love?

Shock.

Long, awkward-ass pause.

I look down at his hands, which are clasped a little tighter than they should be on his knees, as if he's holding on for dear life. Here is my evidence of strong emotion, and I'm satisfied to see it.

I realize now, I came here looking for something more than an end to this thing we've been doing. I want to see him beg for me to stay. And if he doesn't, then what?

"That isn't what I was going to say," he says.

"It isn't?"

He shakes his head, frowning. "I guess it doesn't matter what I was going to say now."

"Tell me."

"I . . . I was going to ask you if you wanted me to take you out there . . . to the trail where she fell."

"Oh."

This is what I am supposed to be consumed with—my sister's death. Still. Maybe forever. I am, sort of. Breaking up with David was supposed to be part of getting on with my life, wasn't it? Making right some of the shit I've done wrong?

"I just thought, maybe you'd like someone to go back there with you. So you could get some closure."

Closure. As if that were something that happens to people like me.

The cliff where Sarah died is the last place I want to be right now, even if I do feel like it belongs to me. I am repelled from it like a burn victim from fire.

"That's sweet of you to think of it. I don't think I can go there now though . . . it's too soon."

"You really want to stop seeing each other?"

I open my mouth to say yes, but no sound comes out.

If I knew what the hell I wanted, life would be so easy, like a menu with only one choice. But it's all the options that trip me up. I am dazzled by the endless possibilities.

I know how to be unhappy. It never feels the same way twice. It is an emotion full of nuance and variety, nothing like happiness, which always feels the same and never lasts long.

"No," I finally say, and it's like peeling back a scab, finding the tender, unhealed flesh beneath. "I don't know why I said that. Guilt, I guess."

He scoots closer, puts an arm around me, and I don't pull away. I lean in, kiss him softly on the lips, as if picking at the scab some more, hoping to see fresh blood.

Eighteen

Sarah

Watching, watching, I am watching life without me go by, an endless movie. I have lost the remote control.

Watching Rachel and David together should be more painful than it is. It should be torture to see her lean in and kiss him now. She is there, and I am not. She still has a life to live, and I don't.

Instead of its feeling painful, it's bittersweet. I wish I could turn back time ten years or more. I wish I could remake our history into one in which Rachel was given what she needed instead of feeling like she had to take it. She used to be a sweet girl sometimes, always mercurial but occasionally lovely, the sister who, when she wasn't being a brat, brought me hand-picked flowers in the hospital and sat beside my bed reading to me from the Laura Ingalls Wilder books, skipping over the boring parts and pausing to make fun of Ma when she acts like a racist.

But slowly, time and lack of attention let Rachel grow

wild—a garden overtaken by weeds. She was always preco-
cious, but once she discovered her power over the opposite
sex, she changed.

Do I regret what I did to her?

Was it revenge for David?

Such questions are not as easy to answer in this strange
afterlife as you might expect.

My favorite memory of Rachel is from our early days back
in Marin, before I got sick.

We shared a room because Asha still slept in bed with our
parents well past her fourth birthday, and Rachel used to
have nightmares about a man climbing through the window
and taking her. Whenever she woke up after one of those
dreams, she would climb in bed with me and ask me to tell
her a story to help her fall back to sleep.

One night, I was tired and cranky from her waking me up,
and I couldn't think of a story. I'd always told her tales of fair-
ies and princesses and magical castles, but this time, I told
her she had to think of her story. She started to cry, but
after a couple of minutes, once she saw that I was serious,
she quieted down.

"Once upon a time . . . ," she said slowly, her voice still
wobbly with tears, "there were two sisters who lived in the
woods. They had no parents, so the big sister, named . . . Sarafina, had to be responsible for both of them."

Rachel nestled up against me, her small knees poking into
my lower back, her hand tangled in my hair, stroking and
twisting it like she always did when she shared my bed. I
sometimes woke up in the morning after Rachel had slept with
me to find random, crooked, little braids all over my head

because she'd put herself back to sleep braiding my hair in the dark.

"Sarafina's sister was named . . . Raya, and one day when Raya was walking through the woods alone, something began to chase her."

I had always kept my stories free of scary elements, not wanting to upset Rachel more than her bad dream already had, so I remember being surprised that Rachel's story included a chase.

"She could hear heavy breathing and footsteps behind her, and she ran as fast as she could all the way back to their cottage. When she got there, she slammed the door and locked it, and Sarafina was inside cooking their lunch.

"'What's the matter?' she asked.

"'Something's been chasing me,' Raya said.

"The girls went and looked out the window, but they couldn't see anything. Then Raya started to feel a little silly, like maybe she imagined the whole thing.

"'Did you see it?' Sarafina asked.

"'No, but I heard it.'

"Just then, they heard a loud thump on the door, and the whole house shook. Raya began to cry, but Sarafina was calm. She went to the closet and got out her bow and arrows. She slung them over her shoulder and climbed up the chimney, out onto the roof of the house. From there, she could see the evil troll that was trying to get in their door, so she took out one of her arrows and shot him dead right then and there. And the two sisters buried the evil troll in the forest and lived happily ever after."

I remember this story so vividly in part because it became

one we told over and over, making it more elaborate and detailed with each telling. I remember it also because it gave me
the unshakable belief that I was responsible for protecting
Rachel from anything that might harm her. I knew she saw
me that way, and I wanted to be that kind of big sister.

But then I got sick, and well, and sick again, and well again.
Hindsight, I know now, is the cruelest view of all. I can see
now exactly how this twist of fate that was my leukemia diagnosis worked its way through my whole family, a disease that
would destroy them rather than me. Rachel, most of all, suffered the damage of it. I'd never be the kind of sister who'd
sling a bow across her shoulder and climb onto the roof to
defeat evil trolls. I was a different kind of sister entirely—and
not what Rachel was hoping for.

I was the sort of sister, ultimately, who was out for revenge.

Nineteen

Asha

I mark time now as what has passed since Sarah's death. There is my life before it happened, and here is my life after. The two parts are so different as to render me into two separate people. Once I was Sarah's sister Asha. Now I am only Asha, a person I never intended to be.

More than a month has passed since Sarah's death now, so the new me, the star-tattooed me, is over a month old, an infant in my grief.

It's Saturday night, and tomorrow is the big ash-scattering event that I am trying my best not to think about. I am sitting on the couch at a party I'm not sure why I've agreed to attend, watching the two people across from me groping and kissing and tangling limbs together. I don't want to watch them, but every time I scan the room, my gaze falls back on the spectacle.

I think I see Sin enter the room, but, no, it's a girl with dark hair wearing a shirt the same shade of green as his.

I want to leave, but I'm anchored to this spot, afraid if I get up, I'll have to see people and talk to people who want to tell me how sorry they are and how great it is to see me out again and how I'm so strong to be moving on and I must be so aware of Sarah's presence all around me, and blah blah blah.

Where is Sin, and why did he leave me here alone? I haven't seen him in what feels like an eternity but is probably more like a half hour. He disappeared with some girl I've never seen before, and I am perplexed that I feel a little jealous. Probably because he's my only friend here. I know some of these people, but they are not exactly my pals.

Sin heard about the party from Tristan, and because Sin's managed to hang on to his mom's van all day, he thought we should drive out here. I came, I'll admit to myself now, partly because I was hoping to see Tristan in some setting other than the claustrophobic space of his house, but no luck.

Now I just want to go home.

I'm tired from not sleeping well lately, and I'm annoyed at Sin for disappearing, and I'm mad at myself for even wanting so badly to see Tristan.

I sip my beer halfheartedly, not liking the yeasty taste of it—not liking beer at all, but someone handed it to me and it gives me something to do with my mouth while I sit here not talking to anyone—when a figure slouching against the wall catches my attention. It's him.

My stomach does a little joyous flip, and I down the rest of my beer in a few long, bitter gulps.

He's talking to a girl. Or rather, she's attempting to dance with him, writhing her body around to an old Outkast song that Tristan is doing little more than bobbing his head to. Not even that—maybe he's just nodding.

I will him to look over at me, and by some miracle he does. His gaze lands right on me, over the dancing girl's shoulder. He doesn't look away.

He stares. I stare. We have some sort of a moment.

I haven't eaten all evening, so the one beer is making me feel a little drunk now, a little less averse to being like the couple on the couch across from me, who have by now advanced from an upright position to a full-on lying-down-on-the-couch-and-grinding-hips-together one.

Tristan says something to the girl writhing before him, then he walks straight over to me.

"Hey. You're here."

I'm not sure what to say to this brilliant observation, so I just try to look bored or something.

"Where's my little brother?"

I shrug. "He disappeared."

Tristan sits down next to me, and my whole body goes on alert to the sensation of his thigh against my thigh, his hip against my hip, his arm now draped around my shoulders.

"Is he going to get pissed off if he sees me sitting here?"

"Maybe." I don't want to consider that right now.

Sin must be busy, or maybe even gone. He's been weird and silent all day, and I almost wonder if he's been mad at me again over the hot-tub incident, but I haven't had the energy to ask.

Some part of me wants to punish him for not letting go of the whole thing, for not understanding, for being so weird about it. So what if I made out with his brother? It's not like Sin owns me.

Or maybe it is.

"Remember when I caught you pulling up your pants?"

"Yeah." My cheeks burn at the embarrassing memory. "What about it?"

"That was kind of hot, walking in on you like that."

"You've already seen me naked." I don't know where my boldness comes from, but I like it.

"You should be naked more often. It suits you."

"It suits you too," I say, sickened by my own lameness.

"I'm opposed to clothing."

"Even when it's cold out?"

"Especially when it's cold out."

I can't think of anything to say to this, so an awkward silence follows. I stare at him. He stares at me. We have another moment, this one far more intimate than the last.

"You don't look like you're having much fun here," he finally says.

I shrug, wishing I had another beer. Something to do with my hands and mouth that won't get me into trouble.

"How about we find someplace a little quieter?"

This is the best idea I've heard in my entire life. I conveniently decide Sin has abandoned me. "Yeah," I say, but Tristan's already standing up, tugging at my hand.

I rise and follow, floating almost. Giddy with my newfound fortune.

"This house," he says as he guides me upstairs, "is amazing. Did you get the tour yet?"

"No. Do you know the people who live here?"

"My mom's second husband."

Sin, in typical fashion, never mentioned this. I didn't know him when his mother was married to either of her husbands, and Sin doesn't like to talk about them much. I recall his saying something about his stepdad being an asshole, but not that he was rich.

This house is pretty deluxe, I notice as we move away from the horde of teenagers. It's kind of a funky hippie place, but much nicer than usual. Trust-fund hippie. The stair railing is some kind of carved wood in a swirling pattern that isn't fancy like in most expensive houses, but is instead expensive looking while still funky. Like some artist was high when he worked on it.

Tristan leads me down a hallway past three or four doors, then to a pair of double doors that he opens into a room lit by a few small, glowing lamps, one on each side of a giant bed. The room has a high, wood-beam ceiling, like a church, and something about the dim lighting reminds me of churches too.

Not that I've been inside many, but I've seen plenty of them on TV. And once, the summer after fifth grade, my grandmother had celebrated Sarah's going into remission with a trip for all of us to Paris, where we'd visited cathedral after cathedral. Mostly I remembered people walking through these supposedly sacred spaces talking on cell phones and taking cheesy pictures. Here, a woman in front of an altar, grinning fakely; there, a guy next to a stained-glass window of a saint loudly speaking Spanish into a cell phone.

This room feels the same to me—the mundane and sacred all mixed together.

But I am only fully aware of my hand in his, growing sweaty. I take advantage of his closing the double doors behind us to wipe my hands on my skirt.

The doors block most of the sound of the party down

below. Now we are in a different world, someone else's bedroom.

"That's better," Tristan says, and I notice finally the sound
of soft music coming from hidden speakers.

Had he come in here ahead of time to set the ambience,
planning to bring someone up here? Me, maybe? Or had
someone else prepared the room for his or her own romantic
encounter? I weigh the possibilities for a moment before Tristan
takes my hand again and I tense up, losing the ability to think
complex thoughts.

"You're not a virgin, are you?"

I was not expecting this question, out of the blue and so
blunt.

I almost point out that I'll soon turn sixteen, as if this is
evidence of anything one way or the other. But I don't. I'm
not embarrassed to be a virgin. I like the possibility of it, the
not-yet-ness of it. It fits me.

Or at least it did until now. I'm here with Tristan for a
reason, for not-yet to become been-there-done-that.

Understanding dawns on his face. "You are, aren't you?"

This is what I've been imagining for a long time, all my
fantasies wrapped up in one guy. And it's nothing like I imagined.

How have I gotten so lucky that he notices me? That he
actually wants *me*? And why don't I feel lucky?

"Yeah," I say, my voice barely audible.

This person I become with Tristan—I barely know her. I
don't know where she's come from, or how she got into my
body. I guess she is the new Asha, the one born after Sarah's
death.

He nods. "That's cool. I'll be right back."

I watch him disappear into the master bathroom, and he returns with a plush burgundy towel.

Then he takes my hand again and leads me to the bed, where he spreads out the towel on top of the white duvet.

"You scared?" he asks as he slides his hands beneath the waist of my shirt.

I am hyperaware now. His touch gives me gooseflesh. He smells like weed and beer, and he hasn't shaved in maybe a few weeks.

"No," I say, though I'm not sure it's true.

I want this to happen, but a nagging something is in the back of my mind. Is this what I've been imagining? What I've been waiting for?

His hand ventures farther north, exploring virgin territory. I want his touch everywhere, and in a few specific aching places, all at once. I slide my own hands up his bare arms to his shoulders, his neck.

There is the sensation of falling, falling fast. I am on the bed. He is on top of me. I am burning all over.

His beard is alternately rough and silky against my face when we kiss, depending on the angle. I wonder how it will feel on other parts of my body. But when he pulls my skirt up, along with my shirt, I wonder if we're going to bother getting undressed for this at all.

I don't hear the door open. I am only aware of it when I hear footsteps. Both of us stop and look toward the sound, just in time to see Tristan being pulled up and a fist smacking into his face.

I look up to see that the fist is attached to Sin's arm.

Tristan goes sprawling backward on the bed, and there I am, my denim skirt hiked up around my waist, my rainbow unicorn panties exposed. I start tugging my skirt down.

I didn't even know Sin was capable of punching anyone. I am too stunned to make sense of it.

"What the hell?" Tristan bellows at his brother.

"What the hell? Yeah, what the hell, Asha? You said you'd stay away from him."

My face burns, nothing like the burning I felt before. Now I am horrified, humiliated, wishing I could crawl under the bed and hide.

Tristan is tugging at the towel underneath me, trying to wipe his bleeding nose, and I move off it.

"You left," I said dumbly.

"I was outside. So that's a good excuse to screw my brother?"

Tristan stands up and heads for Sin. I know they're going to fight if I don't stop it. Jumping up from the bed, I fling myself between them.

"Stop it!" I cry, but I'm not sure whom I'm hoping to defend.

Sin? He's the one being a jerk here. Tristan? He hasn't exactly done anything wrong, has he?

And neither have I.

I think.

Well, except for the lying part. And the sneaking part.

I narrowly avoid a punch in the face myself when I grab Sin and drag him toward the door, but before we make it out, Tristan pushes past us.

"Screw it," he says. "You two can have the room—I'm out of here."

I stop. Watch him walk away. Part of me wants to go after

him, and part of me is relieved to see him go. He slams the double door as he leaves.

I turn to Sin, and he's looking at me as if I have something nasty oozing from my eyes.

"It just . . . happened."

"You *just happened* to fall underneath my brother and your skirt *just happened* to get pushed up to your armpits?"

"Why are you being like this?"

"You promised you'd stay away from him. You *promised*."

His arms crossed over his chest, he is looking at me as if I disgust him, and I can't take much more of it. I just want to leave, storm out of here, get away from him.

But I also don't want to face the party again—or the rest of the world—without Sin.

"Just because I'm attracted to your brother doesn't mean I'm betraying our friendship."

Sin looks at me with an expression of utter disgust. "What friendship? We're not friends. Just stay the hell away from *me*." He turns and storms out, leaving me alone in the big bedroom with the church ceiling.

I sink onto the edge of the bed, put my face in my hands, and cry—really cry—over more loss than I can measure.

Twenty

Rachel

Me and Asha have never been friendly, as far as sisters go. From the time she was old enough to walk, she was grabbing my hair, taking my toys, and generally getting on my nerves in the way only little sisters can.

People say the middle child gets ignored—and that's in a normal family. Now imagine how ignored the middle child gets when the oldest child has cancer and the youngest child is the matching donor. There was no room for me in that medical drama.

Oh, poor me, right? At least I had my health, right? At least I didn't have to get poked with needles or anything like that, right?

That's not how I see it.

If Asha had shown even the slightest kindness, had been even a little bit nice, things might be different, but she's always been a brat, and I've always been the odd sister out. I guess I got along better with Sarah—sometimes—but only because Sarah had so perfected the sainthood act that it was hard to find anything to be mad at her about.

When she was still alive, she and Asha were tighter than tight, always ready to defend each other, always ready to make stuff my fault.

And that's how it was.

But how is it now?

Asha, as a rule, knows better than to ask me for favors, which makes it pretty out of the ordinary that she called and asked me to come get her from this stupid party. I almost said no, but she was crying over the phone, and Asha crying is such an unheard-of event, I came to get her mostly out of morbid curiosity.

When I've parked in front of the house with the address she gave me over the phone, I can see kids inside, talking and dancing. It's a big cedar-siding place that is sort of a Marin County version of modern, with a slanty roof and lots of windows. I scan the front lawn, looking for Asha, because she said she'd be waiting out front, but I don't see her.

Then my gaze lands on a shadow in front of the garage, and I realize it's her. She steps out, her arms crossed over her chest and her shoulders hunched, totally not dressed for the chilly night in a miniskirt and short-sleeved top. She is shivering, and her face is a wreck, all red and puffy from tears, I see as she crosses my headlights. A few seconds later, she's sitting in the passenger seat beside me, putting on her seat belt.

"So what happened? You lost your virginity unwillingly? Drank too much and barfed in front of everyone? What?"

She makes a loud snuffling sound. "Can we just go home? I don't want to talk."

Suddenly, though, I do want to talk. I can't think of anything I'd rather do. I've got her captive here, her only way home, and I have never seen Asha like this.

I look over at her, keeping my expression as serious as I can, and try to sound . . . if not caring, at least not hostile. "I'm your sister, you know. You can tell me what happened."

She looks out the window, shivering and sniffling, and I see her for the first time in years as a scared little girl. I almost feel sorry for her.

"I got in a fight with Sin, that's all. He left me here."

Two drunken teenagers wander past the front of our car, a guy and a girl, heading off toward the backyard, their bodies leaning into each other as they walk. The girl stumbles, lets out a screech, and they descend into laughter.

"Drive," Asha says. "*Please.*"

I back up out of the driveway, then head north toward home.

"What were you fighting over?" I ask once we are away from the house and she's stopped sniveling so much.

"Nothing."

"Doesn't seem like nothing."

She sighs. "What the hell do you care?"

Good point. I don't have an answer at first. I have made it my mission not to care about Asha, but I guess sister stuff is more complicated than that. I have never once in my life thought of Asha as a person aside from who she is in my family—the little sister, the heroic bone-marrow donor, the royal pain in the ass—but seeing her tonight, emerging from the shadows of a strange house, looking like a freaking wreck, she is suddenly this other person I don't know.

And somehow, that tugs at me.

Who is this lost-looking version of my sister?

In the silence of the car, she finally says, "Do you know Sin's older brother, Tristan Tyler?"

"Sure. Who doesn't?"

"Sin caught me making out with him and got mad."

Pulling up to a stop sign, I slam on the brakes too hard. Asha has surprised me yet again. "You and Tristan Tyler? Seriously?"

She says nothing, only glares at me for a moment and looks away.

"What does your little gay friend care if you make out with his brother?"

"He says he's just a big user or whatever."

"What guy isn't?" I try to imagine my little sister with Tristan Tyler.

Maybe she's just convenient, since she's at his house all the freaking time anyway, but she has a lushness about her that I've always envied, if I'm being honest. Everything about her overflows. And the attitude of not giving a damn that she has perfected, it makes her magnetic.

I've always liked to think of myself as the sister who gets all the guys, but I know that in one way Asha has always had me beaten, until tonight. I care if guys want me, and she doesn't.

But this wrecked version of her—she clearly does care about something.

"I hate going home now," she says out of the blue.

"What?"

"Since Sarah died, I don't want to go home anymore. I just wish our whole house would disappear."

I don't know what this has to do with Tristan Tyler and

his lame-ass brother, and I definitely don't want to talk about Sarah.

"Is that why you've been staying at Sin's?"

"Yeah."

"Maybe he likes you," I say, realizing for the first time that Sin doesn't seem all that gay. He's just not all that manly, either.

"Maybe who likes me?"

"Sin."

"What?"

Her dumb act annoys me, and I totally lose interest. We are only a few blocks from the house now, but I don't want to go home either. I can't stand the thought of being in that house right now.

"Never mind," I say.

I can feel her staring at me. "Can we, like, not go home?"

"Where the hell else am I going to take you?"

"I don't know. Denny's?"

"I don't have any money," I lie, knowing she doesn't either.

A minute later, I pull up in front of the house, and it takes all my willpower not to kick her ass out onto the curb and speed away. This sisterly bonding shit is not my thing.

We are sitting in front of the house with the car idling, me waiting for Asha to get out.

"Aren't you coming in?"

"No."

She gives me a look, then gets out and slams the door.

I watch her walk up to the empty house, with its one lamp lit in the window that I left on a little while ago. I know what she wants from me, and I can't even begin to give it. It's not what our family does, right?

We leave each other alone. That's how we are.

Before she has even gotten the front door open, I am driving away. I don't want to watch her walk in, don't want to feel tempted to go in after her, to offer any of the comfort no one has offered me. I have none to give.

I wonder who is out downtown, so I drive down there, not exactly wanting to see anyone, but not wanting to be at home either. I park and wander toward the sound of a band playing at a bar down the street. My fake ID has been proven fake at this particular bar, so unless they have a new bouncer, I have no hope of getting in, but I am drawn to the sound of partying nonetheless. I pass couples leaving a late movie that has ended, and I stop and peer in the window of the bar, seeing no one I know especially well. The bouncer is indeed the same jerk who's denied me entrance in the past, so I sigh and lean on the window ledge.

At times like this, when I don't want to see any guy exactly, I wish I had some close female friends, but I don't. I never have.

There are sort-of friends. Girls I know, hang out with occasionally, but not anyone I'm close to.

The band playing inside is some kind of bluesy rock group that wishes it was still the 1970s, and I get sick of hearing them, so I wander down the street farther to the Blue Diva, a restaurant-bar combo that will let me sit and drink a freaking Coke while I listen to whatever lame band they have playing.

I hear the sounds of tribal dance beats as I near, and sure enough, at the door I see people dancing to a group onstage that's having a serious cultural-identity crisis—didgeridoo, congas, some kind of little Middle Eastern guitar thing, and a singer dressed in sort of Gypsy clothes.

There's no cover, so I go in and sidestep the sweaty dancers, making my way toward the dimly lit bar. I am about to sit down when I feel a hand on my shoulder.

"Rachel!" a male voice says as I turn to see that it's Krishna, smiling and sweaty.

If I had only ever run into Krishna once randomly on the street, I would count it as not exactly eventful, other than that he's freaking gorgeous. Running into him twice though in this town where I thought I knew every hot guy starts to make me wonder what the hell is going on with the universe.

Is it trying to tell me something?

Now I'm starting to sound like my fucking mother, which has to stop.

I am thrilled in spite of myself. Thrilled to see him and thrilled to have the distraction. "I didn't know monks were allowed to go out dancing."

"Maybe not every night, but I believe in getting outside my head and into my body as much as possible."

If only he'd get out of my head into *my* body . . .

"I don't even know what that means."

He smiles that damn Jesus smile again. "Can I get you a tea or something?"

"Whatever you're having," I say, curious to see what he orders.

He asks the bartender for two seltzer waters with lemon, and my brief hope that he's a Buddhist who knows how to party is dashed.

I sit down at the bar, and he takes a seat next to me. He is still wearing a loose white cotton shirt, but his sarong is gone, replaced by a pair of baggy, orange cotton pants. What is it with this guy and the color orange?

I would roll my eyes except he somehow makes the look work for him.

"It's good to see you," he says, and I get the distinct feeling he actually means it.

"You too."

"I've been thinking about you, wondering if you'd come back to the center again."

I shrug. "Maybe someday."

He says nothing, just lets a little silence sit between us that would normally be awkward, but with him it kind of feels okay. Also, the music is loud enough that we have to lean in to talk to each other, and I guess that makes small talk not worth the effort.

I watch the girl onstage, doing some kind of whirling-dervish dance that makes her silver skirt and her long red hair fan out around her. It's actually not that stupid looking. A minute later, the band ends their show, and the sweaty people start sitting down at tables or coming to the bar for drinks. Another band immediately starts setting up, but for now, it's quiet enough that we can talk.

"There's going to be another community meditation and dinner tomorrow night, if you feel like coming," Krishna says.

"I can't. I have a family thing." This is half-true because I'm planning to work an extra shift instead of cooperating with Lena's efforts to get us all standing on the mountaintop to sing "Kumbaya" together.

He nods, which makes me feel like explaining further. I don't want him to think I'm brushing him off, and, okay, maybe I'm hoping to score a little sympathy.

"It's for my sister. We're scattering the ashes tomorrow night."

"Are you ready for that?"

I don't know what to say. Am I?

"Letting go of the remains can be the most difficult part."

"Is anyone ever ready for scattering ashes? You just do it, right? And then it's done. Whether you're ready or not."

"Life is what happens when you're busy making other plans."

"John Lennon," I say with a sigh. "My mother is a huge fan."

"So then you must know that every day, in every way, it's getting better."

How this guy manages to recite song lyrics without sounding like a tool is a testament to how gorgeous he is. Or maybe how sincere he is. Or both.

"What's getting better?" I ask.

"You are."

He says it without any sign of flirting, but I want to lean in and kiss him. I wonder what he would do.

And then I do.

But when I'm like six inches from his mouth, his hand comes up between us and rests on my cheek, right next to my mouth, and he smiles a sad, little smile. Like he's sending me a big fat rejection without even saying a word.

This is not something that has ever happened in the history of my life. It is unprecedented.

"That won't make the pain go away," he says.

"Then you haven't been doing it right."

At this, he laughs, and I am tempted to try again, but he gives my shoulder a squeeze and says, "Come on, let's walk."

Do I dare to hope?

I follow Krishna outside, where the night is cool, a relief

from the stuffy bar full of sweating patrons. We walk away from the noise of downtown, toward a residential area that is mostly dark since most everyone is in bed.

"Do you ever think about how this road goes all the way from here to the ocean?"

I shrug. "Not really."

"And across that ocean is a whole world of people we'll never know, living their lives, with their own problems and worries and pleasures."

He has led us out into the middle of the street, where we are standing now, looking toward the Pacific. But a mountain lies between here and there, which the road goes up and over.

What I don't say is that I am more likely to think about the whole world of people right here who don't give a flying fuck about me or my problems, while I in turn don't care about theirs. I see them come and go from the coffee shop, I pass them on the street, and I am frequently struck by how little we all matter in each other's lives.

We are all just extras in each other's movies. Nameless, almost faceless, our details completely irrelevant.

That's about as philosophical as I get.

"When you scatter your sister's ashes tomorrow night, remember you are returning her to the world to be reborn."

"Right. As a flower or a bird or a flea on some dog's nutsack."

He studies me but says nothing, and I turn away. I start walking up the road, fully intending to leave Lena's car downtown and just walk my ass straight home.

I don't need this shit.

Suddenly, I don't want to be anywhere near Krishna and his load of spiritual crap.

But he follows me. "I understand you, you know. You have a right to be angry."

"What do you know about that? You think I'm going to just meditate it away if I'd only become a Buddhist?"

"No."

"Then what?"

He stares at me calmly. "When I was using heroin, I did it to stop feeling sad, bored, angry . . . I wanted to be numb."

When I try to imagine Krishna as anything but the enlightened being he is now, I can't see it. Part of me wishes I'd known him back then. I could probably have gotten laid with old-Krishna. We would have made a good self-destruction team.

"Are you even tempted by me?" I ask, feeling my burst of anger deflated by his calm.

"What if I was? Then what? Would your life be any better?"

"Definitely."

He grins and shakes his head. "You're lovely."

"I'm not trying to be funny."

"You know, sexual interest in a person is perhaps the basest, lowliest sort of interest. It's like being interested in a toilet because you need to take a piss."

"I didn't know Buddhists used words like *piss*."

He says nothing to this. I guess he is waiting for me to see how profound he's being.

"What if sexual interest in people is the only kind I have?"

"Then you're using it like I used heroin—to numb yourself—because it's easier that way."

"Do you have anything to say that isn't completely full of shit? Because I want to go home and go to bed."

He grasps my shoulders and turns me to face him full on. He is staring into my eyes all intense when he says, "What if I tell you I love you?"

"I'd say I've heard that line before."

"Have you ever loved someone just because they are there to be loved?"

"You know, I was born in a commune, so I've heard this kind of crap my whole life, and just because you say it with a meaningful gaze while standing in the middle of the road at midnight doesn't make it any less stupid."

He lets his hands drop to his sides, closes his eyes for a moment, and nods. Then he puts his hands together in the prayer position and bows his head. "Namaste, Rachel."

I watch him turn and walk away, back toward town.

"That's Hindu! Can you at least stick to one fucking religion?" I yell after him, but I don't follow.

I can't, and I won't.

But I want to.

Twenty-One

Asha

The next day, I do little more than breathe. After the whole Tristan-and-Sin fight—and having to call Rachel to beg her to borrow the car and come get me from the party—I can't bring myself to get out of bed. So I stay in my room, studying the patterns of leaves and shadows in the canopy of trees outside my window as the afternoon light fades to darkness. A thick, knotty branch of a live oak reaches out toward my bedroom window, and it becomes the closest thing I have to a friend.

Beyond it, a group of bay trees looms with the threat of sudden oak death. They are vectors for the disease that is slowly wiping out the majestic oak trees around here. We had a field trip last year where we learned about it, so what happens to me when my best friend is a tree and it dies too?

Lena has left me alone today. Maybe she senses I am not to be fucked with, or maybe Rachel said something about my abandonment at the party in Mill Valley, but whatever. She seems to have given up on making me do anything for now.

Sadly, I was half expecting her to force me to go help scatter Rachel's ashes tonight, so I have finally gotten up, showered, brushed my teeth, made sort of an effort to get dressed. I am wearing jeans and a sweater now, back in bed but ready to go, and I seem to have been forgotten.

The scattering-of-ashes trip is getting started late, thanks to Ravi's arriving an hour late and Lena's yelling at him in the driveway for a while, and then his yelling at her for inviting her boyfriend and refusing to ride with her and her boyfriend to the top of Mount Tam.

Ridiculous that they thought of taking one car in the first place, but such is the state of my sad excuse for a family.

I watch the drama unfold from my bedroom window.

Then I hear Ravi say, "Where are Asha and Rachel?" and I know I'm doomed.

Ravi is nothing if not determined. He may be a half-assed dad to us and a world-class idiot when it comes to choosing women, but when he decides something is going to happen, he is relentless.

I hear Lena say something about Rachel having to work at the last minute and me refusing to go, and then my stomach twists itself into a knot as I hear footsteps making their way closer and closer to my bedroom door.

A soft knock, and then the door pops open. "Asha, it's time to go up the mountain."

I haven't seen Ravi since our lunch, which makes exactly two times since Christmas, but seeing him here in my room brings on a pang of loss for the past we used to share. He was the kind of father who'd swing us endlessly on the swing, who'd help us build intricate, gigantic sand castles that, at the end of the day, we'd all crash into and destroy. He hasn't always been such a dumb fuck.

When I say nothing and make no move to get out from under the covers, he steps inside and comes to the side of my bed, where he sits and places a hand on my shoulder.

He looks into my eyes, and I recall how I've always been told I look like my dad. When I was younger, I wanted to look more like my elegant, blond mother, but only Sarah got that honor. These days, I don't care. Dad's genes are a combination of Irish on his dad's side and Italian on his mom's, giving him green eyes and dark brown hair, with a complexion that never burns but turns a golden color in the summer.

"I'm sorry about that crap with your mother just now. I always think she can't get under my skin anymore, but I guess she still can."

He smiles a tired smile. I shrug but say nothing. I remember that he hadn't wanted the divorce, that he'd argued with Lena that it wouldn't be good for us girls, that we needed a solid family and a father figure and all that, and I realize for the first time that I never gave him much credit for having tried to save things.

"This is hard for all of us," he says. "We've got to come together right now, not fall apart."

They keep saying that. But aren't they the ones who split us all up in the first place?

I still don't speak because all of a sudden I miss Ravi like crazy. I want the old days back, when he was my dad, the guy who tickled me until I cried uncle and taught me to hammer a nail and danced with me to old-school R&B on the radio and picked me up to hold me close after the first time I fell off a bike.

"Asha? I know these past few years since the divorce have been rough, and I'm sorry I haven't been around more. I want to change that."

I nod, afraid now that I might cry. I blink and blink again, forcing the tears away.

"I need you to come with me up the mountain and help us scatter Sarah's ashes." He takes my hand, and I think I will refuse again to go, but instead, I allow him to help me up off the bed. I grab a coat, slip my feet into a pair of sneakers, and I go.

I don't ride with Lena though. Instead, I climb into the passenger side of Ravi's BMW and am grateful to see no ridiculously young girlfriend of his lurking inside.

"We'll go get Rachel and meet you up there in a half hour," Ravi says to Lena through the car window as we drive past her.

"Rachel won't come," I say, but he ignores me.

The coffee shop where she works is only a two-minute drive from our house, and I am amazed when, after sitting in the car waiting for what must have been only a few minutes, Ravi emerges from the shop with Rachel following. She takes off her apron, puts on her jacket, and gets into the backseat.

The car is cool and smells like leather, and when I turn to Rachel in the back, I can barely see her thanks to the dark and the tinted windows blocking out any light from the street. Her face, cast in shadow, doesn't look nearly as angry as I would have expected given the circumstances.

"Will you get in trouble for leaving in the middle of your shift?" I ask, not sure what else to say.

She shrugs. "Ravi knows the owner. He said it's cool."

We ride in an uncomfortable silence for a while, until Ravi glances into the rearview mirror and says, "So how are things?"

He glances over at me and waits for one of us to say something. I hear Rachel sigh loudly. She's not much for small talk.

"Kind of awful?" I say, not sure how else to describe the train wreck that is my life.

"Yeah, for me too."

Since Ravi lived for most of his childhood traveling the world, and then much of his teen years in a commune in Holland with his hippie parents, his voice has a strange accent that is from no country at all but always reminiscent of faraway lands. People ask him where he's from sometimes, trying to place the accent, but he smiles and says he is from everywhere, an answer that doesn't satisfy. Yet he rarely explains further unless they ask the right questions.

"I should have been around more," Ravi says after a brief silence. "And I will be."

He glances over at me meaningfully, but I just look away, out at the hillside passing by the car window, where houses cling precariously to the downward slope. Having him pop up twice now acting all sincere makes me wonder if he's maybe, actually serious.

I am starting to fixate on the purpose of this trip now. For a while I was so startled by my father's abrupt reentrance into my life that I had let it slip to the back of my mind, but now, my stomach is getting so twisted up I fear I might puke as we take each bend in the winding road.

"I don't expect you to believe me," he says. "You have to

understand that after my relationship with your mother ended and Sarah had her relapse, I was so devastated, I got lost in my own sorrow. That's not an excuse though."

After my parents split, Ravi had tried for a while. There has been shared custody and lots of shuttling back and forth between one house and another, and having two bedrooms and trying to remember which house I left my shoes at or my homework or my favorite pair of jeans. Everyone acts like that shared-custody stuff is great for the kids, but mostly it's a lot of confusion and losing stuff.

How many adults would choose to live in one house half a week and another house the other half of the week?

But then Ravi decided to move to the city, and our visits with him became fewer and fewer. We were allowed to choose, and we chose Mom. Not because she was the better parent, but because she was there—where our friends and our school and our home was.

Maybe six months ago, Ravi moved back to Marin because he'd started doing some kind of consulting work that allowed him to work from home, and so now here he was, promising to be our dad again.

I think of Sarah, of how she'd so easily have welcomed him back with open arms. She never let herself get caught up feeling bitter about the way things worked out. I guess that's the only advantage of having cancer—it teaches you every day you live with it that life just isn't fucking fair, and there's not a thing you can do about it, so you might as well just get over yourself and appreciate shit.

Thinking of Sarah—and not just the idea of her—causes me to go so green I start to roll down the window in case I need to stick my head out of it to barf.

"Are you getting carsick?" Ravi asks.

"A little."

"We're almost there. Do you want me to pull over?"

"No. Keep going."

I wonder if Lena has remembered to bring the urn with Sarah's ashes. Forgetting it is just the kind of thing she would do. But around the next bend, our headlights shine on Lena's car parked at the side of the road, and she is standing next to it holding the urn. Standing nearby and talking on his cell phone is Ron, and I decide she is an insensitive bitch for bringing him to this event.

All of us barely know him. He's just the guy who's currently sleeping with my mom—one of a long line of guys—not someone I want present when scattering my dead sister's ashes to the wind. I consider thanking Ravi for arguing with Lena about this, even if he lost the battle, but he has parked the car and is getting out now.

Too late.

From the backseat, Rachel exhales an enormous sigh. "This sucks," she says under her breath, not talking to me.

"Yeah," I say.

No part of me makes a move to exit the car, but Ravi opens my door, extends a hand to me, and again I let him propel me forward into the next steps. Walking up the trail, finding a spot, scattering the ashes.

I think now this is a stupid tradition. Why do we do it? Why not just flush our loved ones down the toilet, for all it matters. I visit the toilet a lot more often than I visit this one spot on Mount Tamalpais.

After extracting me from the car, Ravi does the same with Rachel, and he walks with us up the trail, following Lena and

Ron. He holds my hand as we walk, and I don't remove it because I need someone else's momentum right now or I will not take another step and another and another. Rachel has her arms crossed over her chest, not holding our father's hand but rather watching the trail as she walks, cursing every few feet at the rocks and dips that make walking hard to do in the ballet flats she is wearing.

With his free hand, our father shines a flashlight on the trail so that we can see where we are walking. Ron and Lena have not thought to bring one for themselves, so they are relying on the bit of light they get from us walking behind them.

I notice Lena hasn't dressed appropriately for the terrain either. She is wearing a black, wraparound dress with a black leather coat over it, and knee-high black boots with precarious heels. She struggles as the trail meanders uphill, and Ron has to support her quite a bit in her stupid boots.

Why does my mom need to look hot on this of all nights? Can't she just give it up for one stupid night and allow herself to look like someone's mother? Like three someones' mother?

No, not three now. Two. We are no longer the three daughters of Ravi and Lena, that supposedly golden family we once were. *What a beautiful family,* I remember people saying to my parents again and again when we were younger. Now we are only the broken remains, grotesque and pointless with our missing parts and damaged leftover pieces.

Up ahead, as if on cue, Lena stumbles and nearly falls. In slow motion, I watch in horror as the urn sails out of her gasp and goes crashing to the ground. The metal vessel makes a clunking sound as it hits the ground.

I stop dead still, watching with a growing feeling of nausea as the lid tumbles off and the urn rolls down toward us, bits of . . . of, stuff, falling out as it goes.

My sister, falling out as it goes.

"Oh, God!" I hear Lena cry out as she turns and watches the urn. "Get it!"

My heart lodges in my throat. Ravi, letting go of my hand, springs forward and stops the urn from rolling any farther with his foot. He bends down and begins scooping up what looks like bits of bone and a sort of crumbly stuff that doesn't look at all like ash, putting it back in the urn.

I stand there, so stunned I can't move. A sense of shame rises up next. Like, if *this* is us at our most solemn and dignified, what hope do we even have?

"Fuck me," Rachel says. "This is un-fucking-believable."

For once, she's managed to sum up the situation perfectly.

Finally able to move, I bend over and pick up the flashlight Ravi dropped as he went for the urn and shine it on the place where he is working to fit my sister back into her semifinal resting place.

"Well, I suppose we just got the scattering started a little earlier than planned," Ron says with forced merriment in his voice.

I want to hit him with the flashlight, but instead I just look at Rachel and we simultaneously roll our eyes—the one way we can communicate without fighting.

"I don't want my daughter getting stepped on by goddamn hikers," Ravi mutters.

Everyone is silent as he scrapes up the last bits of Sarah and puts the lid back on the urn. I think she is probably going to get stepped on wherever we put her. Those bone chunks are going to be chewed on by coyotes, maybe even picked up by big, dumb golden retrievers and played with like a fetch toy.

This thought makes me totally want to retch, but then, isn't the whole point of scattering the ashes about letting go of the physical body? Letting it sail away on the wind and go back to nature or some shit like that?

And why isn't the stuff in the urn—Sarah—all burned to ash? Why is she just chunks of stuff now? This is not going to make the romantic ashes-on-the-wind picture we all had in mind, but it is too late to go back now. Inside the urn, Sarah is now mixed with bits of Mount Tam trail dust and gravel that Ravi scooped up into the vase along with her, so we might as well finish the job.

A few minutes later, we find a spot marked by a large, mossy boulder that, I guess, is supposed to help us find the place again if we want to go back and feel shitty about Sarah's being gone forever.

Lena takes the lid off the urn, flashing a dark look at Ravi when he reminds her to be careful, and I think I might pass out. I get all dizzy, and my mouth goes dry. Almost two months since Sarah's death? Is that how long it's been? I don't know, and I am not ready to say good-bye to her. I will never, ever be ready. I think I will lie down on this spot and die with her.

"I brought something I want to read," Ravi says, and he clears his throat as he takes a folded paper out of his pocket and opens it up. "I wrote this a few days after I learned of Sarah's death, but it was too personal to read at her memorial."

My throat tightens, which along with the dizziness and

the dry mouth is not a good sign. I edge over to the boulder and lean against it, trying to breathe. After all the drama of the night, me passing out is a cliché I'm not going to let happen.

Ravi reads, "'Dear Sarah, my beloved first child . . . First children are the ones we must practice upon. Our mistakes becoming small scars on your once-flawless souls, but you bore no marks in spite of all I did wrong. You glided through life as if carried by wings, your smile the most startling beauty I have known. Once you asked me to toss you high into the oak tree in our front yard, and when I jokingly tossed you a few feet, then caught you midair, you said, "No. Higher, Daddy, higher." I told you—'"

He stops reading, his voice choked off by tears, and we all stand awkwardly watching my dad begin to bawl like a baby. It feels like minutes pass as we wait for him to pull himself together, but he doesn't. Finally he chokes out that he can't keep reading, and I think maybe I should volunteer to read for him, but I am still so dizzy and choked up I am afraid any little bit of exertion will have me flat on the ground.

I feel bad for him though, alone in his effort to make this moment perfect. Lena doesn't have the grace to read for him, I can tell by the set of her mouth.

Then, surprising me, Rachel takes the paper from his hand.

She begins to read so quietly I can barely hear her over the wind. "'I told you, I can't make you fly like a bird, darling. But you kept begging me to toss you higher, as if you believed you could soar up into the tree and beyond it, straight to heaven. Now, sweet girl, you finally can. Yours always, Dad.'"

Rachel's hand shakes as she reads. Maybe it's the wind, maybe it's because she is cold, but it's the first hint I have that she might be feeling as wrecked right now as I am. I study her face for some hint of emotion, but Rachel is a master of revealing nothing but contempt for us.

I grip my father's left hand as he wipes at his eyes with the right, and for once I feel closer to him than anyone else in my family. He, the absent one, all of a sudden is not Ravi. He is just Dad, a word I haven't been comfortable with in a long time.

Rachel hands the paper back to him, and he takes a lighter from his pocket and sets the letter on fire. He bends to pick up a small rock, then places the letter on the boulder to burn, pinning it down with the rock. We stand there watching it for a moment, and Lena begins tossing the ashes of my sister out into the darkness beyond the rock, toward the Pacific where Sarah died.

I am standing between Rachel and our father, and I reach for Rachel's hand. I don't remember the last time we've held hands. Probably she will shake off my grasp. But I glance over at her, and she is staring out into the darkness, tears streaming silently down her cheeks. She doesn't pull away.

Our father holds my other hand. The urn is empty now, I guess, because Lena puts the lid back on and grips it against her chest. For those few moments, we are there silent in the dark, the remains of my broken family.

Twenty-Two

Asha

Ravi drives us home, all three of us unwilling or maybe unable to talk now. When we are coming up on the turn for our house, he asks us if we'd like to stay at his house tonight. We haven't stayed there since he came back to Marin, our memories of the back-and-forth of shared custody too unpleasant and our estrangement from our dad too solidified.

"No thanks," Rachel says from the backseat, her voice suddenly full of sarcasm.

I guess we couldn't have hoped those few moments of Rachel's having a heart up there on the mountain would last.

"I'm, uh, supposed to stay at a friend's house tonight," I lie, not wanting to admit to my dad that we aren't quite familiar enough to do that kind of thing anymore without its feeling weird.

"Maybe some other night soon?" he says, sounding hopeful.

"Yeah," I say. "Maybe."

I don't imagine it will happen, since he will probably go back to being his formerly aloof self and I will go back to being one of the two remaining daughters who reminds him too much of everything he's lost.

He pulls into the driveway, and Rachel climbs out fast, saying bye as she goes. Ravi leans over to hug me awkwardly, and I let him linger there. I am trying to get into the spirit of things. He's my father, I tell myself. Not Ravi. *Dad.*

Rachel has already unlocked the front door and gone inside by the time I get there. Lena's car is not in the driveway, but it might not be for the rest of the night if she goes home with Ron the Dick. I go to my bedroom, feeling sick and restless and horrified at the thought of being alone right now, even though the thought of hanging out with Ravi sounded just as bad.

I have only allowed my thoughts to tiptoe around what happened at the party last night. I haven't been able to face the humiliation head-on. But now, with pieces of Sarah drifting around on Mount Tamalpais, I feel as if I am coming apart so completely, what does it matter now? So I made out with Tristan. So Sin hates me now. So my big chance with Tristan is probably gone forever.

So what?

It doesn't matter. None of it matters. Well, except Sin.

I hate the way he treated me, but I did promise him I'd stay away from Tristan. I broke the promise, so I guess he has the right to hate me. I just wish he understood how good it felt to forget for a while, to be distracted by some kind of feelings more real than the feeling of Sarah's being gone, to be consumed by something other than the questions surrounding her death.

If only he knew how hard it was not to know for sure what happened to my sister, maybe he'd understand.

Or not.

From my bedroom window, I hear a car pull up outside, and I see a lowered, black Mercedes in the driveway, its rims shining against the porch light. It's AJ, Rachel's wishes-he-were-black, wannabe-rap-star boyfriend, whom she must have texted on the ride home to tell him to come get her.

A white guy who grew up in Marin, to distance himself from his whiteness he has moved to Oakland, traded in his white middle-class speech for street slang, and his scruffy liberal attire for what he thinks is hip-hop. What Rachel sees in him, I don't know. He's even got a couple of baby mamas, from what I hear, at the ripe old age of twenty.

Maybe it's wrong for me to assume he's a drug dealer, except I've seen him down at the park on two separate occasions leaning into car windows and taking money from people.

Maybe he's selling Girl Scout cookies for one of his two little girls back in Oakland, or collecting money for the homeless, but I doubt it. I watch out the window as Rachel gets in the car, and then they speed off.

I don't know how or when Rachel and AJ met. I started seeing her with him a couple of months ago, but I give them two more months max before they have a screaming argument in the front yard, he punches her in the face, and they are no longer an item.

Why do I think he'll punch her in the face? She will surely say something awful and stupid to him, probably about his kids, revealing her true nature, and she will kind of deserve it. Also, AJ forever has some kind of rap song about bitches and hos and clockin' the bitch and on and on with antifemale rhetoric blaring from his car windows. I'm not sure you can listen to that stuff day in and day out without its seeping into who you are and what you do.

Once they are gone, I feel so completely alone I think the weight of it might crush me. I get up off my bed and pace the room, anxious to be anywhere but this haunted house.

It finally occurs to me that I have to apologize to Sin. I know this, but I don't know if he'll accept it. I don't know if he'll stop being mad. I only know I have to try before I lose my nerve. So I go downstairs and slip out into the night.

I knock on his door sometime before midnight, but no one answers. I know someone in the house is awake because plenty of lights are on, and besides, they're all night owls. Sin never goes to sleep before twelve.

I knock again, then try the doorknob, which turns out to be unlocked. I nearly live here, so no one will care if I just walk in. I ease the door open and call out a "Hello" because I don't want to surprise Jess, who can be volatile.

Her Westfalia van isn't in the driveway, but this doesn't mean she's not home. She sometimes claims she's forgotten where she's parked it, but Sin and I have our own recreational-drug-related theories about why she occasionally returns home without the van and the next day seems confused about its absence.

"Hello?" I call out again now that I'm inside the foyer.

No answer. A light in the family room is on, but no one is there. The house is quiet, until I hear a movement from the darkened hallway and I look.

Tristan emerges from his room. "Hey. It's you." He's turning off his iPod and removing the headphones from his ears, which explains why he didn't answer the door.

I'm instantly torn between wanting to get away from him before Sin walks in, and wanting to see what will happen next. We didn't exactly part on good terms Saturday night, but he doesn't seem to be holding a grudge.

"Where's Sin?" I ask, sticking to the safest topic I can think of.

"Mom needed his help setting up a show in Sausalito."

Oh.

So we're alone.

"Do you know when they'll be back?"

An almost-smile plays on his lips, and I notice the slightest bruise under his right eye were Sin's fist must have made impact before it went on to bloody his nose. "Nope. It's just you and me."

I glance at the door without meaning to.

"Don't worry, I'll only bite if you want me to."

I have no witty comeback for that, but some little frozen part of me melts. I still can't quite believe Tristan Tyler is interested in *me*. At school, I am no one. I am known only for being the sister of a girl who had cancer, and now the sister of a girl who died in an awful accident.

Sarah's sister is how I've always been known, and I've been okay with it mostly because I love Sarah. But now . . .

Now that Tristan sees me, I want to know what it is he's seeing. I want to know what there is about me that might catch his attention. Is it merely my convenient presence, here so much more often now that I can't stand to be at home?

I don't have to respond because he motions for me to follow him to the kitchen, where he rummages in the cabinets until he's found a bag of miniature Snickers bars.

"Want some candy, little girl?"

I'm not sure if I should be offended at the "little girl" part. I shrug. "Sure."

"I have to keep these hidden or everyone else will eat them."

"I thought your mom only ate spinach smoothies."

"That's just what she eats when other people are looking."

I don't quite believe this. If my mom is a size two, then Jess must be a size zero. Or maybe she shops in the juniors' section.

He takes out a handful of candy bars, then slides the bag across the table to me. I grab two, then one more because I realize all of a sudden that I didn't eat any dinner.

"I want to show you something." He nods toward the backyard.

"I've already seen the hot tub," I say, surprised at my own nerve.

He laughs. "That's not what I want to show you."

Oh. "Oh," I say on an exhaled whoosh of air.

That we have been naked in a hot tub together and kissed—that we nearly did so much more than that on his ex-stepfather's bed—seems like a small miracle.

Or does he even remember?

I worry that it was all a crazy dream, or that he was so stoned he's forgotten it happened.

We go out onto the back deck, where Buddha is lying spread out in the moonlight—at a time when any normal cat would be stalking about in the shadows hunting things.

I unwrap one tiny candy bar and take a bite as he points up into the oak tree whose branches shelter the deck. From the branch above us hangs a mobile of glittering silver stars. It looks like a hundred of them, all different sizes, suspended as if by magic from clear string.

"I made it. Thought you might like it since it matches your tattoo."

I don't know if I should attach any significance to this, but I really, really want to. I love the idea that he not only noticed the stars on my ankle, but actually liked them enough to make a matching mobile.

This seems unlikely though.

I decide I'd better not point out that one heavy wind is going to have the thing hopelessly tangled in the tree.

Still, with my head tilted back, staring up at the twinkling stars above me, I feel myself getting swept away by romantic feelings, like a heroine starring in my own love story. Will it end in tragedy, or happily ever after?

He did this for me. I can almost make myself believe it. "It's beautiful."

"Just like you."

I look at him, glad it's dark so he can't see me blushing. Yes, I am lame enough to blush at his compliment.

"I didn't know you made stuff," I say before the full stupidity of the comment sinks in.

"I just do it to annoy my mom. She hates kitsch, says real art is the only thing worth the effort."

"Oh." I'm not sure what kitsch is, but I am chastened enough by my last dumb comment not to ask now.

He takes a step closer to me. "Did my brother ban you from staying here anymore?"

"I didn't think you'd notice I was gone." This comes out sounding more pouty than I intended.

Another half step closer. "Of course I noticed." He reaches out and takes my hand in his as if this were something we do all the time—this touching thing. When, in fact, it's only the third time our bodies have touched. And what do they say about the third time being charmed?

My hand is clammy, but it's too late to pull away and dry it on my jeans. Except, well, this is the point at which I should be pulling away if I'm considering Sin's utter fury at me. Sin, who could arrive home at any moment. Sin, who is, or was, the only best friend I have in the world.

Finally I remember the two Snickers bars in my other hand. "Better eat these before they melt," I say as I tug my hand free and begin working on a wrapper.

He watches. I think *bemused* is the right word to describe his expression when I take another bite of candy bar and look back up at him.

"Are you afraid to be alone with me now?"

"I'm afraid of melted Snickers bars."

"Melted candy bars are tragic."

Tristan and I always have dumb conversations, and I'm not sure this is such a good sign.

I shove the rest of a Snickers in my mouth, thinking this will keep him from kissing me at least for a few minutes. But then I chew quickly because I want him to kiss me.

Don't I?

Isn't that what my every fantasy involves?

It is. Or it was.

Now, I'm just as likely to think about the trees outside my window. Fantasies require too much effort, and more hope than I can muster these days.

Then I recall lying next to Sin in his bed, and how he said

we. I marvel at how something inside me felt as if it cracked open that night, and I haven't been able to put the pieces back together again.

But it makes no sense. It's not like any other feeling I've ever had. I have no name for it. I can only marvel at it when I'm alone, when I have nothing else to think about, feeling around for some clue about what it was, what mysterious fossil I've found.

It's much easier to understand what I feel for Tristan—pure, unabashed lust combined with storybook love—and go with that right now.

And whatever happened with Sin, it might be lost forever.

By the time I finish chewing, I've regained my nerve. "Why did you take me up to that bedroom at the party?"

"Because you looked like you needed to forget."

"Oh."

"Just like you do now."

"Oh."

"And also because you're beautiful."

"You're just saying that."

"I am. Because I mean it."

"How do I know you're not just saying it so I'll let you take me to your bedroom now?"

I'm being coy, and it sounds stupid. It's much more natural for me to act like I don't give a damn, to flaunt the emotional calluses I built up waiting for my sister to die.

"Because I already know you'll kiss me whether I tell you you're beautiful or not?" Somehow he manages to say this without sounding cocky.

"Maybe I won't this time."

Then there is a sound from inside the house.

"I think we have company now," Tristan says as he gazes through the kitchen door, his expression vaguely disappointed.

I want to grab him and drag him away somewhere private, demand to know exactly what all this means, or does it mean nothing at all?

But the instant the impulse arises, it is stomped down by the equally urgent desire for Sin not to see us out here alone looking suspicious. So I muster all my strength and go back into the house.

I am a lousy traitor, the worst kind of friend.

Just as I reach the hallway, I see Sin putting down a box beside the door. He looks up and sees me.

"Hey, I was looking for you," I say, wondering if I sound too defensive.

"Here I am." He glances past me, at Tristan, and his expression changes.

"You set up the show already?"

"It was ten paintings. She didn't need my help."

She, as in Jess, is walking through the door now. "Oh, hi, Asha. How are you *doing*?" She says it meaningfully, as if apologizing for my pathetic life with that one little question.

Before I can answer, she sweeps me up in an embrace that's a little too eager. She must just now have remembered that I'm still in mourning. Now that she's spent a couple of hours staring at and arranging her own art, she's probably in a good mood, ready to acknowledge that other people—and our pain—exists.

"I'm—" I say before the squeeze becomes too tight for me to speak. "Okay," I finish when she lets up a bit.

I awkwardly put my arms around her thin, wiry body. It

reminds me of when Sin had a pet python (until Jess found out and made him get rid of it), the way it would wind itself around me, surprisingly strong and a little unnerving.

She releases me abruptly, holds me at arm's length. "Sin told me you scattered the ashes. Sarah's gone back to Mother Earth, darling. It's the circle of life."

Spiritual lessons from children's movies.

I say nothing at all. Just blink at her, because Jess is unaccustomed to comforting people, and I'm unaccustomed to being comforted. Especially with Tristan and Sin as my audience.

Jess gives me one last meaningful squeeze before letting go and disappearing upstairs to her bedroom.

Sin rolls his eyes. Tristan shuffles down the hallway, back to his lair.

"So why were you looking for me?"

"Do I need a reason?"

"I thought I made myself pretty clear."

"Yeah." I feel my courage faltering now. I hadn't imagined how hard this was going to be. "You did. I owe you an apology."

He stares at me. Through me. Says nothing.

"I'm really sorry."

"Okay, you apologized. Are you done, or do you want to go hang out with Tristan in his bedroom now?"

I kind of deserve that, but I still wish he'd make this easier.

"No," I say, a lame, little protest that hangs in the air between us like a bad memory.

Standing alone together in the kitchen, only a few feet apart, I am aware all of a sudden of how many times we've been closer, lying in bed with our bodies touching, even. During those times, I felt the sort of closeness I had with Sarah. Comfortable, intimate, like a favorite sweater. But now I see there was always something more, a little twinge of energy beneath that comfort.

My mind skims over the idea but won't settle on it. I feel it now, that spark of heat, not like any other feeling I have known.

Sin, with his hard stare, his arms crossed over his paint-stained, gray sweatshirt, is having none of it. "You smell like chocolate." It's an accusation.

I remember the last Snickers bar still clutched in my hand. It must be goo by now. I hold it out. "For you."

He eyes it and makes a face. "It's not even shaped right."

"It melted."

He sighs heavily. "Tristan was bribing you with his private stash, wasn't he?"

Busted.

"No," I lie. "He was just sharing. While I waited for you to get back."

"I bet that's not all he shared."

"Actually, it is." I hold out the Snickers again.

"I don't want your old, melted candy bar."

He turns and heads for his room, and I follow him. I see on the door that the kitten poster is gone now, replaced by one of killer robots.

"What happened to the kittens?"

"The robots killed them." He starts to close the door in my face.

"Sin, please, wait." I stick my hand between the door and its frame so he can't close it all the way.

Through the crack, he glares at me.

"Will you go with me, tomorrow?" I say, playing my final card. If this doesn't soften him, nothing will. "To the spot?"

He knows which spot I mean.

The hardness in his eyes softens a bit, or maybe it's my imagination. For a long, painful stretch, he says nothing.

"Okay," he finally says, annoyance lingering in his tone.

I breathe a sigh of relief. "Do you think your mom would let you borrow her van? Maybe in the morning?"

"I'll just take it before she gets up. Ten o'clock?"

I nod. "Thank you."

In the old days, he would have invited me into his room. I would have spent the night. We would have lain awake taking sips of contraband whiskey and speculating about the sex lives of our classmates.

But something fundamental has changed between us, and I'm afraid things aren't going to be like they used to be anymore.

"I'd better go," I say, wishing I could stay and knowing I can't, even if he did invite me.

I can't stick around, smelling of chocolate, seeing stars whenever I close my eyes, knowing Tristan is right in the next room, possibly wanting me. And all with Sin right here, stirring up feelings I don't know what to name.

So I go. It's painful, and I don't want to be at home, but I have to be anywhere but here.

Twenty-Three

Rachel

I can't stop thinking about all the ways Sarah was brave and I am not. She is really gone now. There is no more of her sitting in the next room, her ghost appearing to me every time I see that damn urn, because the urn is empty now.

But her ghost is maybe still here.

I don't believe in ghosts, but then again maybe I should.

I am haunted as fuck.

That's what I am.

It's becoming clearer to me by the day, because I cannot sleep anymore. I don't want to eat. I just want something to happen that will obliterate my memory.

Or me.

Either one.

Because I apparently don't have the guts to do it myself.

Maybe that's the lack of sleep talking. I have never been the suicidal type. Yet having Krishna leave me standing alone on the street in the middle of the freaking night, and scattering

my sister's ashes tonight . . . it's like all signs point to life as I
know it ending.

And what's a girl to do with depressing signs like that?

So when it is four in the morning and I'm still not asleep,
I instead find myself thinking about Krishna. I sit in bed with
my laptop and do an Internet search of his name and the
meditation center. I find the center's website, which has a
lame-ass bio page for each of its instructors, including him.
In his photo, he smiles out at the camera in that way he has,
as if he is peace itself.

His bio says the same kind of stuff he has already told me,
only less detailed and more fakey-fake, so I click back to the
results page and look for anything else juicier that I might
find about him in less official places. Like, do Buddhist monks
have Facebook pages?

He doesn't, but I find an interview of him on some punk-
rock Buddhism website, which seems like a ridiculous con-
tradiction if you ask me, but nobody has. The interview has a
couple more pictures of him—one in which he's sitting on a
tree stump looking off into the distance, and another of him
laughing as he stands in front of a class of meditators.

I stare at him, try to burn those images into my memory.
Something is seriously wrong with me because I think I'm
falling in love with a guy who has no interest in having sex
with me, or anyone else.

How could this go anywhere interesting?

I read the interview, which is mostly about how Krishna
credits his recovery from his addiction on his spiritual practice, and how he works a lot with recovering addicts, and how
he struggles to stay true to his Buddhist values with blah blah
blah . . .

I stop reading, but then I force myself to go back and pay attention to every last word because I have to know more about this guy who has me up all night and not giving a rat's ass about the other two guys in my life.

Then I find a few other references to him online. Like he was part of a peaceful protest at San Quentin for some guy who was wrongly imprisoned for something, and he is listed in a *Marin IJ* article as a volunteer tutor in a new program for some crappy school in Marin City where the kids don't have books or whatever.

So as far as I can tell, he is exactly what he says he is; not the kind of guy I should be interested in.

Someone to be left the fuck alone.

So why do I want to do anything but?

When I look at the clock again, it's nearly 5:00 a.m. Don't monks get up at the butt crack of dawn to meditate?

I want to see him right now. Seized with a burst of crazy energy, I get up and go downstairs. By some miracle, Lena's car is in the driveway, and her keys are hanging on the little hook by the door. All I have to do is get in the car and go, and I could be at the meditation center in like fifteen minutes.

So I go.

I don't think about it. Don't do anything to my hair or even change my clothes. I don't even have a reason for going, exactly.

The dawn light is just starting to change the sky in the east, but it's mostly dark out. Streetlights are still on, and the town isn't up and moving yet as I drive west. I don't have any kind of plan, and nothing occurs to me as I drive in my sleep-deprived stupor. I don't know how I will find Krishna once I get there, and I don't know what I will say if I find him.

The only thing I know for sure is that I want to see him again.

When I park in the lot closest to the main building, I sit in the car for a moment in a sleep-deprived stupor, and it finally occurs to me that I'm losing my mind. Sane girls don't go out searching for Buddhist monks at five in the morning.

Maybe it's not a question of sanity, though, so much as it is a need to fill up the big empty-ass space I feel inside. Or to crowd out the ugly facts of Sarah's death that won't stop screaming at me every time I let my guard down.

Nothing is sacred anymore.

I'm not even sure what the word *sacred* exactly means, except when I think of life in the commune, which I can barely remember, I remember a feeling of peacefulness. Life made sense. We had a purpose. We knew the rules of the game we were playing.

None of that is true anymore. There aren't any rules, or if there are, no one has told them to me. I don't know of anything or anyone worth believing in, and I'm not sure about the whole question of God.

Is there a God? If so, after what happened with Sarah, I'm definitely going to hell.

I only know that when I'm with Krishna, that feeling of hollowness starts to go away.

Sacred . . . the word, the idea, whatever . . . maybe it applies to him somehow.

But I will have to get out of the car to find out, so I do.

I recall seeing a row of dorm buildings down the path a little way. I hear a few cows lowing in the pasture at the bottom of the hill, but that's pretty much the only sound.

I am never awake at this time of day, unless it's to come

home from partying, and by then I'm always too trashed to notice the peacefulness of dawn or any crap like that.

Just as I make my way up the path from the parking lot, I see two people walking up ahead, toward the main building. The one on the left looks my way, and it is Krishna. After saying something to the other person, he breaks off and heads in my direction.

When we meet halfway on the path, he smiles. "What a nice surprise. I was hoping you might show up."

"You were hoping I'd show up *today*? Before dawn?"

"Stranger things have happened."

He has to be bullshitting me. But this is Krishna, and I don't think he does that sort of thing.

"I'm sorry," I say. "I was a jerk to you."

"You had a hard weekend."

It is so good to see him, but I can't think what else to say. He is wearing his orange sarong again, with another white shirt, this one with red embroidery along the collar. It seems a little fancy for monk clothes, but what do I know?

His hair is pulled back in a little ponytail, and he somehow manages to look not at all tired at this ridiculous hour of the morning.

"Have you been up meditating all night or something?"

"Just for the past hour."

"Where are you going now?"

"Early morning group meditation. Care to join us?"

I feel awkward now. I guess I was hoping I'd have him all to myself for a while. I am definitely not in the mood to face a group of happy Buddhists, but I don't want to say that.

"Is something wrong that you're not telling me?"

I shrug, hoping like hell I don't start crying.

"You scattered your sister's ashes." He places a hand on my arm. "Would you like to talk about it?"

Another shrug.

I think of how Catholics have confession, a little anonymous booth where they can sit and spill all their sins. Maybe that's why I've come to see Krishna—to confess to him my sins, of which there are many. I want his goodness to rub off on me, to somehow wash me clean.

I feel filthy inside.

"I can have someone else lead the meditation session. Come up to the center with me and I'll get that taken care of."

I say nothing, but follow him up the path. A couple of cars are pulling into the lot now, the first to arrive for the class, I guess. What kind of crazy people show up here this early in the morning to meditate? Can't they do that at home?

But I'm here too, and with no real purpose, so who's crazier?

I wait next to the reception desk, still with its job posting taped to the counter, while Krishna talks to a gray-haired, hippie-looking woman about her taking over the meditation session this morning, and moments later he is leading me toward I don't know where.

"Would you like some breakfast?" he asks as we pass the cafeteria.

"No thanks." I'm afraid I'll puke if I put anything in my stomach right now.

He leads me back outside, where the sun is just starting to peek over the horizon. Up on the hill, we have a great view of the sunrise, a slight band of orange blazing in the far distance.

"I'll show you one of my favorite places on earth," he says

as we walk along a path that leads away from the center, toward the woods.

I feel oddly wired, my body buzzing from lack of sleep, my brain hyperalert. I notice every little thing, from the cacophony of the birds calling in the trees, to the feel of the crisp air on my skin, to the spongy texture of the ground where redwood leaves fall again and again. When we enter the woods, it's much darker, and I can barely see where we are going.

Krishna takes my hand to guide me. The contact, innocent as it is, makes me crazed with his not wanting me in any of the ways I want him. He keeps holding my hand until we come to a clearing, where a perfect circle of redwoods stands.

"It's a fairy ring," he says when we are standing in the middle of it. "When one redwood died, these trees formed sprouts from the dead tree stump."

I think of Sarah, of course. Our family isn't exactly sprouting new life from the remains of my fallen sister, and I wonder if it would even be possible for something good to come from all the crappiness that's happened.

"Look up," Krishna says, and I do.

Above us, the pointed tops of the redwoods form a circle. The sun blazes over the horizon somewhere beyond the woods, and a ray of light pierces the forest darkness, glistening on the branches of the redwoods. I feel dizzy, standing here looking up, exhausted, wired, aching, wanting things I can't have.

I start to lose my balance, and Krishna grasps my arms before I fall. He leads me to a tree stump, where we sit down.

"Are you okay?"

"I think so."

"The only way you'll get through this is to go through it."

"What?"

"Have you ever heard that saying that the only way around a problem is through it?"

"No."

"It's the same with grief. You have to let yourself be in it, sit with it, feel it."

"I just got dizzy from not sleeping."

"And you're not sleeping because your sister is dead."

"If only it were that simple," I say before I even realize the words are exiting my mouth.

"Isn't it?"

"She's dead because of me." I'm too exhausted to care about hiding the truth anymore. "It was my fault."

"It may feel that way—"

"No. I haven't told you everything, but if it weren't for me, Sarah would be alive today."

"That's a heavy burden."

I am wildly, crazily relieved that he is willing to accept the ugly truth just like it is, without asking for details, without judging.

But it doesn't change things. I can't bring Sarah back from the dead. I can't put our lives back together. I can't convince Krishna that he should be my latest male distraction from my stupid, pointless life. The list of things I can't do is endless.

Then he does something I am absolutely not expecting.

He slips his arm around me, pulling me close, and presses his lips against my forehead.

I melt into him, let my body mold against his, allow his weight to be what holds me up.

Though just when I am thinking this is one of those brotherly types of embraces, he cups my face in his hand and looks at my mouth as if he's about to kiss me for real.

But instead, he says, "You know I can't—"

I shut him up by kissing him, leaning in and covering his mouth with mine. It's only a short distance, that space between us, and the kiss happens so fast I'm not sure he or I saw it coming. I just knew I had to do it, and I did.

For the briefest moment, I feel him kiss me back, but then he is grasping my arms and pulling away.

He sighs, and I feel so stupid I don't know if I can ever look him in the eye again.

"I'm sorry, Rachel. I shouldn't have brought you here." He sounds genuinely pained, as if he's committed some crime.

As if we both have.

I stand up and stumble back toward the path, turning away as fast as I can so I don't have to see that look of pity in his eyes.

Then I run, hard, fast, stumbling through the woods, as far away as I can get as fast as I can. I don't know if he even follows me because I never look back.

Twenty-Four

Sarah

I am falling.

Falling fast.

I know from the blur of hillside and brush speeding past as I tumble over it, my body skipping and bouncing like a stone. Pain is a vague abstraction, second to the astonishing truth of gravity pulling me down fast, faster.

This is what I remember of those last moments. And then the cold, stinging slap of the ocean coming up to meet me.

I was conscious until then, but the impact of the water knocked me out, I suppose, and my last few memories are either unconscious dreams or the final death throes of my brain. Having never died before, I can't say which.

Next thing I know, I am floating up, up, up. It's a dizzy, weightless sensation.

Not a sensation at all, actually. More of a disembodied consciousness, I guess you might say. I am here, but not here.

Present, but not able to touch or feel. Somehow watching myself come unhinged from life.

I see my body floating in crashing surf, bobbing over waves, bumping against rocks like a discarded toy.

It all seems so impossible, and yet I see it, while removed from the realness of it. I am a nameless, faceless audience member.

How many others are watching?

I don't know, because I am here alone. This, perhaps, is the most disturbing part of my nonlife. I've never liked being alone for long. My whole life, or at least the parts I can remember, I've had Rachel, and, more important, Asha, always near. We were a giggling knot of sisters as small children, never more than a breath away from each other.

Then, after the cancer diagnosis, we started losing the glue that had held us together as a unit of three. Asha grew even closer to me, afraid of our parents' strained expressions and short tempers, afraid to let me out of her sight.

And as Rachel drifted further and further away, the closer Asha and I became.

I now understand Asha and Rachel so clearly. It's like that hindsight's twenty-twenty saying, except in death, it's a million times more true. As if a light has been shined upon all the dark, murky corners of my life.

Wherever I care to look, I can now see. No matter how hard I worked to avoid the truth in life, it's all laid out before me now, facts glaring like neon signs. Here, a sister scared and lonely, there a sister jealous and forgotten, and there again, another sister starring in her own drama, complete with pitiable medical condition and suitably tragic ending.

Except it didn't end the way anyone expected at all.

Twenty-Five

Asha

Next morning, I am lying on my bed, fully dressed, rereading my favorite book in the world, *Cat's Cradle* by Kurt Vonnegut. This is probably the fifth time I've read it, and I am only reading it now because it's easier than thinking about what comes next.

If I put down the book, get up, and go downstairs, I'll have to face my mom or Rachel. And when Sin gets here, I'll have to go with him. I can't *not* go to the spot anymore. Every day I stay away, it takes on more significance, more mystery, fueling more of a sense of dread.

I have to go, and the whole idea is scaring the hell out of me.

When I hear the sound of an engine outside, I sit up and look out the window next to my bed. Jess's Westfalia is in the driveway, so I close the well-worn book, an old school-library copy that I've never returned, and reacquaint myself with the shaky feeling in my stomach.

It's a good thing I haven't eaten breakfast or I might throw up now.

I hear Sin knocking on the front door, then Rachel's voice saying something to him. I get up. Go down the stairs.

"Hey," Sin says, looking ridiculously perky for this occasion.

He's wearing a gray cable-knit sweater that probably belongs to his mother, the most conventional thing I've seen him wear, like, ever. He's paired the sweater with jeans and a white thermal shirt underneath. Without any wacky clothes, tattoos hidden, hair unspiked, he looks completely respectable, like the kind of guy normal parents might be happy to see show up at their door to pick up their daughter.

I'm happy to see him too.

Rachel is slouching on the sofa in the living room now, staring at her laptop computer as she puffs on a cigarette. She's not allowed to smoke in the house, so this must mean Lena is out already. Sin looks from me to Rachel in the sort of significant way that I guess is supposed to urge me to talk to her about the day Sarah died.

I sigh and enter the living room. Rachel doesn't look up until I sit down on the love seat across from her and Sin does too.

"What?" she says.

"We're going out to the coast today," I say. "I was hoping you could tell me if you know anything about . . ."

"Where Sarah fell," Sin finishes for me.

"Why should I?"

I wasn't expecting this question, and I don't have an answer.

"So Asha can see it for herself," Sin answers. "She needs some closure."

I almost laugh at this, but my revulsion over the topic at hand keeps me straight-faced.

"Oh. Well, I don't know. You should probably check the police report, I guess. I don't remember exactly where it happened."

"Didn't you have to go back there and show the police the spot?"

She blinks, exhales some smoke. "Yeah, but I was freaked-out. I don't remember that much."

"Was there, like, some landmark or something? A tree or a plant that marked where it happened?" Sin asks.

She frowns and thinks about this. "I remember walking through some eucalyptus trees, and then we came out on the other side of the woods, and there weren't any trees around."

"About how far from the trailhead?"

She sighs, put out by the inquisition. "I don't know. Just a while. Like after the eucalyptus trees, it wasn't far. Just maybe from here to that house across the street."

Sin and I both look through the front window at the distance she's described, and I try to memorize it.

"Anything else you can remember?"

"What're you, like detectives now?" Rachel takes another drag on the cigarette and exhales at us.

"I guess that's a no."

Sin looks at me, seeing if I'm ready to give up and leave. But I'm not. Rachel always has more to say than she lets on, and I don't mind pissing her off.

I just stare at her for a few long, awkward moments.

She tries to turn her attention back to the computer, but I ask, "Does the spot look like a place someone might fall?"

"Sure, if you get too close to the edge like she did. The hillside was, like, eroding there or something." She frowns again.

My stomach twists into a tighter knot at the thought of Sarah's frail body slipping, falling, crashing into the surf. My eyes sting. Why wasn't I there to protect her? She liked to go hiking with *me*, not Rachel. Why wouldn't she have asked me to go that day?

It all made no sense.

What were we missing?

"Do you remember anything she said that morning before she left that made her sound like she was depressed or something was wrong?"

Rachel takes her time putting out her cigarette on the rim of a Coke can that sits on the end table next to her. "I don't know. I mean, she seemed like she was normal, I guess. She maybe was quieter than usual. . . ."

"Maybe?"

Rachel shrugs. "I can't really remember that well. I've tried, but at the time I just thought it was like any other morning."

"How could it have been like any other day? You never go hiking," I say.

She aims her glare at me, and I see some sort of calculation taking place.

"She asked me to go with her, so I went."

"But *why* did she ask you?" I say before I lose my nerve.

I am treading on dangerous ground now, speaking aloud things we just don't say to each other—that in the pecking order of sisterly affection, Rachel has always been the distant third. That it's hard to believe she would be the one invited anywhere.

Rachel's gaze narrows. "She needed to talk to me," she says mysteriously, and I know she's not going to tell me about what before I even ask.

"About what?"

"About none of your business, *little sis,* so shut the hell up and go away."

"We you guys drinking or something? Getting high?"

She rolls her eyes. "Yeah, me and perfect Sarah were getting our buzz on. That explains everything. Now *go away!*"

Her sarcastic tone isn't enough to convince me they weren't drinking, but . . . the only thing I have a harder time imagining than Sarah and Rachel going for a friendly hike in the woods is them doing it while intoxicated.

A horrible feeling settles in my belly, but I don't know what it means. I look over at Sin, and he shrugs. I take this as my signal that we're done.

I go to the foyer closet and dig around, looking for my hiking boots, but they're not there. Which is weird because I always put them in this closet. Knowing the perpetual wetness on the coast, I don't want to ruin my regular shoes on a muddy trail, so I go upstairs to check my own closet, and there they are, tucked away in the back under an old pair of black Converse sneakers.

The boots are already dirty, the soles caked with a light coating of dried mud from a previous hike, so I carry them downstairs and put them on by the front door.

Sin is still in the living room talking to Rachel, but I don't bother trying to listen in because he'll tell me every detail of what she's said as soon as we're alone again.

I peek in the doorway. "Bye, Rach. We're going out there

now." I'm not sure why I feel the need to report in to her, especially after our not-so-friendly talk.

Instead of answering, she begins typing on the laptop again. Sin follows me out of the house. When we're on the road, heading west out of town, I feel some of the tension drain from my body.

I know I've been stressed about making this trip, but I didn't realize just how much until we go over White's Hill into the San Geronimo Valley, where the last vestiges of city life fade away and the landscape turns to one of alternating redwood forests and cow-dotted hillsides, and the headache I didn't realize I had vanishes.

Sin has some kind of Brazilian instrumental music on the radio, and he's being oddly silent, but I don't feel like talking now either. I don't know what to do with Rachel's claims about Sarah, and I also don't have the mental energy to attempt solving any sort of emotionally fraught riddle. Instead, I sit there with my feelings of dread and stare out the window.

This drive out to the coast is the only time I ever get a sense of what it feels like to meditate. Slowly, it lulls me into a more peaceful, thoughtless state as I take in all the beautiful trees and soaring views, and I begin to feel as if none of the crap in my life matters.

But finally, Sin interrupts my passenger-seat meditation with "So do you want to hear what Rachel told me while you were gone?"

"I don't know."

"She said if we think we're going to find out what happened to Sarah, we're not going to unearth any amazing clues on the coast."

I let his words settle in my thoughts, processing their full meaning one little bit at a time.

What happened to Sarah?

We won't find any clues on the coast?

"So, she's hinting that something besides an accidental fall happened, and that there are clues to be found *somewhere*."

"Or she might just be fucking with us."

"Maybe."

This is a real possibility. Probably the most likely one, given what I know about Rachel.

But . . .

But I fear I am letting the most convenient conclusion prevail.

The truth is rarely convenient, I know. It's often messy, difficult, even unfathomable.

"I think she's just messing with us, honestly, but I thought I should mention it."

"Yeah." I want to return to that place where I feel nothing, so I go along with Sin's assessment of the situation.

"It's hard to believe you have such a bitch for a sister when you and Sarah were so normal."

Were.

I consider pointing out that Sin and his brother aren't exactly two peas in a pod, but I don't want to bring up anything even remotely about Tristan now, not when Sin is actually speaking to me.

"Rachel did kind of get a raw deal," I say, defending her yet again for her bad behavior. "You know, being the third-wheel sister and all."

But Sin has already heard my lame defenses of Rachel's

bitchiness too many times. I can tell he's bored by my not jumping in and trashing her with him.

I'm not sure why I ever bother to defend her. I guess because I know what it's like to be forgotten by our parents. Only I had the advantage of being so close to Sarah, no one could come between us. Except, what if someone or something had? If she'd been having problems, I want to believe she would have talked to me about it. She'd have told me. I can't imagine her keeping anything big a secret.

We reach Highway One and make a left, winding our way through more idyllic farmland, past the bizarrely tiny village of Dogtown, through a eucalyptus grove that, in spite of the lovely familiar scent, I'm supposed to think is evil because it's a nonnative species. Just over the coastal ridge, a wall of fog looms, and I wonder if we'll even be able to see down the cliffside. I halfway hope we can't.

"Don't worry," Sin says, reading my mind. "It'll be sunny closer to Bolinas."

And he's right. When we near the Bolinas Lagoon, the fog has faded into a thin mist lingering over the water.

When we finally reach the gravel road that leads to the trailhead, I feel the tension creep back into my shoulders, my neck, my temples. I try to breathe it away, but it doesn't work. With each breath, my chest feels tighter.

I don't want to see how my sister fell to her death.

I don't, I don't, I don't.

"Stop the car," I say as we bump along toward what I know is the final turn before the trailhead parking lot.

Sin, not the world's best driver, hits the brakes too hard, and we both are jerked forward into our seat belts.

"What? What's wrong?"

"I don't want to go."

Only weeks ago, Sarah was here. Alive. She'd ridden on this same road.

But why? Why come all the way out here when she could have taken a hike only a few minutes from our house on one of her favorite trails? Maybe she was just in the mood for a change of scenery, but something about that idea leaves me just as unsettled as the other details I know about that day.

Sin is staring at me, but he says nothing. He's waiting for me to get my nerve back, I know. He doesn't believe my little freak-out.

"Let's leave. This is stupid. We're not going to figure out anything by going out there. All we're going to see are some trees and rocks and water."

Sin reaches over and takes my cold, clammy hand in his. He leans in close so that I have no choice but to look away or look at him. I meet his gaze, and I blink away tears.

"We're going," he says. "We have to go."

"I meant to bring flowers or something. I can't go without anything to put there at the spot."

"I remembered. Everything's in the back—flowers, candles, a poem she had in the school newspaper."

I'm so stunned I can't think of anything to say. While I was busy trying not to think, Sin was thinking for me. He remembered to do what I should have done, even though I've been an utter shit of a friend lately.

This sullen, weird drama queen who gives me whiskey and tattoos is the one who remembered the flowers.

We, he'd said in his bed with me when something between us shifted, unbalancing our friendship.

Now I know he meant it.

He presses the gas pedal again, moving the van slowly forward as if easing me back into the idea that we are proceeding.

A few minutes later the van stops, and I look up to see the trailhead right in front of us.

"I'm scared." I need him to somehow pry me out of my seat if we're going to go any farther on this stupid journey.

He sighs, but not exactly in an exasperated way. "Do you believe maybe Sarah is somewhere that she can see you? Or, like, know what you're doing?"

"I don't know."

"I do."

This is news to me. In all the time I've known Sin, I've never heard him say anything remotely spiritual unless he's being ironic. "What makes you think that?"

He shrugs. "It's just the way it has to be. What's the point of our ever being conscious if we eventually stop being conscious? It would make our whole lives meaningless if we're just here and gone again."

I'm too sick to my stomach to ponder anything this heavy, so I open my door and start to get out. My mouth tastes like I've been sucking on my house key. The scent of ocean and eucalyptus hits me, carried on a cold breeze, and I'm thankful for it.

"She knows you're here to say good-bye to her," Sin says, and for a few seconds I freeze.

I haven't once thought of Sarah as with me, or watching

me from a cloud above, since she died. Thinking about such things would require totally accepting that she's gone, and I'm not sure I'm there yet.

Or maybe that's why I'm here.

Sin is on my side of the van now. He opens my door some more, takes my hand, and says, "C'mon. Let's go."

Twenty-Six

Sarah

Some truths
we cannot bear to know
and we cannot bear to reveal.
Some truths are the ocean,
and I,
a grain of sand.

My first memory of Asha: she's a baby, maybe eight months old, just getting good at crawling, and soon as Mom puts her down on the floor in our living room, she smiles at me and comes crawling in my direction, giggling wildly all the way.

I'm not quite four, and in my memory I have conflicted feelings about this little bundle of flesh barreling toward me. She's cute, but I almost hate her for that because so far she's taken from me my mom's scattered attention. I remember resenting the way Lena watches Asha as she crawls, smiling like an adoring mother.

"She loves you so much," Lena says to me, and in my little-kid head I am both flattered and disbelieving.

Then Asha reaches my legs where I am sitting on the couch, playing with a doll. She plops back onto her fat baby bottom and grins up at me her gummy, toothless smile. She is delighted.

And I see it's true. It's really true, this little sister of mine loves me like no one else does. Unlike Rachel, who is just as likely to pinch me and take my dolls as anything, this newer sister, from this moment on, is my ally.

Years later, I got my big, bad diagnosis, and the Kinsey family started falling apart, but not me and Asha.

She continued to be my loyal sidekick, and I her doting big sister. I savored the little ache in my chest that came with having someone I loved so completely.

But now I can't take care of Asha, and I am powerless. That ache I once savored is gone, replaced by a cold, horrible understanding of how little we can control.

I like Sin. I like that he's a good friend, that he carries the flowers for Asha, that he's there to see this horrible trip of hers through to its sad end.

I only wish I could be there to help her grow up, guide her away from the ugly, and toward the beauty she might find if she looks hard enough.

Twenty-Seven

Asha

Sin is holding my hand as we make our way along the trail. This would be way too syrupy for us under normal circumstances, but the unspoken rules of our friendship seem not to apply right now. Over his shoulder, he has a backpack filled with flowers and the other stuff he remembered to bring that I didn't.

The air here so close to the ocean is cold and wet, and I wish I'd worn another layer under my sweater and jacket. I'm trying not to think about anything except putting one foot in front of another as we enter the grove of eucalyptus trees Rachel described, but my mind won't stop.

This is the last place Sarah was alive. The idea won't stop assaulting me. I look around, half wanting and half not wanting to imagine what she saw and felt. She always walked around in nature as if seeing trees and birds and water and earth for the first time. But I can't imagine her being like that the last day. If she was happy, or scared, or hopeless—I might never know, and this is the hardest thing to contemplate.

I don't know how Sarah felt at the end.

Sin lets go of my hand and puts his arm around me. "You're shaking."

"I'm cold. And scared."

"I know."

We reach the clearing, but it's too awkward to keep walking with his arm around me, so he lets go, but keeps his hand on the small of my back, and I focus on this. I feel a tiny bit of comfort knowing he's there to catch me if I fall.

Sin stops again. "Okay. We're in the right area."

I look out at the ocean. In the distance, the fog layer is creeping in, but here, the sun is still shining through, and only tendrils of fog reach out over the water. Seagulls screech somewhere nearby, and I see a trio of pelicans swooping low, gliding just above the waves in search of their next meal.

We don't need to guess where Sarah fell because up ahead, on the ocean side of the trail, someone has set up a small altar with her picture in a wood frame. There is a pile of smooth, round rocks, Zen-garden style, some dried-up flowers, and a little votive candle that's already been lit and burnt out.

I kneel down in front of the altar, and my stomach feels as if I've just dived over the cliff myself. It rises up, gets caught in my throat, and I have to try hard to breathe.

The small photo of Sarah is a recent snapshot. She's standing next to a tree trunk, smiling serenely, and whomever she's looking at behind the camera, she loves. I think her boyfriend, David, must have made this altar. The pile of rocks is his kind of thing.

I reach out and touch the photo. The glass is cold, and I don't know why this surprises me. Sin sits down on the ground next to me and unzips his backpack. He hands me a bouquet of mixed flowers, a riot of bright colors that don't seem solemn enough for the occasion, but, I realize, are exactly what I'd pick out if I had been presented with a choice of flowers for no reason at all.

He's taken the time to remove them from the florist's plastic wrap and tie them together with a piece of twine. I place the flowers in front of Sarah's picture, on top of some old ones that have dried up and started to decay.

Then he hands me the poem, which he's written out on a piece of nice parchment paper.

"Want me to read it to you?" he offers.

I shake my head. Sin has seen me at my absolute worst, drunk and puking and looking like hell, but for some reason I can't bear for him to see me fall apart right now.

"I'll give you some time alone, okay?"

I shake my head harder this time. "No, don't leave."

I can hardly look at the poem at first. It's one Sarah wrote a few years ago for English class, called "Take Me Away from Here."

I see the first line, *They call this a place of unbearable beauty,* and I look away. I can't read it. Instead, I tuck it under the flowers so it won't blow away.

Sin sits quietly staring at the altar, and then he stands up and peers over the ledge a few feet away. I haven't looked down there yet, but his doing so compels me to do the same. I cannot stand, so I crawl to the edge and peer down, my stomach doing another tumbling maneuver, bile rising in my throat.

Just as Rachel described, halfway down a black rock is jutting out.

"Are you okay?"

"Yeah." I edge away again, feeling suddenly exhausted but desperate to get away from this spot.

I was expecting this moment to release all the bad feelings I've bottled up, but it hasn't. It's just screwed up. Why doesn't anything make sense? Why don't I feel some wonderful sense of resolution, like I can finally say good-bye and all that crap?

Too many questions, not enough answers.

I'm not sure anything will ever make sense again.

Sin bends over and picks a tall piece of grass, then twirls it absently between his fingers as he stares out at the ocean. I can see he's feeling pretty useless right now, doesn't know what to do with himself.

I sit on my knees again, not wanting to see over the edge any longer, or to imagine how her body might have looked bobbing around down there.

Sarah's picture smiles at me still. I pick it up and look into her eyes, silently ask her to tell me something. What happened? And why? Except she's nothing but a piece of photo paper now. She can't talk.

The person who took this photo can talk though. What does David know? Anything? I haven't seen or talked to him since the funeral, and I don't want to, because he reminds me too much of Sarah when she was happiest, but I will. If anyone knows more about her state of mind before she died, it's him.

"Want to walk a little?" I say as I put the picture back in its spot.

"Sure, if you're up for it."

Sin takes my hand and helps me to my feet, and I follow him north on the trail, away from these questions that have no easy answers.

Twenty-Eight

Rachel

Stupid boy. He doesn't get the obvious truth that is clearer to me every day. He doesn't understand that without Sarah, there is no us. This seems so apparent to me, but to David, it's like I'm the cure to whatever ails him.

He shows up at my work, looking like a lost puppy dog, right at the end of my shift. I am tired, cranky from dealing with rude customers, and David is way down on the list of people I want to see right now. Like maybe at the bottom.

"We need to talk," he says from his position at the coffee bar.

I have been avoiding him, and he knows it. He reminds me too much of me sometimes, the way he could just wreck Sarah's life and go on living like everything's pretty much A-fucking-OK.

I wipe up a spilled bit of cream from the black countertop and don't look at him. When I am finished with the counter, I turn and try to look busy with the espresso machine. I will make one for myself and pretend it's for a customer. I will do whatever I can to keep him from thinking I can leave now.

"Don't you get off work at three?" he calls over my shoulder.

I shake my head no and continue with this all-important task.

"You can't ignore me forever."

He underestimates me. He really does.

"What can I get for you?" I hear Lindsey, my shift replacement, ask him, and then I know my gig is up.

"Actually, I'm just waiting for Rachel," David says.

"Oh, she can leave now."

I want to strangle Lindsey with my apron ties. She smiles at me when I turn from the espresso maker, and I glare.

Why must I work with such freaking idiots?

I take off my apron and have an idea. Maybe it's a good thing David has shown up today. I can catch a ride home with him, and with any luck Lena will be there, and she can experience the joy of seeing us together.

She doesn't know about me and David yet. Not that I have been trying to hide it, but she's been so caught up in her own fabulous problems she hasn't been around enough to notice anything about my life.

This could be sweet.

I am picking at the scab again, and I don't know why I do this shit. Half of me doesn't want anything to do with David, or with what happened before Sarah died, and half of me can't turn away from it.

"Give me a ride home?" I ask, and David nods.

I flash a smile, which I can see immediately confuses him. Even better if he thinks there's still a chance between us.

I never expected him to fall for me so hard, which is why this whole extended breakup thing has been so difficult. I mean, if it was just sex for me, then how could it have been more for him? Stupid question, but still the idea intrigues me.

When we are in the car alone together, he doesn't start up the engine. Instead, he clears his throat and turns to me. "I'm beginning to feel like you were just using me." His handsome cheeks redden a bit.

"Why would you think that?" I'm not ready to give up all my cards. I don't know when David's thinking I love him might come in handy. And *using* is a harsh word. I don't think I was, exactly.

"Were you?"

"Of course not."

"Maybe you just wanted to hurt Sarah. Maybe I was part of your whole sibling-rivalry thing."

I lean over and take his hand in mine. Put on my most sincere face. "No. That's not true. I didn't mean for us to happen. We just did."

He smiles a little at this. "Yeah. Fate, right?"

"Yes."

I lean closer and kiss him on the lips, feeling not at all turned on, yet wondering whether we should go somewhere and get it on before he takes me home. If we've got that vibe about us, it'll only piss off Lena more.

"Can we go to your place for a while?" I say against his lips when I break the kiss.

"It's full of roommates right now, not exactly private. What about your house?"

I shrug. "Sure, we can try there."

I imagine Lena walking in on us. Maybe even in her bed.

All of a sudden I feel as if I'm careening head-on over a cliff, and I can't stop myself.

I'm sitting in the seat where Sarah once sat, with the guy she once loved, and I am both repulsed and exhilarated. I don't know where this flood of feelings is coming from, but I welcome it. It's been a long time since I've felt anything this fucking real.

A few minutes pass and we are pulling into my driveway. Lena's car is there. I am not sure how best to play it, so I figure we'll just have to see how things roll.

"Your mom's home?"

"Looks like it."

"Oh, God. I haven't seen Lena since the memorial."

Right.

I glance over at him to gauge his reaction to this idea. He seems a little on edge now, maybe thinking of his role in the whole betrayal thing.

Good. Let him squirm a bit. It can't hurt.

"Maybe this isn't such a good idea. I mean, does she even know about us?"

I shrug. "Who gives a damn what she knows?"

"I do."

"Well, if you want us to be together, then you'd better get used to her knowing it."

"Right," he says, not sounding too confident.

I get out of the car and stand waiting for him in front of it until he gets his cowardly ass out and follows me into the house. Inside, I can hear Lena talking to someone in the kitchen. I contemplate taking David straight to her bedroom to create some real drama, but I can tell by his reaction that he won't go for that.

Instead, I lead him into the kitchen, where we sit down at the table and watch as Lena turns to see us there. She has her cell phone tucked between her face and her shoulder as she talks while dicing a cucumber on the cutting board.

I go to the fridge and take out two beers, pop the top on each, and hand one to David. I dare her with my eyes to say something when she turns and looks at us for a long moment. She is processing what she sees, but I can't tell exactly what her reaction is, so I take a long drink of the IPA I'm quite sure she didn't buy with me in mind.

"Look, I'm going to have to call you back," she says into the phone. "Someone just arrived."

After saying her good-byes and setting aside the phone, she turns to us. "Hello, David," she says evenly. "It's good to see you."

"Hi, Lena, good to see you too."

"What's brought you here?"

David's face goes white, and he looks to me for help.

"Actually, Lena, David and I have been seeing each other." As soon as the words are out of my mouth, I wish I could take them back.

All the satisfaction I thought I'd get from twisting the knife is just an ugly, little feeling. Lena's expression goes from confused to angry in the blink of an eye.

Inexplicably, I think of Krishna, and I feel like an utter, absolute shit.

"Seeing each other?" She says the words slowly. "I don't understand."

I can't say any more. I don't have the heart. I don't know why I was stupid enough to come here with David now, so soon after we scattered the ashes. Suddenly I hate myself for it. I want to be anywhere but here.

David looks at me again as if I might explain, but I can't make my mouth form words.

"It's kind of, uh, unexpected, I know," he says.

Lena looks at me, and her expression hardens. "How could you?"

How could I not? is probably the better question.

Lena picks up a glass from the counter, looks as if she will throw it, then slams it down. It shatters, and her hand begins to bleed.

I am frozen, watching her.

"Oh, crap, your hand," David says, springing forward to grab a towel.

Lena backs away from him. "Get out of my house." She clutches her injured left hand with her right.

He stops, makes a gesture of surrender, and starts backing away.

Still frozen, I know one thing for sure—I don't ever want to see him again. So I guess we are breaking up for real now, but I don't bother to follow him out the door.

Asha

I was lying in bed halfheartedly reading my English homework—incomprehensible Faulkner—when Rachel and David pulled up in his car.

I have never seen the two of them together before, and the incongruity of it startles me for a moment. Maybe he bumped into her in the coffee shop, I think, and turn my attention back to my book, determined to stop drifting off and start sorting out all the different characters in the novel and whether any of them are likable enough to keep reading about. So far, every character in *As I Lay Dying* is pretty awful, and I'm not a big fan of the whole death theme, given recent events, but I'm sure the teacher didn't have me in mind when she selected this book.

I don't wonder about David and Rachel again until I hear Lena's raised voice and the sound of glass breaking. Soon after, David walks back out to the car, and I sit up, watching him intently, wondering.

Him and Rachel. Rachel and him, together. Why?

What besides *me* could have gotten Lena mad enough to raise her voice like that?

She and Rachel don't fight, at least not since Sarah's death, because Rachel has become the oddly obedient daughter lately. She goes to work, she comes home, she tests no limits other than smoking and drinking in the house.

I don't know why.

David pulls his car out of the driveway and heads east toward his place, so I make a decision. Now is as good a time as any to talk to him. I will ride my bike to his house and find out whatever he knows.

I put on a pair of black Converse and an old hoodie, pull my hair back in a ponytail, and creep down the stairs as quietly as I can, hoping to avoid any unnecessary talking to Lena now when she seems to be on a rampage.

I pause at the bottom of the stairs, where I can clearly hear voices in the kitchen.

"—don't understand how you could do that," Lena is saying. Silence from Rachel.

"Is this some kind of mutual-comfort-in-grief relationship?"

My stomach sinks. Rachel and David are *dating*?

"Whatever," Rachel says. "I guess. We're not a couple. We're just, like, *whatever*. Friends now. Like you said, the whole grief thing."

Something about the tone of her voice sets me on edge. What she's saying isn't the whole story, but Lena rarely chooses to question our lies because it's easier not to.

Lena sighs. "It can't lead anywhere positive. You have to know that. The karmic debt you'd owe—"

"Oh, what the fuck ever! Don't start in on my karmic debt. We're just hanging out a little is all!"

I hear a chair scrape on the floor, and a second later Rachel rushes past, out the door, never noticing me at the bottom of the stairs eavesdropping.

I watch her walk down the sidewalk, heading west toward the center of town, and decide I'm still safe to try talking to David now. I wait, holding my breath, hoping Lena stays put, and a few moments later I leave too.

It's a short ride to his house. My eyes water in the cool breeze on this windy day as I pedal up the hill. I have never talked to David on my own.

I never saw in him what Sarah saw. I mean, I guess it would be normal for me to be a little jealous or whatever, since she started spending more and more time with him, but I mostly just thought he wasn't good enough for her.

Then again, what guy *was* good enough?

I am both relieved and nervous when I see David's car parked in front of his house. I lean my bike against the front porch and climb the steps to his door, my nerves jangling in my stomach, but before I can knock, he is standing at the screen staring out at me.

"Oh, hey," he says, sounding weary.

"Hi, David."

"I was just at your house."

"So was I."

"Right. So you heard? Sorry about that."

"About what?"

"That whole scene, your mom's hand . . ." He trails off when he sees my look of confusion.

I think of the broken-glass sound, Lena's raised voice. "I'm not here about that," I say, hoping he'll relax and see me as an ally long enough to talk to me about Sarah.

"Oh. Do you want to come in?"

I glance toward the sounds of talking and a television inside. "Could we talk out here?"

"Sure." He steps out and lets the wood screen door slam shut behind him.

He sits down on the top step of the porch, and I sit next to him. I think of the last time I was here, a few months ago, when I'd come to wait for Sarah to drive me to a dental appointment.

The thought of this turns my stomach. Another mundane detail of my life, forever rendered pointless and horrible by my sister's death. Will I think of her every time I go to the dentist? Every time I see this house? It feels like nothing can ever matter all that much again.

Or like it shouldn't matter.

None of it.

"I miss her a lot," he says, his thin arms in a gray flannel shirt, resting on his knees.

I think of Rachel and him together earlier. How much is a lot?

"I've been thinking about the time before she died," I say, "and how she died, and I guess I keep wondering what really happened, you know?"

The air between us shifts.

"What do you mean? She slipped and fell. Rachel saw it happen."

"Why was she there with Rachel, though? Do you have any idea?"

He shrugs, and one of his knees begins to bounce. "Not a clue. I mean, I just figured they felt like going on a hike together."

"They never went on hikes together," I say, watching him.

"Really? *Never?*"

"Never. Except for that day."

"Hmm."

"Do you know if Sarah was maybe upset about something?"

He shakes his head. "No, nothing that I know of."

I sit and stare over at him, hoping he might come up with something if I wait long enough, but he doesn't budge.

"So," I finally ask, "why were you and Rachel together this afternoon?"

"Oh, that. Well, you know, now that you mention it, Sarah could have been upset about, um—"

He glances over at me, but when our gazes meet, he stops talking abruptly, leaving the statement ambiguous.

"What do you mean?"

He looks away, out at the street, and sighs. "It's just, we . . ."

I hold my breath, unable to fill in the blank for him. Whatever it is he's going to say, I don't think I want to hear it, even if it's the answer to the questions I have.

"We weren't getting along so great at the end, is all," he finally says.

"Why?"

He shrugs. "It's kind of hard to admit now, after, I mean, you know . . ."

"What?" I say when he doesn't continue.

"I wanted to see other people, and she didn't."

Did those other people include Rachel?

No.

Who would do something like that?

Even if he would, I can't believe Rachel would betray Sarah in such a shitty way. Not even she was that low.

I swallow the dryness in my mouth. "Do you think she was depressed about that?"

He shrugs. "She was just upset with me was all."

"Were you trying to break up with her?"

"No. I just wanted to have, like, an open relationship."

"Right. Like that ever works." I am disgusted on Sarah's behalf, but I contain myself. I try to imagine Sarah wanting to kill herself over this unbelievable shit of a guy, and I can't. She wouldn't. She was too smart for that.

"I'm really sorry. About everything."

I don't know what I was hoping to hear from David when I came here, but it's not his pathetic apology.

Suddenly, I feel too antsy to sit still, too pissed off by this conversation to stay for another second. I stand up and descend the stairs, grab my bike, and start walking it down the driveway.

David says nothing as I go.

I feel as if an unspoken question hangs in the air between us, but I'm not sure what it is, or if I want to know the answer.

Twenty-Nine

Sarah

I am selfish. I am a coward. I am anything but a saint.

I deserved the cancer I got, only in reverse.

The punishment before the crime.

Except it wasn't enough.

I will need to explain some things, but I still don't have the words for most of it.

Especially not for Brandon.

He was the kind of kid you meet on the Northern California coast. Creative, slightly adrift, educated in a halfhearted way. I know some things about him now that I didn't know then. I know that his mother loved him dearly, that she has never recovered from his death, that his father, an alcoholic, is sunken deeper into his disease since the accident. I know they are troubled by the lack of closure to the case. They want to know who killed their son. They want someone to pay.

They deserve that.

I see now how much more selfish I could be than anyone ever thought possible. That's the thing about being the good sister. People overlook too much. They forgive too often. I didn't deserve the mark of sainthood just for having once been sick.

Thirty

Asha

Back at school again. Permanently this time, I suspect. A truancy officer has gotten involved, and I'm tired of battling Lena anyway.

I'm in English class with Ms. Abel. It is, or was, my favorite class, back when favorite classes were a thing I had. I loved to read and write and analyze. Now I forget what it's like to love doing things. I want to remember, but the feeling eludes me.

"Asha," Ms. Abel says to me when she looks up from her desk and sees me sitting there waiting for the bell to ring to start class. "Could I speak with you for a moment?"

I go over to her desk, and she has this look on her face. "I know you're having a very difficult year."

I look down at her hands. She's holding my poem about dead people's things. I didn't use to write poems—it was something Sarah did—but now it feels like the only thing that will come out of me when I pick up a pencil and try to write. It's the first thing I've turned in for weeks. I keep thinking I'd better start doing some makeup work, but all that comes out of me are fractured words and phrases when I try to write whole sentences and paragraphs. Not literary analysis. Not five-paragraph essays.

"This isn't exactly the assignment I gave you, but it's a very good poem."

I look into her eyes, then back down at the paper. It's wrinkled, written in purple ink on a scraggly piece of notebook paper.

"I want to help you pass this semester, so I'll give you a bit of leeway on the type of assignments you turn in. Does writing help you process your grief?" she asks in a careful voice.

Process your grief. It sounds like something that happens at the Department of Emotions. If I fill out the right forms and turn in the proper paperwork to the correct department, in six to eight weeks all will be well again. I'll get an official certificate in the mail making it so.

I shrug. Shift my weight from one hip to the other. I've never been all that friendly with Ms. Abel in spite of my love of the subject, so I don't know what to do with her personal questions. It feels like she's peeking into someplace private.

"What if you spend some time just writing whatever comes out? And you turn that in for some credit?"

I think I can do that, so I nod.

"Good. And I was wondering if you might like to read this poem aloud to the class. It's so moving, I was hoping your classmates could hear it."

"No." I shake my head, blushing already. "I can't."

"Would it make you feel uncomfortable if I read it?"

Most definitely, but I'm too flattered by her compliment to say anything.

"I understand if it's too personal, but I think it might be cathartic to share it with the class."

Cathartic? I remember this word from studying the Greek tragedies. It's like when watching a sad movie makes you cry and you get out all your sad feelings that way. I don't know if I'm ready to let go of any feelings, but something about the idea of everyone else hearing those words . . .

I guess I like the thought, because what is a poem without an audience? "Okay."

Ms. Abel smiles. "Thank you for sharing it. I'll read it at the start of class."

I go to a desk in the back of the room and slump down in it, feeling shy now that I know what she's going to do. Sin walks in, and like always lately, he is careful not to look at me.

Nothing has changed since our drive to the coast. He was so sweet and thoughtful that day, but afterward, we are back to this. The cold war, or whatever it is. He is still mad at me, even if he says I'm forgiven. He still doesn't trust me, still thinks I'm a skank for messing around with his brother. He hasn't said it out loud, but I know how he thinks.

Our friendship's vanishing before my eyes leaves me feeling so empty I'm afraid I will collapse in on myself, like one of those buildings in Las Vegas that's being demolished so as not to fall on all the others around it.

How does he even know I'm here if he isn't looking? He must catch a glimpse at the doorway so he knows where in the room not to look. Or maybe he just senses my presence because we were so close. He should know where I am just by scent, or vibes in the air, or something.

I watch him sit in a seat three rows over, five desks up. Not beside me like before. I study the back of his head. He put some kind of purple tint in his hair, but you can barely tell. Jenna Carson sits down beside him, laughing at something that must have happened in the hallway, and I look away. Down at my notebook. I take out a pen and start drawing a black swirl, doodling without thinking.

The class fills up and Ms. Abel is talking about expository essays due Friday. I don't remember this assignment, but I will do what she asked. I will write down something, whatever comes out, and turn it in. I'm not sure I care about passing tenth-grade English, but I like the idea of seeing what comes out of me. I like the way I felt after writing the poem—sort of clean—and I want to feel like that again. It's as if I'm grasping some little part of Sarah when I write.

"Before we get started on today's reading, I have something special to share with you," Ms. Abel is saying.

I feel my face start to burn. I should have told her not to say it's *my* poem, I think in a panic.

But then she already knows, because she says, "One of your classmates has written a poem that is quite good, and I've asked permission to read it aloud to all of you."

She is using her Very Serious voice, the one that makes everyone get quiet and listen. I've always wondered how she could do this, because it's not a stern voice. It just has some quality that makes kids shut up and take notice. People glance around to see if they can spot whose poem it could be. It's

pretty unusual for Ms. Abel to compliment anyone's writing—
she's an old-school teacher, stern and quick to point out errors—
and even more unusual for her to want to read it aloud.

She clears her throat and begins to read my words:

In a room that's silent now,
This is all that's left behind:
A jewelry box
A journal
A pair of jeans
An unmade bed because she hated making the bed
A cell phone that doesn't ring
Everyone knows not to call
And the battery is dead
An alarm clock glowing red: it's 3:29
Or 4:15 or 1:25 or any number at all because
Time is the thing that matters least now.
The coroner cannot give the exact time of death
Though we all want to know—
Was it dark, light, morning, night?
Perhaps daytime, they say, at high tide
When the water would have covered the rocks
A kindness to spare us, or the truth—
It doesn't matter because
Time has ceased to pass since
And no detail like the time of death can
Erase the fact of an empty room
That holds the things she left behind.

She uses just the right tone of voice, careful and with no
emotion to get in the way of the words. But you can tell she's

touched by it. She looks sad as she's reading. I feel my eyes well up with tears, and I blink hard, then swipe at my cheeks before anyone looks back at me.

When she finishes, people know it's my poem of course. Some kids turn and give me kind of sad or understanding looks, and I feel awkward from all the attention, so I start doodling again. What I don't expect when I look up again, when Ms. Abel has moved on to asking everyone to take out their copies of *As I Lay Dying*, is to find Sin staring at me. He's turned sideways in his desk, and I don't know what the look he's giving me means, but then he looks away. Five minutes later, a text causes my phone to buzz.

I take it out of my pocket, careful to keep it in my lap, and read Sin's message: *u r beautiful. I want us to not b mad at each other.*

My heart swells up so much I can hardly breathe. I will stay away from Tristan for real. I will never touch him again, so long as Sin and I can go back to the way things were.

I text back, *you 2 . . . and me 2.*

I watch him read the message and slip the phone back in his backpack.

The rest of the class period is agony. I try to pass the time by paying attention to the book, but Faulkner is so hard to understand, and the class discussion is too much to follow. I just want to put my head down. I start writing in my notebook, thinking I will come up with something else I can turn in for a grade. I write about what I remember from the first few chapters of the novel, about my confusion with the stream-of-consciousness style—while writing in my own stream-of-consciousness style—and this passes the time.

When the bell rings, my chest goes tight, and I look over

to see if Sin is going to wait for me. He does. I feel this huge relief, like crazy just-got-pulled-back-from-the-cliff relief.

"Hey," he says. "Good poem."

"Thanks."

"What are you doing after school?"

"Lena wants me to clean out Sarah's room."

Apparently, we are not one of those families who will keep the room as a monument to the last day Sarah spent there. No, that is not the Kinsey way. We will transform the room into a meditation space for Lena, or perhaps a yoga studio, or a stylish yet comfortable guest suite.

"Ah. The inspiration for the literary work?"

"Sort of. I mean, I go in there and try to put stuff in boxes, but it's hard. I don't know what to keep, what to give away."

He pauses, as if considering his options. "I'll help."

This is the best idea I've heard since, like, forever. "Okay," I say, containing my joy in a careful voice.

"Come on." He gestures for me to follow as he heads for the door.

I trail after him, kind of breathless with relief that we are talking again. Sin isn't mad at me anymore. This fact dances and tumbles in my head, whirling like a little kid trying to make itself dizzy. I had almost given up hope. But there he is, his thin back leading me down the hallway, toward our lockers. I have to make sure I never, ever, ever lose him again.

And I realize something. That sense of danger about our friendship, it's mostly because I need him so much in order for me to stay sane. It's because in this vast world of unreliable people, he is the one I know I can rely on.

• • •

I have not ventured into the dark, hidden places of Sarah's
room before. I have stuck to the safe territory—the tops of
dressers, the bookshelves. It feels wrong to invade her privacy,
even though she is gone. Is there even such a thing as privacy
for the dead? I think so, I decide, as I sit on my knees on the
floor of the closet and pull out pairs of shoes.

I want to know what happened the day Sarah died, but
I'm not sure I want to know what might be hidden in the truth
of it.

Having Sin here gives me confidence, but still this process
makes me want to throw up. The idea that her feet will never
fit into this pair of sandals or that pair of boots . . . it's further
and further proof that she will not be coming back anytime
soon. Or ever.

Sin is going through a dresser, placing items of clothing
into a box. I don't want to see any of it, because every time I
try to give away a shirt or a pair of pants, I think maybe I
should keep it and wear it myself if I ever lose ten pounds.
Then I think, no way, I'd be depressed every time I saw the
stuff. Then I think, but if it's gone, I won't have that little piece
of her.

And I get nothing done.

The shoes are not so difficult since I can't very well turn
my size-nine feet into size eights.

After working my way through all the shoes, I pull out a
shoebox from the bottom of her closet. I can tell by the weight
that it doesn't hold a pair of shoes, and besides that, it is deco-
rated with little pen-and-ink doodles of swirls and stars and
hearts and animals. It looks like something Sarah might have
done in her middle-school days, which means this box has

been around for a while. The brand of shoes it once held has been obscured by white cardstock glued to its sides and top.

Sin is still busy sorting through Sarah's clothes, folding them all carefully and placing each piece in a cardboard box that says FARM FRESH on the outside.

I try not to look at the stuff as he puts it in the giveaway box because then I recall different times she wore a certain shirt, a certain pair of jeans. And what if someone else wears her stuff? They won't even know anything about Sarah when they do, won't know she's gone, which bothers me. I think maybe we should burn the box of clothes when it is packed. Maybe Sin shouldn't be folding it all so carefully, but I don't want to commit to doing one thing or another, so I say nothing.

I open the box, feeling guilty as I do so. Inside are some letters, a couple of rocks and seashells, a journal I am careful not to open, and beneath all that a blue shirt folded up. I recognize it as one of Sarah's. It's a delicate silk tunic edged in crocheted lace. I don't know why she would keep it in here. Maybe she was trying to hide it from Rachel, who borrows and ruins things, but it isn't Rachel's style. I take out the contents on top of the shirt, then the shirt itself. From within it falls a piece of newspaper folded up small.

When I hold up the top, I can see that it is streaked with stains, brownish in color, like old blood. Was this why she'd hidden it? Was she too in love with the shirt to get rid of it after she'd ruined it?

But . . . it doesn't look like it has even been washed. Like no attempt has been made to remove the stains.

Sin notices and comes to take a closer look. "Is that blood?"

"I don't know." The hairs rise on the back of my neck.

Something isn't right. Or maybe I'm prone to thinking the worst, now that the worst has already happened.

I imagine possibilities. Stomach cancer. She could have been vomiting blood. Maybe she didn't have the heart to put us through it all again.

He bends and picks up the piece of newspaper. As he unfolds it, I see that it's one section of the *Marin IJ*, folded small. The cover section. On the cover is an article about the hit-and-run accident that happened in February, in which a guy who'd been hitchhiking along Highway One had been killed. The car that had struck him—and the people in it—had fled the scene and hadn't been found.

"Let me see that." I take the paper from Sin.

He is frowning in a way that makes me nervous.

"Do you think . . ." He begins to ask, but doesn't. He knows better than to complicate matters right now.

I don't think.

No. Absolutely not.

Hearing footsteps in the hall, I look up to see Rachel standing in the doorway, just home from work and still wearing her black barista apron. She eyes the article in my hands curiously. "What's that?"

"Nothing," I say, not wanting to betray Sarah's secrets, even if I don't yet know what they are.

She comes closer. "Let me see."

I ignore her outheld hand.

But she needs only to look over my shoulder to see that it's an article about the dead guy. His name was Brandon Ashcroft, a guy from out of state who'd been backpacking along the California coast.

"So what's all this?" Rachel asks, looking at the box of stuff I've been going through.

"I don't know."

She surveys it all. "Come on, Nancy Drew. You can figure it out."

"What are you talking about?"

"You found Sarah's private stash. This is where she keeps all her deep, dark secrets."

"It's just some old stuff," I say, but Rachel picks up the stained shirt and cocks an eyebrow at me.

She has this look in her eyes, like a snake preparing to strike. "Was *this* in the box? With *that*?" She nods at the article, sounding calmer than the situation calls for.

I say nothing.

"So what?" Sin asks. "Do you know something we don't?"

Rachel expels a breath of disbelief and drops the shirt on the bed, rolls her eyes at us, and walks out.

"Idiots," we hear her say on the way out the door.

My stomach twists and turns. Shadowy, ugly possibilities dance around the edges of my thoughts, and I don't want to consider them.

But it's all so obvious. Maybe Sarah was there when that guy died. Maybe she knew what happened. Maybe she was involved in what happened, if the shirt had anything to do with it.

Why wouldn't she have said anything though?

David springs to mind. Had she been protecting him by saying nothing? Had *he* been driving the car that killed the hitchhiker?

No, she was too honest. She'd had come forward, no matter the cost.

I'm pretty sure.

Sin picks up the shirt and folds it into a small square, which he puts back into the box. Then he takes the newspaper and does the same. Each item I've scattered on the bed, he places carefully back into the box, then he puts the lid back on and places the box inside the larger cardboard box of stuff we plan to keep. But what if Mom sees it? I think but don't ask.

He looks at me carefully. "Maybe you should keep this stuff in your room."

"What about Rachel?" I love that Sin knows what to do without having to ask.

"She could have already come in here and gone through this stuff if she'd wanted to find something."

Nothing makes any sense. What does Rachel know that she isn't saying? And what does any of it have to do with anything?

I don't want to think that the most obvious explanation could possibly be true, and I'm not sure truth is what I want to find anymore.

Maybe Sarah left this stuff here because she wanted me to find it. Was it supposed to tell me something she never had the courage to say?

"Do you want to take a break?" Sin asks.

"Yeah . . . no. I mean, I don't know."

"Let's take a break."

"No, we have to get all this sorted. What if there's more . . ." *More stuff hidden* is what I intend to say, but the words stall out on my tongue.

He watches me as I turn and start pulling out the drawers of Sarah's nightstand, looking for I don't know what. My insides are tightening up and hardening now. I pull out entire drawers and dump their contents on the bed. Bottles of nail polish mingle with papers and jewelry and pens and earrings and all the other random crap that accumulates in a drawer. Something inside me feels monstrous and scared and out of control now. My hands are shaking.

Sin sits down on the end of the bed and picks up a folded piece of paper, opens it, and reads it. Then he sets it aside and does the same with another piece, and another. He understands now that we are no longer sorting a dead girl's stuff into what to keep and what to get rid of.

We are looking for answers I'm terrified to find, while I am sure I can't let anyone else find them first.

Thirty-One

Sarah

Little sister.
Flesh of my flesh,
Bones of my bones,
Heart of my heart.

She found the box that tells the tale I could not tell.

At the top of the list of things I wish I had never done, I struggle to order the events. Which one thing is more awful than the next?

Here is the dirty secret, the story for which I have no pretty words.

Something changed about David. I can't say when, but I knew things were different between us, and I made the mistake of asking him about it on the way home from a party. We'd been in Point Reyes Station, at the house of someone who was celebrating the release of an album I can't even remember. We'd both been drinking, he more than I.

I should never have agreed to drive, but I did. I knew I was more sober than he was, and I'd thought . . . only two drinks.

I'd had two drinks. Maybe three. More than enough for a girl like me who almost never drank.

I was angry at David for seeming distant, so I asked him what was wrong, and he told me. All about Rachel, and him, and how he was in love with her.

It made terrible sense. Perfect, horrible sense.

The hills were dark, like sleeping creatures spread out around us on a cloudy, moonless night. This is what I remember most—how black it was, how lightless. Wisps of fog hung around us, covering the darkness in gauze.

Why was I driving? I asked myself so many times. I should have pulled over, insisted on walking, anything. I should have, and given another chance, I would have, but I didn't when it counted.

Fate. That's why. I understand now that it was time for me to meet mine.

I started crying as David talked about his feelings for Rachel so openly, you might have thought he was telling a friend and not the girl who loved him like a puppy dog.

I cried, and I looked at him across the darkness of the car, and I never saw the hitchhiker.

Not until he was in front of the car, so close there was no swerving away.

Too late.

I remember only the screech of tires, the unfathomable thud of metal against flesh, the shock of a body against the windshield of the car.

I remember a frozen moment of surprise, feeling as if time had stopped.

The next moments were a blur of terror. I don't recall opening the car door or getting out.

He is lying on the cold earth, amid the wild wheat growing at the side of the road. I feel as if I am moving in slow motion as I go to his side and kneel down there. I am having too many thoughts at once—is he alive, and call 911, and what have we done, and it's my fault, and it's David's fault, and why were we even arguing, and God this can't be happening, and what will happen to me, and will I go to jail, and what if he's really dead—

"Check his pulse," David says, standing over me.

My hands shaking, I try to find an artery in his neck, but I can't, so I try his wrist. I feel nothing.

Most frightening is his stillness, which is not the stillness of the living.

I glance up at David, and he understands.

"Fuck!" David says. "Fuck, fuck, fuck. This is bad. We could go to jail for this."

Not *we*. *Me*. It's me who would go to jail. I am the driver. I am the guilty one. I think of the beers I had at the party, and maybe I felt okay to drive, but maybe I wasn't.

No, I definitely wasn't okay to drive.

"I'll say I was driving," David says, "so you won't get in trouble."

I shake my head. Whatever else he's done, I'm not letting him take the fall for me. I know without thinking that I couldn't live with that. "No," I say, on the verge of tears.

"Let's just go. There's no real damage on the car that wasn't already there. Let's go before someone drives by and sees us here."

I look down at the guy. He's our age, blond, good-looking. I cannot believe he's died right here, right now. I wonder about CPR. Would it help? I've taken a class, but in my terror I can't remember a single thing about it. Can you give it to dead people?

There is so much blood. I think it's coming from his head, mostly. On his face, his clothes, his hair.

It's on me too, not sure how it got there.

I place a hand over his mouth, beneath his nose, to see if I can feel any breath, but no. He is so still, something about his face totally different from that of someone merely uncon-scious.

He is inanimate. Whatever made him alive has gone. In that moment, I wish I knew what his eyes looked like before his death. I have only a flash of an image of him, just as we were about to make impact, shock registering on his face. That tiny bit of horrific memory doesn't tell me what I want to know.

I cannot think what else to do, so I stand up and look at David, trying hard not to cry, not to fall apart.

"He's dead. There's nothing we can do," David says. "Come on, let's go now while we still can."

And so.

We go.

In the moments and hours and days that follow, we never decide upon a strategy. Our strategy is simply to pretend the accident never happened. We never speak of it out loud again.

Although I know David has checked already, I do look the next morning at the front of the car, but its old chrome bumper looks the way it always has, and the dents and the rust on the hood do not appear any different from how they did the day before.

Days and weeks pass, and the news of a hitchhiker killed by a hit-and-run at first dominates the papers and local TV, then fades when there is nothing further to say. I begin to sense that we will get away with what we have done—what I have done—but this doesn't ease my conscience. It only makes me feel worse.

Yet what haunts me most, what consumes me day and night, invading my every thought, are the stories of Brandon himself.

A sense of guilt like the weight of a mountain settles over me. A feeling I know I will never outlive.

I find a story in the *Marin IJ* two days after the accident, with a picture of Brandon, his senior photo, in which he looks not quite clean-cut, but nice. His hair comes to his collar in the photo. It is wavy and dark blond, and he is smiling as if thinking of some private joke. His eyes though, his eyes are what keep me studying the photo again and again. I can see the life in them, the spark, the essence of who he must have been.

That is what I stole from him.

When I sleep, I dream about him. In my dreams he is my lover, my fiancé, my secret crush, my husband—any or all of these, depending on the particular dream. I wake up feeling in love and happy, then I realize he is gone. Not just dead, but dead because of me, and I feel worse with each waking.

So disturbed by my dreams, I am afraid to sleep.

I try to imagine his parents, his life in Boulder, Colorado, where the news articles say he was from. I think if I can reconstruct him in my mind, I will stop having the dreams, but no.

It seems so unfair that after surviving cancer, after beating the odds doctors said were nearly impossible to beat, the legacy I leave is to take someone else's life. If I had died, Brandon would have lived. This fact plays over and over in my head, rarely giving me more than a few minutes' relief.

It's as if by surviving, by cheating cancer, I have paid the debt with Brandon's life.

As time passed, David and I barely talked. I didn't see him after he dropped me off at home the next morning. I'd slept at his place because his roommates were all out, so we could claim to have been there earlier if anyone ever asked. But no one did.

After that night I didn't see any point in trying to make our relationship work. He wanted to be with me, but he also wanted to be with Rachel, and I wasn't going to stick around and let him decide whom to choose. I was surprised to feel so little anguish over what I knew was the end of our relationship, but then, Brandon was lurking in the corner of my every thought.

Brandon, gone but haunting me.

I didn't talk to anyone about the accident, or the breakup, not even Asha, from whom I had never hidden anything. And I thought David would never speak of it either.

Then came the hike with Rachel, when I learned that he had told at least one person.

Thirty-Two

Rachel

I try not to think about Krishna. I really try.

I do have other problems far bigger than him, after all. Keeping it on the down-low is like my full-time job these days. Hiding shit from AJ isn't easy when he comes around because he's used to girls trying to cheat on his ass.

He likes being with me because I'm different from them. But I don't like to think of what he does with all those other girls when he gets back to Oakland. I figure me keeping something extra on the side is okay since I know he does it too, even if he doesn't admit it.

When David was the only other guy in the picture, it wasn't that complicated. But how the hell do I explain Krishna to AJ? I don't, because no way he's going to believe I'm hanging around with some celibate guy. He doesn't even know there's such a thing as guys not wanting to have sex. That shit doesn't exist in his world.

These days I've got crazy skills for cheating. One thing's

for sure though—it's tiresome. I just want to not have to re-member what I told to who and when and why. I want to not have to sweat it every time I walk around town with some-one, worrying the other guy's going to see. That shit isn't fun. Not one little bit.

So here's where it all went wrong. I get a text from David while AJ is using my phone to call his brother because he got his phone shut off last week for not paying his bill.

The text says, *I miss u. When will I see u again?*

Motherfucking fuck fuck fuck. That's what I think when I hear the little incoming-text-message beep.

AJ looks at it, and he gets this look on his face like some-body just ran over his dog. "Who the fuck is David?"

First I think of lying, but then he starts scrolling back through the old messages from David that I haven't deleted in a couple days. I always go back and delete them before I see AJ, but he showed up when I wasn't expecting him and . . . oh, shit, he's going to kill me.

He's going to kill me and David both, and maybe that's for the best, right?

I don't deserve to live anymore.

"Who the *fuck* is David?"

Then I know I've waited too long and nothing I say now is going to get me out of this. "He's my, uh, my sister's boyfriend."

"Your sister's boyfriend," he mutters as he reads message after message, and I'm trying to remember what they say.

These past few days we were talking about where to meet, definitely not when Lena's around, and I don't want to meet him, but I never say that. But did I say anything stupid? Did I say words like *love,* like *want,* like . . .

"You're fucking this guy." He looks at me like he's either going to smash my face or the phone or both.

Shit.

This is the part of playing with fire where I get burned, I realize as my brain fails to produce any suitable lies that might get my ass out of this spot.

"I'm not," I say, sounding unconvincing. "He's just been wanting to hang out a lot since Sarah died. He's lonely."

"Lonely motherfuckers don't text my girlfriend how they're missing you and shit."

He begins typing a text back to David.

Oh, God.

"What are you doing?" I consider snatching the phone from his hands but suspect he will lay me out with one punch if I do, and I want to keep all my teeth.

"I'm telling this dude to come over here right now."

"AJ! He's grieving. What are you going to do? Kick his ass for texting me?"

"Yup." AJ has finished typing and hits send.

Panic sets in and I have no idea how I will get out of this now. I consider running into the house and using the phone there. But AJ will surely follow me.

"You're making a big deal out of nothing," I say.

"We'll see about that shit, won't we?"

"I need to use the bathroom." I head for the front door.

"Don't even think you're gonna go in there and call the motherfucker."

I hear the beep of another incoming message, and I stop in my tracks.

AJ looks at the screen of my phone and smiles. "Homeboy's

gonna be here in five minutes. Damn. He must be grieving awful bad."

I head for the door again, but AJ follows. "Can't I go to the bathroom in private?"

"Sure. I'm just going to make sure you don't make any phone calls while you're in there."

"With what? A bar of soap? You've got my phone, asshole." I roll my eyes and give up the fight for now.

Inside, I close the bathroom door in AJ's face, but he stays right there, listening and talking at me through the door. "Don't you know you can't play a player, girl?"

I consider climbing out the window, but what would be the point? I can't escape AJ forever. Might as well face him down now, I guess. I sit on the toilet with my jeans around my ankles and pee to buy myself some time to think.

Maybe when David gets here, he'll see the angry boyfriend and know it's time to lie through his teeth. But what if his whole free-love attitude gets in the way?

Then I think, okay, so what if David does come here and AJ beats his ass? What then? Maybe it solves all my problems . . . gets me away from David and gives me a good reason not to keep playing with that book of matches.

But then what happens with AJ? I don't like the idea of his dumb ass telling me who I can and can't see. Part of me is afraid of him though. Afraid of what he'll do when he gets mad. Then I realize again that I'm about to find out exactly what he does when he gets mad.

I sigh and flush the toilet. Glance at the window, my last chance of escape.

When I open the door again, AJ is right there in my face,

leaning against the doorframe. He doesn't move when I try to get past him. I glare up into his dark green eyes.

Before I can think what to say, the doorbell rings, and my heart sinks to my ankles.

AJ lumbers down the hallway to the foyer and opens the door, filling it with all six feet and a few inches of himself in his black leather jacket and sagging jeans. His shoulder-length cornrows give him a scarecrow appearance against the outdoor light. I can't even see David on the other side of the door. I can only hear him say a confused "Uhhhhhh . . ."

"You David?" AJ asks, real cool.

"Yeah."

"You the motherfucker ballin' my bitch?"

No guy has ever called me his bitch before, and I feel the urge to hurl the Buddha statue sitting on the hallway table next to me at his head.

"What? What is this? Who are you?"

AJ steps aside and I finally see David, his brow all scrunched up.

"David," I say, my voice shaky, "AJ saw your text and thinks we've been sleeping together, but I've told him we haven't."

This sounds even more fake out loud than it did in my head.

AJ shakes his head and steps outside onto the porch with David, who stands there like an idiot.

I want to scream at him to run, but I am also curious to see what happens next.

"I'm sorry," David finally says. "I didn't know you and Rachel were exclusive."

"You mean you didn't know she was my bitch?" AJ says, all up in David's face now.

"Back off, man," David says, all calm.

"Who you telling to back off?" AJ pushes David, who stumbles back and loses his balance.

He lands on his ass, and before I can do anything, AJ is on top of him, throwing punches at David's head. All I can see is a blur of fists and black leather, and I realize I have to stop this before someone is seriously hurt. *Someone* meaning David.

"AJ!" I screech, but he doesn't respond, so I hurry out the door and try to grab AJ's fists before they make contact again with David's now-bloody face.

"Stop! Stop it!" I yell. "You're going to get in trouble with your PO!"

This mention of his parole officer jars AJ out of his frenzy, and I wish I'd thought of it sooner. He clambers to his feet, dusting himself off as he stands over David on the ground. "Stay the hell away from Rachel. You hear me, white boy?"

David says nothing, pushing himself up on his elbow and wiping at his bloody nose and swelling lip.

I see a flash of my future, me unable to have any fun as AJ intimidates every guy who ever comes within a mile of me. I can't live like this, especially not when I know AJ isn't exactly faithful over on the other side of the bridge.

In the fight, AJ dropped my phone, and I bend over to pick it up off the porch. The glass screen is shattered now. I stare at it, unable to think what to say or do.

I don't know how my life got like this.

I should have ended it with David already.

Should have.

I should have done so many things.

"Look, man, I don't want any trouble," David finally says, then pauses to spit out a mouthful of blood. "I'll let you and Rachel work out your problems on your own. You don't need to worry about me."

David struggles to stand up, and suddenly I don't want to see him go. I want to run after him as he makes his way across the yard to his car. I want to climb into the passenger side and ride away from here.

But this, I know, is my problem—wanting what I shouldn't want.

David glances up at me when he reaches the car, and I can see by the expression in his eyes that we are done. Whatever I used to see there that let me know he wanted me is gone. Probably for the best. It's what I've wanted ever since Sarah's death, right? To somehow get rid of this weird thing I have with him?

Then why do I feel such a loss now?

As he drives away, AJ is glaring after him. Then he turns to me. "Bitch, we're through. I don't hang with hos. You want to be a player, you go play some other chump."

He looks at me like I'm a piece of dogshit clinging to his shoe. Then he walks out to his car in the driveway and drives away. I am numb as I watch him go. I don't dare to call after him because I know I'm getting off lucky. He could have done to me what he'd just done to David, and I can't say I wouldn't have deserved it.

But now I am, without a doubt, alone, and alone is something I don't know how to be.

Thirty-Three

Sarah

When Rachel volunteered to go on the hike with me, I should have known something was wrong. She was not a hiker or a nature lover. But here in this ever-after place, I've had plenty of time to play the day over and over in my mind, and I see no hint of her having intended me harm from the start.

I wanted to get out of town. I was depressed, I see now, though I didn't realize it then.

When Rachel saw me putting on my hiking boots, she asked me if I was going to go for a hike in the nature preserve down the street from our house. I told her no, I was going to try to find a ride out to the coast, maybe borrow Lena's car.

"I've got her keys for the day. Why do you want to go out there?"

"I just feel like it."

She shrugged. "I could give you a ride."

"*You* want to hike?"

"Sure. I've been eating too many goddamn bagels at the coffee shop. I need the exercise."

I hadn't really talked to Rachel since finding out about her and David. I guess when I thought about what had happened to Brandon, my own sister betraying me didn't matter that much. Nothing much besides my own despicable actions mattered to me in those final few weeks.

Surprising myself a little, I agreed to go with her to the coast.

I waited for her while she changed and put on a pair of hiking boots that looked like they belonged to Asha. Probably Rachel didn't own a pair of her own, since they didn't usually have flashy buckles or four-inch heels.

The car trip felt like a ride in a coffin. Rachel turned on the radio, fiddling with the stations since only a few came in clearly out this way, but I heard it all as if from far away. I was wrapped up inside myself, withdrawing from the conversation I knew hung in the air between us like a bad smell, because I had nothing to say.

No, not exactly true. There were so many things I could have said—should have said—but I had no energy for any of it. My thoughts moved as if through mud, and the blood pumping through my veins felt the same. I was slowing down, like a toy with a worn-out battery.

It was my first time riding along Highway One since the accident. When we neared the place where I had struck Brandon, I felt myself coiling tighter and tighter inside, the energy of the place reaching out and threatening to choke me. And me with no energy to flee from its reach.

Although my memories of the night were made hazy by

fear and darkness, the exact location was easy to spot. Someone had set up a memorial near the roadside, with a cross and teddy bears and flowers.

These forlorn objects, already starting to look weathered, were out of place surrounded by the beauty of the hills and the sky all around. They signified nothing so much as how all we ever love and possess will fade to dust. All our silly belongings and attachments—they come to nothing in the end.

Brandon, an entire person wiped away from this earth in the space of a breath. All the care that went into making him, growing him, keeping him fed and safe and loved and entertained and educated. I could see his mother, holding him as a warm, hungry newborn in her arms, gazing into a new face she imagined would grow up, become a man, have children of his own, maybe even take care of her when she got old.

I imagined the stories read on warm laps, the diapers changed, the first steps taken, the meals of spaghetti and meatballs or grilled cheese, the baseball games, the first kiss, first awkward date, first time with a girl, family movie nights and camping trips and all the imperfect moments that make up a childhood, and a life.

Then I had come along.

What loss could I ever feel now that would make up for the life I'd taken away?

I should have known when Rachel slowed down the car and glanced over at me as we passed the cross that something was not right. She was not the type to notice or linger over roadside memorials.

"That must be for the guy who died in the hit-and-run," she said oh so coolly, as if she had no idea about the truth.

Oh, had I ever learned the dangers of arguing while driving, so I kept my mouth shut. Easy enough when I was coiled so tightly inside, breathing was all the effort I could manage.

The farther from the spot we traveled, the more I itched to get out of the car, to get away from Rachel. It was a mistake to have come with her, I knew already.

David was lost to me, Rachel was lost to me, and Brandon was dead. Brandon, whom I didn't know but so desperately wanted to have known, was a beacon of light I couldn't see through the fog. I could only imagine his brightness in the distance, a point I blindly traveled toward.

Everything about my life felt stolen.

As if poking at an open wound, I pictured Brandon hitch-hiking that night. Tried to imagine what he had been doing in the hours and days before his death. In a news article I had perilously, stupidly saved, he was said to have been traveling up the California coast, camping and hiking and wandering. He'd been a college student but had dropped out for a year to travel, said his parents in the article. His major had been pre-med. So he was like me in that way, interested in medicine. He might have gone on to save many people's lives, if he had lived.

Why had he been hitching a ride so late at night? The articles never mentioned. He could have been out at a bar or a party—maybe even the same party we'd attended. I tried to remember if I'd glimpsed his face in the crowd of people, but I couldn't. I would never know if he'd been there, or if things could have been different if somehow even one moment before the accident could have been changed.

I recalled the crushed guitar that had been strapped to his back lying by the side of the road, and I wondered if he'd been a good guitar player.

I tried to imagine what it would have been like to kiss him, allowing myself to believe for a moment that I could breathe life back into him with my slow molasses lungs.

In the dark, lonely cave of my mind, a whole living Brandon took shape. Particular details of him, vivid to me as the day outside. The rough stubble of his unshaven cheek against my skin, the oily male scent of his hair, the salt and sweat taste of him when we kissed—this is what I focused on, as if imagining him could undo all the wrong I'd done on this dark road.

How would Rachel react if she knew my thoughts? But of course I didn't dare speak. Couldn't speak. Wouldn't break this spell even if I could have.

Instead, I closed my eyes and tried to lose myself in these memories that weren't.

"Where do you want to hike?" Rachel asked sometime after we'd turned south.

I knew the trails from countless hikes, and she didn't. I had a favorite trail that wound north along the coast, overlooking the ocean. "Keep driving this way," I said, my voice a strange artifact of my old self, the one who got into the car a half hour ago. "There's a place we can go that I haven't been to in a while."

At the end of a long gravel road was the trailhead, populated by a few parked cars and marked by a couple of signs explaining where we were and how long the trail was. I had been here a few times before with David, in what felt like another lifetime, and the almost-forgotten memory of his leading me into a tuck-away meadow and laying me down on the grass was nearly enough to trap me in the car.

But there was Rachel, standing outside, looking at me

through the windshield with the expectation that we would do what we'd come here to do. And for the first time I thought to wonder, what is it really that we have come here for?

Between the dark deeds that lay behind us and between us, I could not see any good that would come.

Yet I got out of the car, and for that I have only myself to blame.

A heavy fog had settled over the coast that day, keeping the air cool and damp. Around us, pine, redwood, and eucalyptus trees towered like silent, grasping giants. I could smell the ocean but couldn't see it yet, and I longed for a view that wasn't socked in by fog. I had hoped to be able to look out at the ocean and see a dazzling blue horizon, something vaster than my own problems. Instead, I had only this silent, looming gray that felt too much like the feeling in my chest.

Underfoot, the trail was soft and a bit muddy from a rainstorm two days before. I inhaled the scent of eucalyptus and sea air, trying to calm myself and find the sort of peace that hiking in this quiet wilderness had always brought me. But Rachel's presence did not invite calm. I could hear her tromping along behind me, breathing heavily even though we weren't moving fast or uphill.

I led the way along the trail until we were well past a man and woman who'd been headed in the opposite direction. My heart thudded in my chest, its beat somehow feeling too fast and too slow. When we were alone on the trail again, I could feel Rachel dragging like a weight behind me, and I slowed down until she was by my side.

In the cold, dank forest, I could no longer see any reason to hide from the truth. And maybe, if I was honest with her, I could make some kind of good come of all this bad. Maybe

I could make things better with Rachel, if nothing else. Maybe that was the universe's reason we were here alone together now.

"David told me about the two of you," I said carefully, forcing the words out in an even stream in spite of myself, not wanting her to know how much she'd hurt me, or at least the former me who had cared.

"Oh." She looked at me with a flash of defiance. "I figured he would. He never was interested in sneaking."

This little shared intimacy—Rachel's knowing what David was or wasn't interested in doing—should have hurt more than it did. Instead, I felt as if the fog all around us had seeped into me, leaving my emotions blurry and muffled.

"We broke up. Did he tell you that?"

Her expression gave away nothing. "I heard all about your fight."

The fight.

We had only one argument—that night in the car.

He wouldn't have told her. But then, I'm not sure I knew anymore what David was and wasn't capable of doing. Maybe he would have.

I felt myself speeding up on the trail, a cold truth chasing me.

"I know all about it," Rachel said, struggling to keep up.

I glanced back at her and her calculated indifference.

When I said nothing, she continued, "I even know about Brandon."

I stopped. Let the cold truth catch me where I stood, let it seep in and fill me with a new kind of numbness. My life as I knew it was ending right here in the forest. No, it had already ended, but I was only now fully understanding.

Rachel knew.

She *knew.*

What could I do with that knowing except obliterate it?

She gazed back at me with contempt. Rachel hated me, and I deserved it. I was exactly the kind of person she knew I was.

"What did he tell you?" I asked in a voice I didn't even recognize as my own.

"You killed that guy, Sarah. He told me you were driving the car."

This was the moment I deserved. I knew it. When I left Brandon there on the side of the road, I gave up the right to ever feel good about myself again. I knew that then as I know it now.

I couldn't think what to say in my own defense.

"You killed him, and if the police find out, you'll go to prison." She said it all calmly, matter-of-factly, as if we were discussing my having gone to the store to buy milk and bread.

For a second, I considered lying and saying David had been the driver. I wanted to believe he deserved it, for betraying me not once but twice with Rachel. But I couldn't. I just stood there, defeated, filled with loathing for myself.

It was a relief to have someone else know the truth. I got to see how it felt to be accused and to be convicted of a crime of which I was guilty. It made my decision easier, that's for sure.

But Rachel didn't stop there. She kept on talking about the accident. She wouldn't let it go. She took pleasure in knowing how thoroughly I'd ruined my life, and I began to feel a creeping sense of wanting to exact my own revenge.

There. I said it. It's true.

Even my death was a cruel act. Not to myself, but to my sister. To everyone I loved and still love.

Is there any greater shame than that?

But there is also comfort in being able to stand at a cliff's edge and feel no fear. There is a sense of freedom I have only known in that one brief instant before death. Perhaps cancer prepared me for the eventual reality of death, but only this total annihilation of my former self freed me of fear.

When I stood at the precipice, I looked down at my toes. Only a step farther and I would be in the air, a sheer drop so far down to the ocean below. It was a very high tide, because from the other times I'd been to this spot, I knew the ocean was concealing a narrow, rocky beach. Wind whipped my hair, and I felt Rachel's presence nearby on the trail. When I glanced over my shoulder, she was sitting on a rock and tightening her bootlaces, seemingly oblivious.

It was the perfect moment, I decided there and then. Rachel deserved to see this happen. She would be my witness, and at least in that way, in my death, I would exact the tiniest bit of revenge. Let my death be permanently imprinted on her memory. It was only fitting.

So you see? I am reprehensible.

I closed my eyes and thought of Brandon, and the light of him began to take shape.

I looked back at Rachel one last time, making sure she saw me. "Good-bye," I said, so softly she might not have heard.

Good-bye, sister, good-bye, trees, good-bye, rocks and ocean and breeze. Good-bye, everything.

I'd never been confident about diving into pools, but this time, I let myself fly free. I simply dove. Down, down I fell, as the water rushed up to meet me.

Thirty-Four

Rachel

I can't believe Lena has managed this. We are at an actual family dinner, which she of all people has orchestrated. Asha, the new rebel in the family, is here. She seems to have taken a shower, combed her hair, put on clean clothes, even. I try to imagine what Lena could have said to get her here, but I can't. I will have to drag Asha into the bathroom later and get her to tell me.

I didn't have a lot of choice. Lena told me she'd buy me the boots I've been lusting after in the Anthropologie catalog if I showed, so okay, fine. I can sit through a one-hour dinner for a pair of boots that would cost me a paycheck and a half working at Sacred Grounds.

We sit in the dim yellow light of La Table, a new restaurant that tries hard to be hip and local and fresh, with a menu that has stuff like organic, artisanal feta cheese made of milk from a goat down the street named Bacchus, or whatever.

There's shit like microgreens on the menu too. Does that mean we'll need a microscope to see our salads?

I have never been here before but have wandered by and viewed through the window middle-aged couples looking either bored or engaged in conversation and well fed. It's the kind of place our mother does not take us.

To my left, Asha has the edgy energy of a meth addict aching for her next hit. I doubt this is her problem though. She is too fleshy to be on meth. Also too steadily morose.

Tension is in the air, like something is about to go down, but I don't know what. We are all being stiff and polite, and when we have placed our orders, Lena clears her throat and my eyes land on the huge-ass diamond ring she is wearing.

This, she hasn't explained.

"Ron and I have some big news for everyone, so we wanted to bring us all together tonight to celebrate." She pauses and smiles at everyone. "We're getting married!"

Somehow, I thought this would never happen. There have been boyfriends, sure, but no one stupid enough to take on a woman with three daughters, one of whom had medical bills out the ass. But now that daughter is gone, and everything has changed so much I can hardly recognize us.

When we say nothing, she continues, "We're planning a wedding for early fall, but in the meantime, I know you'll want to hear how this all affects the two of you."

She'd better not expect us to change our names. I don't even know what Ron's last name is, and I sure as hell am not going to call him Dad. I stare daggers at Lena.

"Maybe you should have talked to us about that *before* you decided to get married," Asha says under her breath.

"I'm sorry, what was that?" Lena asks.

"Nothing." Asha sighs.

"I've thought about this a great deal, and I don't think I should go on living in a house that reminds me so much of Sarah. It's not good for my healing process."

Oh my fucking God. I eye the fork, wondering if I have the nerve to fling it at her head.

"So what? We're moving?" Asha says, her tone making it clear exactly how she feels about that idea.

"I'm going to move into Ron's house," Lena says. "It's a two-bedroom though, and he uses the second as his office, so we were thinking, perhaps . . ."

"Perhaps," Ron cuts in, "you'd like to strike out on your own, either at the current rental house or elsewhere."

I blink at this, none of it making any sense. My brain hasn't caught up with the meaning of the words.

"Or," Lena adds, "you could move in with your father now that he's back in Marin."

"Those are our choices? Ravi or the street?" Asha says, her voice rising, and I can tell she's very, very close to making a scene.

My feral cat of a mother is kicking me out of the house. That's what I finally realize.

I am not sure who to hate more—Lena for making this decision or myself for not being thrilled at the idea that I am set free. No option of living at home now, so that should be a good thing, right?

Then why do I feel like total crap?

I look over at Asha, who is seething. What does she care? She doesn't want to live with us anyway—and she manages not to half the time.

Lena is saying something about starting a new chapter of

our lives or some shit, but I can't focus on her words. I want to push the table over and storm out of the restaurant like the star of some reality-TV show, but it feels like lead weights are holding me down, pressing me into this chair.

I look over at Ron, who is busy texting on his phone. Texting? Right now, in the middle of our big family moment? I'd expect that of myself or one of my friends, but not of a guy my former-hippie, antitechnology mother is about to marry. I feel like everything I thought I knew is suddenly wrong, like all the rules of this stupid universe have been rewritten.

My gaze falls again to the huge diamond sparkling on her ring finger, and I see a glimmer of the truth. Lena has full-on sold out. She has been bought for the price of a two-carat rock, and she doesn't need me anymore. I'm not a part of the new Lena Kinsey–de Graas life story. I'm only going to get in the way, like one too many hyphenated names she will need to drop to make room for the new.

"What if I don't want to move?" Asha says, her eyes darker than usual as she glares at Lena now.

"Darling, we all have to make adjustments to this new situation. I simply can't continue living in a house that reminds me so much of Sarah."

Ron looks up then. "Like I said, there is the possibility of you and Rachel remaining at your mother's house, if the two of you can pay the utilities and half the rent. I'd be willing to chip in the other half. It would be cheaper than remodeling my current house."

Something about this idea makes me want to puke.

Me and Asha, living on our own? A sixteen-year-old and an eighteen-year-old? Even I think this idea sounds stupid.

Neither of us knows how to cook anything besides a grilled-cheese sandwich. Lena's selling us out for this moron?

"Oh, right. I'll just quit school and come up with a thousand dollars a month, no problem," Asha says as she lets her fork clatter to the plate.

"I don't even earn enough to buy groceries," I squawk, sounding like an idiot.

The rent on our house is two thousand freaking dollars a month, and that's a bargain in our town from what I can tell.

"It could be a good education in money management," Lena says. "Now that you're eighteen, you can work full-time. It's a chance to learn what it takes to budget and plan."

I can learn what it takes to live in a homeless shelter is more like it. Already I am regretting having lost both David and AJ in one fucked-up day. At least I could have lived with one of them, maybe, and then I start calculating what it would take to get either of them back in my life in a serious way. Except I don't want to move to Oakland, and I don't like David enough to live with him.

"I'm moving in with Sin," Asha announces. "And you don't need to call me your daughter anymore since you have no idea how to behave like a mother."

With that my little sister stands up and sends her chair flying backward, startling everyone around us in the restaurant. She heads for the door, and I watch her for only a moment before I realize I want to follow. For once, I feel nothing but admiration for Asha and her relentless anger.

I stand up, and Lena looks at me with thin, pinched lips. "Sit down, Rachel. We will discuss what your options are."

I feel a giant *Fuck you* hovering on my lips, but I don't say it. Instead, I drop my napkin in my plate of pasta and walk away.

Outside, I see Asha standing at the stoplight waiting to cross the street. It's not a terrible walk, the two miles back to our house from here, unless you are wearing freaking four-inch platform heels like I am.

"Asha, wait!" I call out.

She turns and stares at me, no particular expression on her face. But when the light turns green, she does wait as I hurry over to her. I stop at the corner and take off my shoes, figuring it will be easier to walk barefoot.

"I hate Lena," she says quietly, not one little bit of emotion in her voice.

I wish I knew how she did that. "I'll walk with you."

"I can't believe they're doing this."

"I can. We're not exactly the perfect fucking family, now are we?" My voice sounds all choked up, which is embarrassing as hell.

Maybe this is the first time I am admitting to myself that my big sister is truly gone. There is not going to be a Sarah around for me to resent ever again. There is not even going to be the memory of her getting in our way if Lena just leaves behind our family home and goes to live with some new guy.

Whatever we were, whatever shaky, fucked-up little bit of a family we made, will be gone for good.

We are walking along a side street headed back toward what will soon no longer be our home, and I realize that I want to tell Asha what happened. All of it. It doesn't matter anymore anyway. There's nothing for me to hide now that I don't have a family left to protect from the truth.

I am so much worse than any of them think, but Asha,

who doesn't give a damn, I can tell. She'll understand, I think, after the way she glared at Lena in the restaurant.

"I need to tell you something," I say.

She doesn't respond. Just keeps walking, staring straight ahead.

"Remember when you asked about how Sarah died?"

It is easier to say this in the dark, her walking beside me so that I don't have to look into her eyes and see disgust.

"What?" she says so softly I can barely hear her.

"She didn't slip," I say, for the first time aloud. "She jumped."

Asha stops, so I have to turn and look at her. I see the devastation in her gaze and feel all of a sudden like the biggest shit in the world. I never realized until now, I was sort of protecting her by not admitting that part of Sarah's death.

"What do you mean she jumped?" she says with such vehemence, she sounds like a different person.

"I mean, she jumped. On purpose."

Asha's expression is utter confusion. "How can you be sure? You *saw* her?"

"I was watching. I didn't expect her to do it, but she . . . She stood for a long time watching the surf, and then she dove off the cliff. On purpose."

Asha's face crumples in a way I'd never before seen. She clutched her hand against her stomach, and then, seeming to regain herself for a second, she says, "You're just saying this to hurt me. Sarah had no reason to commit suicide."

Before I can explain any more, Asha turns and starts to run. Not wanting to go where I'm going, and not wanting to return to Lena and Ron, she chooses a third direction, down into the drainage ditch that lines the side of the road. It's a steep drop though, and after only a couple of steps, she cries out as it sounds like she loses her balance and falls the rest of the way down.

My stomach falls with her. I'm not ready to lose another sister, and while she's probably fine, I feel crazy panicked.

"Asha?" I call. "Are you okay?"

I start to make my way down to her, but it's pitch-dark and I can't even see where she has landed or where to step on my way down. "Asha?" I call again, holding my arms out for balance and cursing every time I take a step, as brush pokes into my bare feet.

I hear nothing from down below, and I start thinking of snakes and bugs and shit. I hate nature, in spite of my hippie upbringing, or maybe because of it. Now Asha is rustling in the brush, or at least I hope it is her.

"Please just say you're okay."

"Fuck you," she mutters.

With the sound of her voice, I am able to make my way over to her. Thank God I didn't slip, because I would fucking cry if I ruined my dress, but when my shin bumps against something solid, I lose my balance before I realize it's my sister I've fallen on.

"Shit," she says as I fumble to climb off her. "Get the hell away from me."

"Let me help you out of here." I reach for her.

I don't usually touch my sister, not if I can help it. But now I am all of a sudden realizing she is the only one I've got, maybe the only family I've got, and I need to start figuring out how to get along with her without being a bitch all the time.

"I said get the hell away from me," she shrieks, and starts clambering out of the ditch. I try to stand up to follow her, but I'm beginning to think this is a bad idea.

Yet, I don't want to be left alone here in the dark, so I start crawling back out as best I can without dragging my dress on the ground.

"I need to talk to you," I call after Asha, but then I can hear footsteps on the pavement and I know she is running in the direction of home—or at least the place we once called home.

I chase after her for a while, but she disappears into the night, and I eventually give up and walk the rest of the way home. Finally I find her at the house. She could move a lot faster than I could in my bare feet, and she has already gotten a bag mostly packed with her stuff by the time I walk into her bedroom.

"Asha. Please just listen for a minute. I did something to Sarah. I have to tell you so you'll understand."

She stops and looks at me then, her face expressionless.

This is probably as much attention as I'm ever going to get, so I start. "That shirt you found in Sarah's closet, and the newspaper article?"

Asha stares at me, says nothing.

"She was in the car that hit the guy. She was driving."

"You're lying," she says, but she sinks onto the edge of the bed as if I've pushed her.

"I was sleeping with David, and he was so freaked about the accident, he told me about it. I'm the only person besides them who knows."

"Maybe David was driving. Maybe he lied."

"I thought of that too. But here's the thing—I went hiking with Sarah to confront her about it, and she admitted everything."

Asha just continues to stare at me, silent.

"I don't know why I wanted to confront her. Now I wish I hadn't."

"You were sleeping with David," she whispers as if she's just now finding that part out.

"David is a douche bag. He didn't deserve her." I don't know where these words have come from, but I know they are true the moment they've escaped my lips.

"You did it to hurt her," she says.

"Not exactly."

"Then why?"

"I guess I just did it because I could."

"Great reason."

"I'm sorry," I say, the words flat and so profoundly inadequate I almost laugh.

"Why are you telling me this?" Asha stands up and shoves the last of her clothes into her bag and zips it up.

"Because you want to know what happened."

"It's not like you."

"No, I guess not."

Asha says nothing, but she sinks back onto the bed beside her bag.

"She was depressed," Asha finally says slowly, as if she's figuring this out for herself. "That's why she didn't talk to me."

I shrug, a spike of jealousy shooting through me. And I, the evil-bitch sister who practically pushed Sarah off the cliff, if not with my hands then at least with my words.

"It's my fault," I say for the first time out loud. My voice kind of cracks, and I start to cry.

Big sobs escape my throat, but Asha just watches me, silent.

"It *is* your fault," she then says. "If you hadn't slept with David, if you hadn't gone with her on that hike just to make her feel worse, she'd still be alive."

And with that she stands up and leaves the house, leaving me to my pathetic sobbing.

Thirty-Five

Sarah

Deserving is a strange idea, or at least that's what I used to think. Who ever gets what they deserve? And how much of our lives do we spend expecting the deserving to get their due reward? I used to be at peace with the idea that it rarely happens, the reward thing. Did I deserve to have the combination of genes and bad luck that meant I would have cancer?

Maybe I did.

Maybe fate works backward, and what I was being punished for hadn't even happened yet. The more I think about it, the more I think that's just how it is. We never know if we're going to get our good luck now or later, or bad luck later or now or yesterday.

Thirty-Six

Rachel

I thought saying it out loud would help, but it doesn't. I thought seeing Asha hate me, despise me, know me for the horrible person I am, would start to set things right. But instead I see that I am only crushing her too. She doesn't have the strength to hate me the way I need to be hated. She's already broken.

I stare out the door that Asha has slammed. After a minute or two or three, my phone buzzes, and I see through the shattered glass on the screen that it's David sending me a text: *I left a package of your stuff in the mailbox. I guess this is good-bye.* I throw the phone against the door. It breaks into pieces and falls to the floor.

I stand up and go to the door, lock it. I go to the front door and lock it too. I am alone here now, and I hate this house. I have hated it ever since our dad moved out. It reminds me of everything bad that has ever happened. I wander from room to room, not sure what I'm looking for. In Lena's room, the curtains are pulled aside and light from a streetlamp pours in. The bed is unmade, and I sit down on it, where I can smell the faintest scent of Lena, something that once comforted me. The sheets are pale green and soft, Egyptian cotton. Expensive sheets, because Lena spares no expense on herself. I try to remember the last time I ever slept in her bed. It had to have been before Sarah got sick. I was little, had a nightmare, and crawled in with her, between her and Dad, and felt safe there.

Some part of me wishes I could do that now. I want Lena—the old Lena—to hold me tight and make me feel safe again. This is the stupidest thing I could ever think, because she is long past seeing me as one of her children, as someone to take care of. I learned long ago that if I wanted to survive, I would have to take care of myself.

On her nightstand is a book of Buddhist meditations, with a piece of yellow paper sticking out. I open the book to the marked page, and on the paper is scrawled Ron's phone number and address. She has only been with him a few months, and already she is rearranging her life, pushing us away to allow space for him, pretending our past didn't happen.

That's probably where she is right now—still with him, making sure he doesn't forget her before they say their vows of for better or for worse and all that. She's at that age where she knows she won't be attractive to men much longer. She's still pretty, but so many younger women, girls like me, are waiting to take her place.

I go into Lena's bathroom and open the medicine cabinet, where bottles of Percocet and Vicodin—Mother's Little Helpers—wait in their orange prescription bottles. I take the Vicodin bottle, open it, and fill a glass with water. I should have a more creative idea than this, but I dread the thought of pain. I don't have Sarah's courage to dive off the nearest cliff I can find. I just want right now, more than anything else, to go to sleep and not wake up.

The crazy thing is, I miss Sarah. I want to go wherever she is, be there with her in the nothingness. Why did it take my sister's dying for me to realize I love her?

My whole family had been shaped by the ugly deformity that comes from knowing a young person is about to die. Life reveals itself then to be the unfair, cruel, relentless joke that it is. When our family first found out about Sarah's leukemia, I didn't understand for a long time. I remember being vaguely titillated by the drama of it, even wishing I were the center of that drama. Life, I thought at first, was made all the more meaningful by big stuff happening, like death.

In a way, my first instinct had been right. But that wasn't the only truth.

I carry the pills and the glass of water into my bedroom because I don't want the scene of my last moments to be in Lena's dingy, orange seventies bathroom. I want to be in my own bed.

I lean against some pillows, sitting up so I can down a few pills at a time, gulping water between each palmful of pills. Maybe thirty are in the bottle. Enough to do the job, I hope.

When I've taken all the pills, I hide the bottle under the bed so that no one will see it right away and call an ambulance. Better if they think I'm just sleeping and leave me alone. I'm not one of those lame, half-assed suicidal girls who just wants to be found, to get lots of attention, to have my "cry for help" heard.

This is not a cry for help. Let's be clear on that, at least.

My death may not be as dramatic as Sarah's, but we have already established that between us three sisters, I am not the good sister, or the brave sister, or the strong sister. I am the cowardly one.

Asha

When I am halfway to Sin's house, the shock of Rachel's words has started to wear off, and I begin to accept that what she's told me is true. It makes more sense than I want to admit. Sarah had grown quiet, I think, in the weeks after that hit-and-run. I thought it was just one of her withdrawn periods that she went through now and then, but now I see what it must have been.

I try to imagine how horrible and alone she must have felt, but my anger at her for not telling me what was going on gets in the way. Then I think how she would never have wanted to burden me with such an awful secret, and I know exactly what she was going through. Sarah always tried to be the big sister, even when she was the one who needed caring for.

Unlike Rachel.

Rachel. Stupid, selfish, vindictive . . .

And yet, she told me the truth. She sounded sorry.

Sorrier than I've ever heard her sound.

I shouldn't have left her like that. I shouldn't have left at all, not now. It's not what Sarah would have done.

I turn around and go back.

Thirty-Seven

Sarah

What does forever look like?

If you vanish from the earth but are still a part of the universe, what does that mean?

Do you wonder?

My whole life I wondered, how do we know the difference between reality and a dream?

And what if our dreams are a window into another world, an afterlife that exists even as we live?

As if I have been trapped in a nightmare and begin to awaken, a world starts to take shape around me. It is a universe of my own making, a place of dreams and memory.

No longer am I suspended in that white, San Francisco fog of a dream.

I begin to sense myself becoming.

Becoming what, I don't know. Not at first. I only know I am lying in a bed in a dark, familiar room, and bright light pours in from a window nearby. From where I lie, I can see blue sky, and my heart leaps at the idea that perhaps . . .

Perhaps it was all just a terrible dream.

Perhaps I have been made new by that hellish sleep, given a second chance to do it all again. To live a life illuminated by the mistakes I almost made.

I sit up and a familiar cover falls away. It is a pale blue blanket I loved as a child, a blanket that feels a lifetime apart from me. I grasp its satin edge and marvel at the presence of it for a moment, before turning my attention to the rest of me, whole again.

Or perhaps always whole. Perhaps still the Sarah who almost jumped but didn't.

I am wearing the blue tunic I bought at Second Chance, the local thrift shop. Bloodstains streak the front of the top, marring its once-delicate perfection, and I only observe this, feeling no sense of its ultimate meaning. It is blood I recognize, but I simply note its presence.

The room too I begin to recognize. It is the bedroom I shared with my sisters in the earliest years of my memory, right before we left the commune. On the wall is a small painting of a bird that feels like a fossil of the girl I once was. My heart aches now to see it.

In the far corner is Rachel's bed, and just to my left, Asha's crib, that she rarely uses with its giraffe-print sheets. Neither of them is here though. I am alone in the room, and I have a feeling I should be getting up, finding someone now.

I stand up and marvel at the fact of my body. I am whole. My chest moves in and out with each breath. My limbs feel strong and whole.

Here I am. Wherever this is.

I go to the door, then down a hallway I remember only vaguely, passing one closed door after another. I feel only slight curiosity about what I might find behind each door, because the one I am truly interested in is straight ahead. It's the front door of the trailer that my family once shared with another family.

I grasp the cool brass handle and turn it, memories dancing at the edge of my mind of other times I opened this door long ago.

Outside, the light is blindingly bright, so bright that at first I can't see.

I squint and cover my eyes, waiting for them to adjust to the brightness, and after a few moments, I can see that I am, perhaps, on the ranch where our commune was once located. It is more of a desert than I remember, but some buildings are familiar.

The more I look around, trying to orient myself, the more I see that the ranch is eerily different from the one I recall. Not different in big ways, but in little things. Aside from the stark, flat desert landscape, the buildings are neglected, dingy, suffering from what looks to be many years of abandonment.

I move without any sense of deciding to do so, my bare feet stepping on the hot, dry, cracked earth without feeling any pain.

The sound of a badly played guitar disturbs my thoughts, and I look to see a figure hunched over a guitar, sitting under a tree across the long, wide courtyard.

The tree has no leaves and therefore provides no shade

from the harsh sun. It is a gnarled, old mission fig tree that I remember vaguely having eaten fruit from as a kid. No fruit here now.

And since when do figs grow in the desert?

As I come closer to the figure, I realize he is the person I am here to see.

It's Brandon.

I halt in my tracks, but he looks up and spots me before I can think what I will do or say. He seems to recognize me instantly.

He stops torturing the guitar and waves me over. I close the distance between us, trying to think what would be appropriate conversation, but before I can speak, he does.

"Do I know you?"

"Not really." I'm surprised at the sound of my voice, which emerges without my having willed myself to speak.

He squints up at me, as if trying to place my face in his memory.

"You're the girl who was driving the car, aren't you?"

His voice has a soft, gravelly quality, and his eyes . . . I finally get to see what they look like. Gray-blue, they remind me of the ocean where I spent my final moment of life. They contrast with his golden skin and blond hair in such a way that makes them almost startling to behold. He is beautiful.

I'm sorry I killed you comes to mind as perhaps what I should say next, but it seems ridiculously inadequate.

He looks much more alive than he did the last time I saw him. He is whole. Intact. Not exactly alive, but here with me. And we are whatever we are together.

"Yeah," I say. "That's me."

"Hi," he says, not smiling, but not looking hostile either.

"I . . ." My words freeze in my throat.

"Yeah, I know. It was an accident, right?" He doesn't seem angry, but . . .

"I'm sorry."

"It happens."

"Yeah."

"This is awkward."

No kidding.

Slowly, I sit down beside him on the dusty ground.

I notice bloodstains are on his clothes too. They're dried to a brownish color, just like the stains on my shirt.

"How long have you been here?" I ask him.

He shrugs, looks down at his guitar, which I notice now has two broken strings, but isn't crushed the way it was at the side of the road. Maybe it's a different guitar. Yes, it must be. Guitars don't travel into the afterlife, right? But then, why would our clothing come with us?

None of this makes any logical sense.

"No idea," he finally says. "It's not very easy to keep track of time here."

I wonder why we are in my past—the ranch—and not his. Does he see the same surroundings I do?

He plucks at the guitar, which is completely out of tune. "I used to be able to play this thing."

Not sure what to say, I cross my hands in my lap and study him. He is the first dead person I've gotten to see up close in this . . . wherever we are.

"So how did you die?" he asks.

"Suicide."

A hot wind blows my hair into my face, and I push it back from my eyes. Nearby, a couple wanders between buildings, arguing about something. The woman looks as if she's about to cry.

"Why'd you kill yourself?" he asks.

I shrug, not sure what to say. Will he be flattered if I admit it's because of him? Or will I just sound like an idiot? And does it even matter what I sound like now?

"Guilt?" I murmur, half hoping he won't hear and won't ask again.

"About?"

"Oh, you know, running down an innocent hitchhiker. Stuff like that."

"You shouldn't have killed yourself on account of me. I mean, no sense in both of us being dead, right?"

I stare at him, utterly without a response. He can't possibly be for real, and yet, he looks serious.

He strums the guitar one last time, then sets it aside. "This thing got trashed in the wreck when you hit me."

I take another look at it and see that the body of the instrument indeed has been crushed and awkwardly repaired with duct tape. So there are adhesive products in the afterlife?

The shirt he was wearing was this stained shirt he has on now. The jeans, they're the same too. Against the tree leans the same grungy, green backpack he'd been carrying that night. What's in it, I wonder, that's so important he still has it now?

"So . . . this place, wherever we are. You can't get a guitar fixed here?"

"You don't know where we are?"

"You *do*?"

He laughs. "My family's Catholic. Of course I know where we are—purgatory."

I frown at this. "I don't believe in purgatory."

"You don't have to believe in it to be here. You can call it whatever you want, but we sure as hell aren't at the pearly gates of heaven."

"No." I look around again at this eerie setting, this scattering of trailers in the desert with the too bright sun and the wind and the heat and us wandering, lost souls.

I don't know what to call this place, but it's a ghost town for sure. Or something like one.

"So what do you do here all day?"

He shrugs. "Not much. There aren't any cars that seem to work, or if they do work, they break down after a mile or two. And we're in the middle of this desert without another town for I don't know how far—maybe there aren't any other towns."

"But—" I can't even think what I want to ask next. I am still consumed with the horrible feeling I'm stuck in a dream that I can't wake from. And then I think, oh, no, what if he's here only because I'm here. What if he's just a figment of my dead imagination? Is that possible?

What isn't possible in this weird place?

"What did you do to end up here?" I ask. "You know, instead of heaven or hell?"

"You think we're being punished?" He seems to be considering the idea for the first time.

"Aren't we? You're the one who's Catholic."

"I said my family is. We never went to church, and I didn't really believe in any of it until . . . well, until this."

Brandon stares at me for a moment, as if debating whether to tell me something. Then he stands up from the dusty ground and offers me a hand to do the same. "Come with me," he says as he helps me up.

He sets the broken guitar aside next to the backpack. Then he takes my hand again and leads me across the courtyard, toward a building labeled 3013-C in black block lettering done with a stencil. This is not something I remember from the ranch days. It's new.

I'm a little freaked-out by the feel of Brandon's holding my hand. It's oddly intimate for two dead people.

"What is this place?" I ask as we enter a side door and stand in the darkness.

He doesn't answer, and slowly my eyes adjust. I look around and see that we're in a room full of bookshelves. Rows and rows of them. Brandon leads me across to a shelf and pulls out what seems to be a random notebook.

"Open it to any page," he says.

I do, and I find myself staring at a report I wrote in the sixth grade about ancient Egypt. It takes me a minute to recognize it, but when I see my name in the upper right-hand corner, in that loopy, unsure script of an eleven-year-old girl, I know.

"Try another page," he says.

I flip to the back of the book and find a picture I drew a couple of years ago in life-drawing class. A woman sits with her knees pulled up to her chest. She's naked, but in profile; the most obscene thing about her is the rolls of fat that form at her rib cage. Nothing else is much visible in her position.

"Oh, God," I whisper. "I hated this drawing. What's it doing here?"

He pulls another book from the shelf. This one I even recognize the cover of. It looks like a diary I kept when I was maybe fourteen and fifteen. A purple paisley pattern decorates the cover of the journal.

"Recognize this?"

I am sick with recognition. I don't want to revisit this part of my life, these intimate details, in front of a stranger. It all feels too surreal to have presented to me right now, when I am reeling over so many things at once.

"Too much to take in?"

"Yeah, sort of." I put the journal back on the shelf. "But how did you know this would be my stuff?"

"It belongs to whoever picks it up. If I pull one off the shelf, I see whatever is from my past. Somebody else does, they see their stuff."

"But . . . this is the exact journal I used to have."

"It only looks like that to you, not to anyone else."

"But . . . why?" Why any of this? Why us, here, together now?

"That's the question we all have to answer. Right?" He looks at me as if I must know.

Do I know anything? Did I come here to find Brandon, or to ease my guilt?

Maybe both.

Maybe.

It's the new yes and the new no.

Thirty-Eight

Asha

I have not been in a hospital since Sarah was sick. The antiseptic odors that don't quite hide the smell of sickness give me a queasy feeling that I instantly associate with Sarah. I keep reminding myself that I am here because of Rachel.

Rachel.

What if she dies too, and I am an only child? What kind of crazy hell would that be?

I texted Sin during the ambulance ride, and now he comes shuffling down the hallway, looking more bewildered than I feel. The fluorescent, overhead lights make his skin look pale green, and his hair looks as if it hasn't been washed in a while.

"So what happened?" He sits down in the hard plastic, brown chair next to me.

"She took a bunch of pills."

"Suicide? Rachel?" He frowns. "I thought she loved herself too much for that."

I am not in the mood to laugh, so I sigh instead. I will explain it all later, maybe in the light of day.

I don't know where Lena is. And I don't know where Ravi is. I have tried to call and text them both, but they forget to turn their phones on, or forget to charge their batteries, or whatever.

Why is it when there is a crisis, only one person is sitting beside me? How did a sixteen-year-old cross-dresser become the most responsible person in my life?

Anger makes my chest tighten. I don't want to be here right now. I don't want to lose another sister.

When I found Rachel, she was so knocked-out, I knew something was wrong. No way she'd just decided to curl up and go to sleep after everything that went down tonight.

I tried to wake her up and couldn't, and then I called 911. Then I found the pill bottle while I was on the phone with the operator.

I felt so numb, like this was just the kind of stuff that happens to the Kinsey girls now. We kill ourselves. It's a thing we do.

Later, in the ambulance, I watched the EMTs monitoring her vital signs, and I wanted more than anything else I have ever wanted for them to make Rachel live.

She is the piece of our family that never quite fit, but now I see everything everyone could have done to make her fit in. And I want to do my part of it.

Sin puts his arm around me and I lean over on his shoulder and close my eyes.

I don't know how long I have been like that when I hear the click of heels hurrying on the tile hospital floor, and I can tell by the footsteps that it is Lena. I look up and watch her approach, her designer bag bouncing at her blue-jeaned hip. Her face is pale, and she seems to look past me without seeing me at first, until she stops and sits down on the chair next to mine.

"When will they let us see her?" she asks.

At first, I don't know who she's talking about. *See who?* I almost ask.

Which is stupid. How could I not know? But events are slow and jumbled in my mind, and I feel as if we are living in a hellish loop of Kinsey girls dying. Am I next? Should I want to be?

Rachel. Of course. She's talking about Rachel. But then I realize I've been asleep, because when I look at the wall clock, it's just past two in the morning now, and I don't know why my mother's hair looks so good, why her lipstick is perfect. What has she been doing that she just now heard my messages?

"Where were you?" I blurt without answering her, angry at her for not looking as if she has stumbled out of bed like a normal mother would have at this hour.

"I was at Ron's."

This explains nothing, and she knows it.

"He was having a party, for our engagement. I was going to invite the two of you after dinner. I tried to call you but the cell reception is bad at his house."

As I sit up, peeling myself off Sin's shoulder, I try to imagine what a party at Ron's place would be like. A bunch of aging hippie types trying to pretend they're still twenty-one. I've seen it before. My parents used to have such parties, at which no one minded when us kids got drunk too. At which couples who didn't belong together disappeared into bed-

rooms and emerged later, rumpled, still drunk, maybe to find
a spouse waiting, maybe not.

My mom is not rumpled, and this brings me some vague
sense of relief. I want to believe she's past all that crap. But
why should I care now, at this late date?

I realize with a jab of pain in my gut that she's nearly the
only family I have left.

"Rachel's sleeping," I finally say. "They pumped her stomach. We're supposed to wait out here, but I can probably take
you in to see her."

I don't mention that I'm terrified of the hospital room,
that it reminds me too much of the years we spent in them
with Sarah, that just the smell makes me feel like I'm going
to throw up. She probably knows. She was there too.

"God," she murmurs. "What was she thinking?"

I don't answer. Instead, I glance over at Sin, whose expression is totally neutral. He is like Switzerland sitting there in
the queasy glow of the fluorescent lights. Then I rise and lead
Lena across the hall to the room where Rachel is hooked up
to a heart monitor and an IV drip of something. She is asleep.

Lena's face goes white when she sees Rachel. Her mouth
is stained black from whatever they used to pump her stomach.
She hardly looks like herself. Rachel, always the prettiest, the
tallest, the curviest, the shrewdest, is lying there limp and
half-dead looking, and it's very, very real. It's not a bad dream.

Lena places a hand on Rachel's arm and sighs, but instead
of feeling comforted that Lena is finally here, I want to slap
her hand away. I want to scream and rage and break the expensive hospital equipment surrounding us.

"Excuse me, are you a parent?" a nurse says as she enters
the room.

Lena, with a more official audience now, visibly crumples. She nods, her shoulders sag, and her face transforms into that of a grieving mother. Only now do I think to question her lack of emotion before. Would it have been wasted on me? I wonder.

The nurse glances at the monitor Rachel is hooked up to, then at me. Her expression carefully neutral, she places a hand on Lena's arm. "Your daughter is going to make it through this, Ms. Kinsey."

"What did she do?"

"She took what looks to be about thirty tablets of Vicodin."

Lena gasps, but it sounds fake to me. Probably she is registering that it was her Vicodin, that she will have to buy more from wherever she gets her endless supply.

"We can't know for sure about liver damage until test results come back, and it's possible there may be some mental impairment if the brain was deprived of oxygen for any length of time."

"When will you know?"

"She should be waking up soon, and then we'll have more information. Let me know if you need anything—just ring the buzzer there."

When we are alone again, Lena wipes away the dampness on her cheeks and settles into a chair next to the bed. She stares at Rachel's sleeping form for a few moments, then digs her iPhone out of her bag and checks it for messages.

Rage fills my chest, so that I can barely breathe. "How can you just sit there and look at your messages? Did Ron send you a text to see how your kid is doing in the hospital? Why isn't he here too, if he's supposed to be marrying you?"

Lena blinks at my outburst, then drops her phone back

into her purse and sets it on the floor. "What is the matter with you?"

"Rachel nearly killed herself tonight, and you act like she just sprained her ankle. What's the matter with *me*? What's the matter with *you*?"

"I'm not going to talk to you when you're being so hostile."

"Yes, you are—"

"Why don't you go outside and cool off. Rachel doesn't need this kind of energy when she's trying to heal."

"You've barely looked at her since you got here." I feel tears coming now, but I'm not going to fall apart. Coming faster than the tears are all the things I've failed to say for way too long. "Do you even care how screwed up she is? Do you?"

"Asha, now isn't the time—"

"Do you know she slept with David? She knew it would kill Sarah, and she did it anyway."

"You're being hysterical." Lena's face is a calm mask, and I want to say something that will shatter the calm.

I think of telling her the rest of it, about the argument between Sarah and David, the accident with the hitchhiker, Rachel's cruelty on the hike, Sarah's suicide, but I can't. That's Rachel's story to tell now.

My voice must have gotten louder than I realized, because the nurse appears again. "Is something wrong in here?"

"No," Lena says.

"Yes," I say too loudly.

"You'll have to keep it down. If you can't, I'll need to call security."

"Call security," I say, my whole body shaking. "Tell them she's the problem. Tell them it's her fault Rachel took all those pills."

The nurse takes my arm with her cool, strong hands and attempts to lead me from the room. At first I won't budge, but she applies a gentle pressure to my lower back, and I allow her to take me into the hallway, away from Lena, who is only staring mannequin-like from her place in the bedside chair.

"I know it's very upsetting to find your sister like that," the nurse is murmuring, but she doesn't know the half of it.

How could she know?

I hear footsteps coming down the hall toward us, and I look up to see Sin carrying a bottle of Coke and a bag of chips.

"Asha, come on." He reaches out a hand to me.

So I do the only thing that makes sense now. I take his hand and let him lead me away.

Thirty-Nine

Rachel

Holy freaking hell, my throat hurts. I open my eyes and try to sort out where I am and why I feel like such crap. It all starts coming back to me. The day, AJ and David's fight, the dinner, the confession to Asha, the pills, the darkness.

It didn't work.

I must not be brain-dead, because I'm lying here thinking, right? And I can see that I'm in a hospital room.

I don't know if I am disappointed or relieved. I feel like my brain is stuffed with cotton, like I can't make it work at its normal speed. I close my eyes again against the horrible overhead light, and I am all of a sudden shocked at myself.

I screwed it up.

But I hadn't planned it, and I wonder—I guess I will always wonder—if Sarah did plan it. Had she known ahead of time what she was going to do? I have spent all this time thinking no, she hadn't. She'd done it only because of me, because of what I said, because of my betrayal.

Now though, now that I know how quickly life can seem not worth living anymore, I am not so sure.

Maybe, like me, she hadn't so much planned her death as wandered into it after a few bad turns.

God, I feel like crap.

I hear the door open. "Rachel."

It's Lena's voice. I look toward the sound, and she sits down on the edge of the bed. Her mascara is streaked like she's been crying, and I see her eyes well up.

Like, all this grief is for me?

For real?

Hard to believe, but I am groggy from whatever the hell they're pumping into the IV in my arm, and I do believe it.

"Can you hear me?"

I nod.

She takes my hand in hers. Her skin is cold, and I stare down at the big-ass diamond ring glittering on her finger.

"How do you feel?"

I try to croak out an "Okay" but my throat is dry, and talking hurts more than I expect. It comes out more like a whisper.

I look up to see her watching me. Was she the one who found me? I have questions but don't feel like asking them right now.

"Oh, Rach, why?"

Where to start? I am so tired by this question, I close my eyes and hope she'll just go away. I want her here and don't. The sad thing is, I don't know who else I'd even want at my bedside right now.

David? No.

AJ? Hell no.

Ravi?

Asha?

Krishna pops into my thoughts. It wouldn't be so bad if he were here right now.

Instead, the door opens again, and Asha walks in. "You're awake."

She sits down on the edge of my bed. She looks like hell, like she hasn't slept, and I guess that's the problem. She hasn't.

"You scared the crap out of me." She places a hand gently on my thigh. "Please don't do that again."

My throat constricts then, and I just nod. I realize she is the person I want here right now, and I'm glad she is.

"Seriously, however bad things seem? It's going to get better."

Lena clears her throat softly. "Asha, do you mind giving us a little privacy? I need to speak with Rachel alone."

Asha looks from Lena to me. I get a feeling maybe she's worried about leaving me alone with our mother, but I am too tired to wonder why.

"This isn't the time for any dramatic moments, Lena," she says finally.

Lena simply stares at her, saying nothing, and I do start to wonder what's already gone down between these two while I was taking my little vacation from life.

Asha sighs and gets up off the bed. "I'll be right outside if you need me," she says to me, and this, somehow, is the most comforting thing I've heard in a long time.

When we are alone, Lena bites her lip and gives me a long, meaningful look. "I feel like I did this to you. I know the news about my engagement wasn't very well timed."

All of me gets very still, wanting to hear what will come next. Maybe she is waiting for me to give her some response because she starts looking a little uncomfortable, but I still don't speak.

Finally she says, "I feel like you always got lost in the shuffle. You deserved more from me, Rachel. I want you to know that I know that."

I can't keep looking at her. I look down at the ring again instead. White gold, solitaire cut, ridiculous bling on her skinny hand.

After a while she squeezes my arm, sighs, and stands up to go. I try to think of something to say, but I can't think of anything now.

Apparently, neither can she, because she leaves without saying another word.

I lie there staring at the door, with its long, narrow window of people passing by, for I don't know how long. When I am about to drift off to sleep, a guy enters the room with a clipboard in his hand. He is wearing a button-down shirt, a tie, and khakis, but no doctor's white coat.

"Hi, I'm Dr. Raymond. I'm the psychologist here at the hospital." He extends his hand for me to shake with my non-IV hand, and his grip is big and meaty.

He looks down at his clipboard for a few seconds, then back up at me. "So, Rachel Kinsey, how are you feeling?"

"Awful."

He sits down on the chair closest to my bed and nods. "You had quite a close call there, didn't you?"

I shrug.

"I'm here to talk to you about what happened and what

drove you to attempt suicide last night. Do you feel up to talking right now?"

"Sure." My throat finally loosens up enough for words. "Might as well get it over with."

"Your mom tells me you lost your sister recently to an accidental death?"

This, I wasn't expecting him to bring up. I have told Asha the truth, but telling the whole world that it wasn't an accident freaks me out, so I say nothing.

"Can you talk to me a little about that?"

I think of how heavy this secret has been to carry around, and I think of Krishna again for some reason, how he seems to see through me, and how good that feels. Maybe that's how I want it to be from now on—me completely see-through, hiding nothing.

"I was there when it happened."

"That must have been very hard for you," he says softly.

Yeah. Hard. That's one word for it. "The thing is, it wasn't an accident."

Now that I've said it aloud, there's no taking it back, and I feel more relieved than I expected.

"What do you mean by that?"

I take a deep breath. "She jumped. I saw her do it. And I couldn't tell anyone. I was too afraid."

He nods and scribbles something on his clipboard. "Tell me more about that."

How do I tell this guy the whole messy story? I can still see the scene so clearly in my head—when I try to go to sleep at night, when I wake up in the morning, it's always there.

So I just tell him.

I tell him about me and David, and the hitchhiker, and the hit-and-run, and how Sarah had been driving, and how I was talking to her that day on the trail, making her feel worse and worse about what she'd done.

By the time I have said it all out loud, I am stunned at myself, at all the decisions I could have made along the way to change things.

I could have been a good sister for once. I could have left things alone with David when I'd seen how he wanted me. Then they wouldn't have been arguing that night driving home from the coast, and Sarah wouldn't have been distracted, and she wouldn't have killed Brandon.

And after, even after all that had happened, I could still have chosen not to be a raging bitch about the whole thing. I could have tried to help Sarah instead of hurting her more.

"It sounds like you're carrying a heavy burden on your conscience." Dr. Raymond makes another note on his pad.

"No shit," I whisper.

"What do you think you could do next to relieve some of that burden?"

"I guess I could let the police know about the accident, but then that would get David in trouble."

"Do you believe we should have to face consequences for our actions?"

"I just tried to kill myself, didn't I? That seemed like a good consequence for totally fucking my sister's life."

"Perhaps David needs to face the consequence of covering up the accident. Would you agree?"

I shrug. "I guess that's not my problem."

"You're right, it's out of your hands. And for yourself, perhaps there's a better outcome than you committing suicide?"

I say nothing.

"What do you think that might look like?"

I'm getting kind of sick of the psychology talk, which reminds me of the stupid sessions Lena use to make us attend after the divorce. But I think of Krishna then, of what he would do right now, and I decide he'd go along. He'd cooperate. He wouldn't tell this guy to go screw himself.

So I go along because Krishna is maybe the first person I've ever met who makes me feel totally quiet inside.

"Maybe I try to make up for what I did wrong?" I finally say.

"Can you think of any ways you might go about doing that?"

"I guess . . . tell the police what I know? And tell my family."

"That sounds like a good start. Anything else?"

I try to imagine what my life's being okay would look like, but I can't. I just picture me feeling like shit, knowing I have to live with the fact that Sarah's life ended because of me. I didn't like her when she was alive, but now that she's gone, all I can see is what a petty, selfish brat I've been all along.

"I don't know."

"Who are you closest to in your life?"

"No one." The truth is like slapping myself in the face.

I'm not close to anyone because I've treated everyone around me like crap. But I think of Asha, and I guess she's the one, however not-close we may be.

"No one at all? Not even a family member?"

"Maybe my little sister, Asha, but, like, we're not really close."

"Is that something you'd like to change?"

Fuck this, is what I think. And then, no, that's the kind of thinking that got me here in the first place. I want to do something different.

"Yes," I say.

"Do you have any friends?"

"Not close ones. I've been too busy with guys."

"Tell me a little more about your relationship with Asha."

And I do. I tell him the whole sad tale of our lives leading up to now. As I talk, the obvious trend emerges—the middle-child cliché—that I have always been jealous of how close Asha and Sarah were. I always wanted that kind of sisterhood with them, and I always felt like the odd one out. By the time I am done talking, I know what I have to do.

I couldn't be a good sister to Sarah, but maybe, if Asha can forgive me, I could work on not being such a bitch to her.

Forty

Sarah

I feel Rachel near.

She is a soft breeze rustling my memory.

Then nothing.

She is gone again.

Brandon is still at my side. We are outside now, in the shade of a building, sorting through a box of toys that belonged to Asha.

My sweet little sister. She is not the squeaking, furry mouse toy or the wooden blocks with the paint chipped and fading. She is not any of these old bits of the past, yet I feel as if to let any one of them go will be to lose her forever. I touch each one, hold the toys close, reverently as if cradling a newborn baby in my hands.

Brandon watches me. "It's not me you're here for," he finally says.

"What do you mean?"

"You're not here for me."

I look at him, surprised now, because I remember I did feel as if I had someone to find, as if I was here for a reason.

"I've been waiting for you. But you, you're waiting for someone else."

He's been waiting for me. I take this in. "How did you know?"

"Know that you'd be coming?"

"Yeah."

"I didn't know."

"Rachel," I whisper. "She's not coming."

"Who's Rachel?"

"My sister. She was there when I died."

"I guess that's the thing—we wait for the ones who saw us pass on."

Pass on. Such a strange phrase, I used to think. I hated when anyone would refer to the possibility of my passing on from cancer. And now, I see it is truer than I ever imagined.

We do pass on.

"She's not coming," I say again.

He nods, as if he agrees, even though he can't possibly know. And I put down the toy block I've been holding, the letter *A*.

She's going to be okay.

Maybe they all are. I don't know. And that's the thing—I have to stop wondering, because it's not my business anymore.

Leaning forward, I kiss him softly. So soft it might not have happened at all.

The light around us grows brighter, and brighter still, until everything around me begins to fade away. I feel Brandon's hands on mine, and then I feel them slip away. It's not a sense of loss though that fills me.

It's light, peace, a feeling of forever.

Forty-One

Rachel

My first day home from the hospital, I am not sure who I am anymore. I feel as if I have been hollowed out with a rough tool, and an inflated, jittery balloon is in my chest where my heart should be. I am raw inside. Everything hurts, but if you asked me to point to what's bothering me, I can't.

Lena, put out by the idea that she has to be around watching over me, making sure I don't try to off myself again, is downstairs in the kitchen slamming cabinet doors, rustling around. I can hear her talking on the phone, making some kind of plans.

I fall asleep, and sometime later I wake up and hear Ravi's voice downstairs. Our father, who was apparently in New York for a business meeting when the shit went down, has flown back here and is downstairs?

Yes, he definitely is.

I hear Lena sounding annoyed again. Then the front door slams, her heels click-click to the car, and I hear the sound of her car driving away. I don't bother getting out of bed because of the raw feeling, and I am so, so sleepy. I cannot imagine what the fucking point is of anything at all. I shut out whatever dumb advice the psychologist gave me because it's all too much right now, and I put my head under the pillow and wish the world away.

But after footsteps on the stairs, and a tapping on my door, Ravi's voice is calling for me, and then his weight is on the edge of my bed.

"Rachel, my sweet girl." He rubs his hand along my shoulder.

He has not called me his sweet girl in forever. I lie still, waiting to hear more.

"I got here as soon as I could. I'm sorry it took me so long."

My response is to keep breathing, in, out, in, out. It's all I can think to do.

"How are you feeling?"

Something about his tone wakes me up a little. "Like shit."

He laughs. "That's my girl."

When he pushes the pillow aside from my face, I let him, and I can see he's been crying. His eyes are red and puffy, the way they were at Sarah's funeral.

I wonder how much he knows now, but that's not a question I have the energy to ask or even wonder for long.

"I'm going to stay here tonight. I can sleep here in your room, or downstairs on the couch, wherever you'd like, okay?"

This idea, of my dad sleeping here to watch over me, more than anything else that has happened since the day Sarah died, levels me. Would knock me down flat if I weren't already lying in bed.

I feel so much grief I can hardly catch my breath to brace for it. I let out a strange, desperate sound as it hits me.

He rubs my shoulder some more. "Does that mean you want me downstairs?" he says in his signature wry tone, so much sweeter than I deserve.

"No," I manage to choke out.

"You want me to sleep in your room?"

The state of my throat, closed off to words now, forces me to nod yes.

"Good." He sits there for a while, not saying anything. Then: "I'm going downstairs to find some tea. Can I make a cup for you too?"

I nod again, and I feel his weight disappear from the side of the bed. His footsteps trail out my bedroom door and down the stairs. I guess he left my door open because a few minutes later I don't hear anything but sense the presence of someone in the hallway.

It's Asha, I guess, because who else would it be? I don't have the energy to look, but whoever it is keeps standing there, so finally I peer over my pillow, and I see my sister standing in the doorway, her arms crossed, her eyes hollow and tired looking.

"Hi," she says, but doesn't step inside.

I guess she's waiting for an invitation. I can't remember the last time I allowed Asha to set foot in my bedroom, but when I look back at the past ten years, during which we went from being sisters to enemies, I can't quite imagine what she did that was so awful. I know she didn't deserve to be shut out. Maybe I did, but not her.

"You can come in."

I remember now how she acted at the hospital—concerned,

protective—and I wonder if she's always been that way and I just never noticed.

I wonder who she is. And who I am, this strange, new postapocalyptic creature who can't get out of bed.

Pushing myself up onto my pillows, I sit up with a great effort and wrap my arms over my chest, draw my knees up close. Asha sits down on the part of the bed that's empty now. She grabs a throw pillow and leans back against it, making herself at home.

Then she says nothing, and I am so grateful to have her there, silent, not trying to turn this into some kind of fucking lesson or sisterly moment or whatever.

I slide my cold, bare feet down until they are wedged under her hip, using her to warm them, something I haven't done in more years than I can count. She says nothing about this selfish, little intimacy I've offered, only closes her eyes and takes a deep breath, as if she's settling in for a nap.

I stare out the window into the darkness, at the shadow of a tree branch swaying in the wind. I can't see stars from this angle, only the darkened hillside and the horizon just above it, which is shadowed by clouds that reflect moonlight.

This reminds me of the last time I looked at the sky, in the early morning with Krishna, the sun rising and me a weak, slithery thing only wanting darkness. But Krishna is the opposite of darkness, I understand now. He is light, kindness, hope. It sounds dumb, but it's true.

"Have you ever met someone who seemed too good for the world?" I ask Asha.

"Sarah," she says without a moment's hesitation.

I think of the car wreck, the dead guy, Sarah's secret, but

I know in the end, Asha is right. Sarah had a goodness in her that maybe started getting rubbed away by all the world's rough edges, but it was there, blinding sometimes and often more than this younger sister could bear.

And Krishna, coming into my life just as Sarah left it—I wonder if it has something to do with my universe trying to find a new balance. Trying to fill the dark corner left by Sarah's absence.

"There's someone I'd like you to meet sometime," I say. "He kind of reminds me of Sarah. I think you'll like him."

Asha looks over at me, frowning a little. "Who is it?"

"Just a friend." The phrase feels strange on my lips. "He teaches meditation at the Buddhist center."

"Oh."

"I'm not dating him," I say, thinking this will lend weight to his relevance in our lives.

"Where did you meet him?"

"Outside the coffee shop after work one day."

The way he arrived in my life, I almost wonder if Sarah put him there to save me from myself, but I don't say this out loud. Crazy to think, but nothing anymore is what I used to think it was, so why not?

"I even went to the meditation center with him." I want to make it clear to Asha that I'm not as predictable as I used to be, that maybe some part of me is worth believing in.

"To meditate?" I can tell she's trying not to sound too disbelieving.

"Yeah. It was kind of . . . cool, I guess. I should probably go more—I mean, I will go. If you ever want to go with me . . ."

"To meditate?" she says more carefully, as if talking to a crazy person who might stab her with a fork if she makes the wrong move.

"Yeah."

"Okay." Half her mouth curves into a smile, as if she finally accepts that I'm serious and not deranged. "Why not."

I wonder where Krishna is, what he's doing, what he will say if I tell him about my suicide attempt.

No, not if.

When I tell him.

I will definitely tell him, not for sympathy, but for some sense of light. It will be like shining a light in the dark places, making that slithery, hidden part of myself retreat, maybe for good.

"I'm sorry we shut you out," Asha says into the quiet.

"Who shut me out?"

"Me and Sarah. I mean, if we ever did, I'm sorry. I think sometimes we were just this whole world, the two of us, and you were left on the outside."

I blink at this. Shouldn't I be the one apologizing? Hadn't I just been thinking about how I'd shut out Asha for all these years?

"I just . . . Sometimes I think you got kind of forgotten by everyone, and it wasn't fair, you know?"

This idea, what is and isn't fair, almost makes me laugh. Since when was anything fair, aside from cookies divided equally among kindergartners?

I open my mouth and say the first thing I can think of. "Sarah would have wanted us to forget about all that, don't you think? She would want us to get over it and try to, like, get along, right?"

"Yeah," Asha whispers. "She'd like that."

So I think that's what I will do. I will get over it, whatever *it* is, and I'll try to lead the life Sarah should have been alive to see.

Hope, a feeling I barely know, creeps up on tiny mouse feet.

Forty-Two

Asha

Big changes are afoot in the Kinsey household. Instead of us giving up our childhood home, Ravi has decided to move in with us. He says it's past time he started taking a more active role in our lives, and for once I believe he means it. Well, I believed it when he started moving his stuff in and sleeping in Lena's old bedroom as of last week. He's even talking to the owner of the house about us buying it after all these years of us paying rent and pretending we're above responsibilities like home ownership.

Lena has moved most of her stuff out and into Ron's house, where she is living now, and other than the awkwardness of the situation, I think this is an improvement.

No more fights with Lena, and Ravi has instituted family dinner nights. He also doesn't allow me to sleep at Sin's house, so all of a sudden I'm home at dinnertime and required to cook two nights a week. After much eye rolling from me and

Rachel both, we are getting used to the routine. I am learning to cook, and I make the two things I now know how to make— pasta primavera and spaghetti carbonara. Ravi talks to us about our days, and because he's home all the time with his consulting work and isn't out dating anyone, there is no get-ting anything past him.

Rachel is still Rachel, but I think she is trying to be better. Three weeks since she OD'd, and she has been ridiculously nice to me, considering. Ravi bought her an old beater Honda that she can drive to and from work, since she's taken a job at a Buddhist meditation center, of all places. The car has gone a long way toward winning her over, and I think being around all those Buddhists is mellowing her out a bit.

School is out as of yesterday. I somehow made it to the end of the semester without failing any of my classes. I got straight courtesy D's, but whatever. I guess I'm grateful.

Lately, I'm starting to think the thing we should all be trying to be isn't happy or entertained or excited or whatever. It's grateful. For everything.

Summertime, and the living is easy.

Not exactly, but Sin has planned a beach day for us, and we are best friends again. Just like before.

Sort of.

We have just pulled Jess's van into a parking spot in front of the tennis courts in Bolinas, and Sin is rummaging around in the back gathering a picnic basket and blanket and stuff while I stare out at the sea. It no longer looks as ominous to me as it did a month ago. Now it's just the Pacific again, as dangerous and beautiful as it ever was.

Same as it ever was.

This is my first time here since visiting the spot where Sarah died, and I am beginning to feel a nagging sense of . . . something.

A little bit of truth trying to work its way into my consciousness.

"Hold this," Sin says, snapping me back into the real world.

I turn my attention to him and he is handing me a large beach towel. I'm not sure we've ever gone anywhere so well equipped as we are today.

I take the towel and he shuts the van.

He is looking at me so strangely, I start to feel panic rising in my chest. He's going to tell me something awful.

"What?"

He frowns but says nothing, a line forming between his eyebrows that I've never noticed before.

"Nothing, just . . . Let's find a spot so we can put all this crap down."

We trudge toward the beach access, down a concrete ramp with graffiti-covered walls, and out into the sand. To the left, the beach is dotted with couples and families who've staked out spaces, and after about fifty feet of walking south, we find a suitable spot and plop all the stuff down.

I struggle to spread out the blanket so we can sit on it, but the wind has other ideas. Finally Sin intervenes and puts the basket on one end so we can pin down the other corners with ourselves and a pair of shoes.

"Okay, that's about all I've got in me. I need a nap now." I lie back on the blanket and cover my face with my arms, letting the sound of the crashing waves fill my head. For a few minutes, I think of nothing else.

Then Sin nudges me with his foot.

I peek at him from under my forearm. "What?"

He gives me that weird look again, like he has something to say.

It's been weeks now since I've given any thought to Tristan, I realize. He's just faded away, like a craving for some junk food I no longer like once I've had my fill. So I don't think Sin could possibly be mad at me about Tristan anymore.

"Let's walk," Sin finally says.

Oh, God. Not the walk. Anything but the walk.

"Is something wrong?"

Instead of looking at me, he looks out at the horizon, that place where ocean meets sky. A ship, mysterious and unreachable in the distance, is the only object visible besides the sky and the ocean.

"Not exactly." He takes my hand in his.

He pulls me forward, toward Bolinas Lagoon and the view of Stinson Beach that always makes me feel like I'm looking across at another reality. Bolinas is the hidden beach, the hippie beach, the grungy, graffiti-tagged, naked-surfing beach, while Stinson is the clean, perfect Marin County getaway for city people looking to escape the fog and have a day in the sun. The two are separated by a narrow channel of water and yet are worlds apart.

I let him lead me, and then I catch up so that we are walking side by side, hand in hand. This is not the first time we've held hands, but this time it feels different.

This time, I know my feelings for Sin aren't as simple as they are for any other friend.

My eyes well up with tears that are in no way due to the light wind buffeting us. Pampas grass juts out from the hillside, swaying and looking far prettier than the destructive invasive species it is. I sometimes wish I hadn't taken science classes so that I could just look at things and think they're pretty and that's it. Sort of how I feel about my relationship with Sin. I wish I could just not understand it. Just think it's great and that's it. No complications, no deeper veins of complicated emotion.

Up ahead, someone has built a sort of tepee out of driftwood bleached almost white from the sun. It is set back near the hillside, protected from the surf and the high tide. Sin leads me to it, and we crawl inside. The pieces of wood that form the walls leave gaps, but it is still a cozy little place with a view straight out to the sea from its doorway.

We sit cross-legged inside and say nothing for a minute.

Then Sin says, "Do you remember when we met?"

Of course I do. Freshman year, first day of school. "Ms. Godby's class," I say. "You were sitting in the aisle across from me, and you told me you liked my shoes."

"I wasn't exactly being honest."

"You didn't like my shoes?"

"Not really. I just wanted to have something to say to you."

"Why?"

He shrugs. "I liked the way you sat there writing in your journal, not noticing anybody around you."

"I noticed people. I was just too scared to look up."

I am staring at a little pile of rocks and shells someone has made near the entrance of the tepee. I reach over and pick up a tiny crab exoskeleton, entirely intact somehow, its delicate legs and claws unbroken. I hold it in the palm of my hand and marvel at its beauty.

"You were so pretty," Sin says.

My stomach leaps. He's never complimented me like that before. Never commented on my appearance at all, other than to critique my outfits.

He picks up the crab from my open palm and studies it. "Do you ever think maybe Sarah's been reincarnated as something else by now? Like maybe she's a crab, or a seagull or a new baby somewhere."

"A seagull? You think my sister came back as a *seagull?*"

He shrugs. "She always liked them."

"She was crazy."

"She just didn't believe in speciesism."

"What?"

"Like racism, but for animals."

I laugh for the first time since we've set foot on this beach, and something hard and cold inside my chest melts. I start to relax.

"I don't think I believe in reincarnation," I say, because it's impossible for me to imagine Sarah as anything but Sarah.

"I do, because I always feel this really strong sort of kinship whenever I see an alligator lizard. I think I used to be one in a past life."

"So of all your past lives, the one and only that has stuck with you is the time you were an alligator lizard."

"Yep."

"You're crazy too."

"I try."

I close my eyes and try to imagine where Sarah might be right now, if there are such things as souls or heaven or hell or reincarnation. I imagine her watching us now. I try to feel her presence in the crashing surf and the wind.

And for the first time, I think I do. I think maybe she is

whatever and wherever I want her to be. She is inside of me, and around me, and she is the crab Sin is placing back in my palm now, and she is the grain of sand clinging to my skin. She is everything and nothing, just as we all always have been and always will be.

"I have something for you." Sin takes a package out of his pocket, a little, blue velvet bag. He hands it to me.

I set the baby crab aside, then tug at the drawstring to open the bag. Inside is a bracelet made of beautiful glass beads, some swirls of color, some spotted, some translucent.

"I made the beads in Jess's glass studio."

I look up at him, and I don't understand the emotion I see in his eyes.

"It's so pretty," I say, then distract myself from the awkward moment by attempting to put the bracelet on, but my fingers fumble over the tiny clasp.

He stops me when I'm clearly not getting it right and secures the bracelet on my arm. When his fingertips graze the inside of my wrist, I feel it all the way in my core.

"The beads are good luck because I blew positive vibes into the glass."

I laugh, but I stop when I see he's serious.

I feel my cheeks get hot because he keeps looking at me like he has something big to say. Feeling foolish, I look back out at the ocean and watch a surfer, his black wet suit glimmering in the sun as he skims a small wave. I've never tried surfing because I hate the cold Northern California water and the idea of sharks lurking beneath the surf. Great whites actively hunt this part of the coast, and it's not uncommon for surfers to be attacked, but there's never been an attack at Bolinas Beach. For this reason alone, I will occasionally swim in the water here on the hottest summer days.

But this beach feels safe for other reasons too. It's the beach of my happiest memories, the beach where Sin and I come when we're bored, where we lie in the sand for hours reading to each other and talking about nothing and everything. I guess, now that I consider it, this has become our place.

"Asha?"

It's rare for him to speak my actual name, and I look up, startled.

"Aren't you going to say anything?"

"About what?"

"The bracelet."

"Oh! Sorry. I mean, thank you. It's really cool."

For a moment, his face darkens, and I know I've said something to hurt his feelings.

"I know we're like best friends and all," he says slowly. "But what if we weren't?"

"I'd die. I can't lose you and Sarah in the same year."

"That's not what I mean. What if we were, like, not *just* friends?"

"What do you mean?"

He sighs, and a pained look crosses his face. "When I said I wasn't into girls anymore, I wasn't exactly telling the truth."

"You weren't?"

"I was just, I don't know, kind of confused."

He's stopped wearing dresses and other girlie stuff, I realize. I hadn't noticed until now, but pretty much all he wears these days are normal guy clothes.

"Confused why?"

"Because you were so clearly into Tristan, and you were the only girl I wanted to be with."

He says it like it's the most obvious thing in the world, and like I'm a fool for not knowing. And maybe I am.

I think of all those times we shared the same bed, all the countless hours we've spent together, and me clueless as I could possibly be about Sinclair Tyler.

I look at him, and for the first time I start to see him for who he is, and not who I need him to be.

"Say something!"

"I love you," I say before my brain has even decided to speak the words. My heart has taken control of my lips, and there's no stopping.

He looks stunned. "You do? Like a friend, you mean?"

"No. Yes. I mean, I love you like a friend, and I love you like I love you."

He scoots over so that our legs are tangled together and our lips are only inches apart.

"You mean like this?" He kisses me.

It's not a kiss like any I've ever felt before. It's warm and slow, and it holds a question between us that I know I have to answer. I feel my whole self melt against him, and I can't compare this feeling to anything in the history of my life. I am visiting a new world, embarking on I don't know what.

When we stop kissing, he looks at me for a while, and this time it's this sort of soft, blurry looking that I can't turn away from. It's like we're seeing each other for the first time, but we already know all the details. He's always been Sin to me, funny, weird, quirky Sin. My best friend. But now he's this other guy. He's the one I love, here with me all along but somehow brand-new.

"The reason I got so mad about Tristan is because of this."

I don't need him to explain that "this" is the feelings that have been growing inside of us, like a baby in the months before the mother's belly is big. Still small and secret, but no less real.

"I know," I whisper, and it's true that some part of me did know before the thoughts had even formed.

"I guess I didn't want to admit how I was feeling and risk us not being friends anymore."

"Yeah."

I blink away the tears that are no longer threatening to form a downpour. I could explain them away as being because of the wind, but I don't need to.

"I was stupid. I mean, I don't know what I was thinking doing anything with Tristan—"

"Never mind about him. It's over, and I'll kick his ass if he ever tries to touch you again."

I smile, knowing he's not joking but also aware that it won't be necessary. Tristan has returned to his old self, unaware of my existence, as it should be. He is his own universe, and I don't want or need to be a part of it anymore.

"Are you still afraid of what will happen if we are a couple and then it doesn't work out?"

He shrugs. "Not anymore. We can just go back to being friends, right? It's not impossible."

"But what if we hate each other?"

"We've gotten past me hating you before."

I smile, remembering with a pang how awful it felt to have

him angry at me. There will be more moments like that if we become more than friends.

But then, there is no if. It's happened, whether we meant for it to or not, and now there's only the chance to try to see what happens next.

I take his left hand and hold it between my hands, warming it and noticing the way his long, slender fingers brush against my wrist again.

"You're the first person I've ever said that love thing to, you know."

"The first guy you've ever loved? Or just the first one you've told?"

"The first guy I've ever *loved*, of course."

"I know. I just wanted to hear you say it."

He leans in close again, so I can feel his breath on my cheek. "The feeling is mutual."

For the first time since Sarah died, I know she is with me. Not in that cliché watching-over-me-on-a-cloud kind of with me, but with me in this feeling that washes over me. She is everything I have ever known about love, and she's taught me how to know this feeling now.

Picking up the tiny crab shell, I cradle it in my hand for a moment, then crawl out of the tepee. When I reach the water's edge, I say good-bye, and I toss it into the fathomless, blue ocean.